The Wedding Con

The Wedding Con

Love is in the Air Romance

Janine Amesta

TULE
PUBLISHING

Dedication

To my friend and favorite librarian, B, who's always been a huge champion of romance books.

And to all other librarians who are out there fighting the good fight. Thank you for continuing to make libraries a magical place.

Author's Note

As with most of my books, while there is humor within there's also serious topics discussed. If any of these topics are difficult for you to read, please feel free to set the book aside for your own mental health. There are references to past parental death, financial scams, a manipulative parent figure, some misogynistic language, homelessness, suggestion of a male providing sexual favors in exchange for safety and comfort, lying and conning people, parental neglect, feelings of abandonment, parent in prison, and some physical shoving. There's also some strong language and open-door love scenes. But even with all this, I always guarantee there's a happy ending waiting for you.

Prologue

Two-and-a-half years ago

I F JANE AUSTEN had taught Naomi Moreno anything, it was to watch out for the George Wickhams of the world.

The first time she saw Boone-whatever-his-name-was-Reyes, he'd been sitting at her mother's dining room table. She'd been instantly struck by his handsomeness—like a car crash. And, like a car crash, she didn't enjoy how discombobulated it made her.

Naomi was annoyed to discover she wasn't immune to a good-looking guy, especially one with wind-swept, chestnut-colored hair. Each strand inherently fell in a way to be both unfussy and purposeful. His facial features were clean, sharp, and like a damn cologne model in a monochrome magazine ad.

This had to be the first warning flag.

As *Pride and Prejudice* had demonstrated, the George Wickhams of the world were no doubt always incredibly good-looking. It made it easier for them to worm their way into people's lives and get impressionable young women to run away with them and ruin their reputations.

When his golden-eyed gaze landed on her over the coffee steam as he took a sip from a mug, it set her so on edge, she became convinced the breakfast burrito she'd slammed down that morning wasn't digesting well. Either it was the extra spicy chorizo or it was him. For her health, she should avoid both in the future.

He regarded her with a smirk as though they already shared inside jokes, inside schemes, or any other type of inside activities people did together. She didn't appreciate the presumption, glaring in return. The slant of his hooded eyes reflected mischief at this response. Boone reminded her of an animated, street-smart alley cat, one who could talk his way into and out of trouble as easily as one would put on or take off a coat.

Warning flag number two for those keeping count, which she definitely was.

A big red asterisk went beside his face in her mind, making an addendum that this guy was trouble. He had charm and knew how to use it, which put him further into the George Wickham category. Jane Austen knew a fuckboy when she saw one, and so did Naomi. She wasn't proud to admit these exact attributes used to work on her, mostly when she was silly, flighty, and not yet sixteen. At twenty-four, and with a struggling family hot-air balloon business to worry about, Naomi was no longer interested in the type of trouble she imagined a guy such as Boone could provide.

With the sudden passing of her father, Robert, she became all too aware of how vulnerable she, her mother, and her two sisters were. How they could be seen as easy targets to people who knew the patriarchal head of the house was gone and no longer offered male protection, as backward and unfair as this was. The Moreno family had no one but themselves to depend on to protect them in a world that had become more precarious. Her mother, Elena, and younger sister by a couple years, Hailey, refused to realize the seriousness of their position. Naomi's much older sister, Selah, was level-headed and mature, a natural captain of the group, but she had a lot on her plate with the business. As such, Naomi took on the responsibility of keeping the family safe herself. She would do anything to keep it that way.

It was unfortunate then that her first real test, since Robert's passing, she'd already failed. The evidence of this was in the form of Boone, who was in her family home, drinking from one of her mother's treasured mugs. Naomi was the reason he was there.

To be fair, she'd only talked with him on the phone before. There was no way she could have known about his discombobulating handsomeness. The single hint being the pleasant, smooth tone of his voice, one that might be described as hypnotic.

Her mistake during their phone interview was learning a small amount about him while prattling and revealing too much about herself. This was obviously the wrong way to conduct an interview. Lessons were learned. She blamed it on inexperience and being a middle child. She was so used to being invisible and ignored, when given the opportunity, she'd become too eager to make herself seen.

Feeling embarrassed and thinking Boone had seemed harmless and nice enough on the phone after he'd patiently listened to her ramble about everything, she'd invited him to meet the rest of the family, and . . . well, here he was.

She wasn't sure she could describe him as simpering and

smirking and making love to them all, but there may have been *some* of this happening. He flattered her mother about the coffee and homemade cinnamon rolls she provided. He played into Hailey's vanity by telling her he could see she was the influencer type. He even appealed to Selah's practicality by assuring her he'd be available to work whenever, regardless of the hours or the small amount of pay they could offer.

At the end of it all, the only one growing wary about Boone was Naomi, putting her as the odd person out at this interview. While he did attempt to throw some nice words in her direction—he said her voice fit her face, whatever the hell that meant—she hadn't softened. It didn't matter what he said or whether he studied her with those dynamically inquisitive eyes, as though he were a safe cracker trying to discover the perfect combination to unlock her, Naomi didn't care. She was too worried she'd invited a fox right into their safe and cozy henhouse and, if this was the case, she'd never forgive herself. She, of all people, should know better.

"Really, Naomi? What's wrong with you?" Hailey said after Boone had departed and Naomi floated the idea they rescind the offer, and find someone else to be part of the chase crew for High Desert Tours.

"There's no reason to get our heart set on the first guy that comes along. I'm just not sure about him." Naomi didn't want to bash him if she didn't have to and hoped her gut feeling would have been enough to check the rest of the family.

Her younger sister rolled her eyes. "God. Stop. I can almost guarantee the next one won't be as hot as this one.

Have you seen the guys we come across around here? Why would you be against that?"

"Because none of us are going to be dating him, so why does it matter? This is about the business and that's all we should be considering. Right, Selah?"

If anyone would support her, it would be the eldest Moreno sister. "Sure. Of course. That being said, he seemed okay. Besides being a little bit of a smooth talker, I don't have a problem with the guy—at least not enough to tell him, 'never mind,' and he can't have the job. Maybe if we had a bunch of possible candidates, we could afford to be picky, but the sooner we fill this position, the sooner we can reopen. There needs to be a minimum of three of us during setup. And if Hailey won't—"

"I'm definitely not chase crew material," the youngest sister said with a flick of her curly brown hair. Her sister had never chased anything, let alone a hot-air balloon.

"Yeah, exactly," Selah said flatly, not finding Hailey amusing. "So we need someone to help us, and it's probably best if that person has"—she made a vague hand gesture over an imaginary body—"muscles like that. As strong as I want to say we all are, that fuel tank is heavy and awkward to get in and out of the gondola."

Her sister was correct, but Naomi remained disappointed to be losing the argument. She was also annoyed both of her sisters noticed how attractive he was. Not that this was a big secret. His good looks would only be hidden if he was completely undercover in disguise.

"Ay, mijas, he was so strong and handsome. And such a sweet, nice young man," their mother interjected. Of course,

Elena would feel this way. She only saw the good in someone and had a habit of adopting stray people, feeding them until they were full of love and food. No one would be more appealing than a good-looking, street-smart alley cat, who looked as if it had been a while between home-cooked meals.

"Okay, can we just slow down a minute and talk about this?" If Naomi brought in some logic, maybe they'd see past the beautiful facade.

"You don't like him?" Elena appeared genuinely shocked. "I'm surprised at you. Why are you being suspicious and mean? I didn't raise you like that."

"I—I didn't say I didn't like him. I just want to make sure we're being smart. And I would hope you'd think that you raised me to be smart."

Elena didn't have an answer to this, but smiled and patted her daughter's hand.

"Can everyone calm down?" Selah said. "We can all have a voice. Naomi, what exactly don't you like about him?"

With the floor to air her concerns, Naomi was put on the spot. She realized being against a guy who made her stomach nervous with gut rot, due to an overabundance of charisma, was an odd argument. Let alone bringing in Jane Austen, her intuition, and anything else that was ridiculous. But this didn't mean she didn't have something.

"For one thing, when I talked to him on the phone, he'd told me he'd come from Bakersfield." This was one detail she'd gotten from their phone conversation, and she'd made special note of it at the time because she had thought, *Welp, here's one more Californian trying to move their way into Central Oregon.* "And, Mom, he mentioned to you that he'd grown up near Medford." She noticed he provided this detail after Elena had shared she'd lived in this exact city before moving here with her sister. Her mother had taken this tidbit as proof that Boone coming into their lives was kismet.

"That could be . . . a misunderstanding. Or you're remembering it wrong." Selah might be willing to overlook some things if it got the business running as soon as possible. "Bakersfield. Medford. He can be from the moon for all I care."

"I just find it a weird thing to lie about. And then his name—"

"Oh, god, Naomi. Again?" Hailey groaned, dropping her head backwards.

When Boone had handed over his Oregon driver's license for Naomi to make a copy for employee paperwork, she'd first noticed his picture. It seemed the DMV camera had given him, and only him, a glamour filter because his picture was amazing. The next thing she noticed was the name "Boone" hadn't appeared anywhere on the card. Instead, the I.D. was for Jonathan Henry Reyes.

Oh, uh, sorry. I thought your name was Boone, she'd said at the time.

If this was some kind of incriminating evidence, he hadn't blinked, wasn't fazed in the least. He switched to an easy smile, one perfectly white and straight, like a toothpaste commercial. *Childhood nickname from my parents. You know how it is. I've had it for so long that it feels like my real name. Maybe someday I'll tell you about it.* He'd thrown a cute wink at Elena, who giggled.

"Having a nickname doesn't make you a criminal. Gah!

Be so for real with me right now, Naomi," Hailey said.

Logically, Naomi knew her kid sister was right. These were simply a few more red flags to add to her imaginary folder of suspicious things. If it were just these two items, perhaps Naomi would have felt differently, less responsible for protecting her family. She wished she was being ridiculous, so she could drop it and go along with the decision as easily as the rest of the family without concerns.

The problem was, there was a secret third reason—one shifting her opinion from indifference to definitely against Boone. It gave her enough red flags to make them into a pile of confetti.

Except she was afraid to give voice to the reason, to tell her family, in case it opened a whole can of worms regarding Robert. She wasn't sure she wanted to risk changing anyone's opinion about him when his character had ascended to the level of sainthood, something her beloved father deserved despite his flaws.

While Robert's poor financial situation, both personal and business, had become known to them soon after his death, Naomi had more knowledge than the rest of them about how it came to happen. And, also, how she hadn't done enough to stop it. He hadn't listened to her, and she hadn't pushed him hard enough to hear.

The people he *had* listened to, over his own flesh-and-blood daughter, were the money "influencers" he'd studied on YouTube. At the time, Naomi had been living at home and would read novels in the same room where her father would sit in his recliner, watching on his tablet with the volume almost at max levels. In most circumstances, she would have left, the environment too distracting for reading, but she'd stayed, growing curious about the videos he'd watched.

She didn't think much about it at first, but became concerned as her dad got sucked down the rabbit hole of the YouTube algorithm, featuring questionable characters with no verified credentials. Personalities, who threw out advice on investments and making money, as if only rewards awaited them and not consequences. Her father, who'd always been the smartest, kindest man she'd ever known, was suckered by the foxes. No matter what she said to warn him, that these influencers weren't necessarily safe, it didn't matter. He didn't listen because he knew best. Perhaps if she'd been as respected as Selah, things would have been different, and Naomi almost brought it up to her.

But then Robert had died.

There didn't seem to be any point after that. Their situation couldn't be changed, except to turn it around and save High Desert Tours. Naomi willed herself to forget about it, and let Robert claim his sainthood. He still deserved it.

Except during the interview, Boone had said something that had brought it all back. A motto often said by one of the YouTube personalities her father had frequently watched—a phrase innocent on its own, but which turned her stomach with distrust. Boone may have not been the person in those videos, but why would he know this phrase? Why would he say it? Maybe it was silly for her to attach so much importance to it, but she didn't care. The association was close enough.

Although, Naomi couldn't reveal this without also exposing Robert's mistakes. She decided to keep her mouth shut, and this was why she was ignored once again and outvoted. Boone was hired.

It didn't matter because, at the end of the day, Naomi vowed to never let her guard down.

She'd keep an eye on the fox herself.

Chapter One

"ENJOYING THE VIEW?" Naomi didn't have to look up from her phone to know Boone was studying her—something he did often. It was as though when she'd committed to keeping an eye on him, he'd made the same one regarding her.

Not that there was a lot in their view to enjoy this mid-May day. The old farm field on the Moreno land in Terrebonne had been reclaimed by Mother Nature years ago. The land, filled with High Desert native plants, was mostly brownish yellow with a smattering of wild sage and the craggy juniper trees in the distance. It acted as the perfect landing spot for hot-air balloon tours piloted by Selah. Naomi and Boone, as the chase crew, spent a lot of time together, sitting in foldable camping chairs as they waited for the balloon's return trip.

In the two-and-a-half years they'd worked together, Boone had yet to do anything her sister, Selah, would classify as fire-worthy. Naomi sometimes wondered if she had been wrong about him all along. On the other hand, he was an individual who enjoyed sharing the most fantastical stories of his past with her. Why he continued to lie to her about the silliest things that didn't even matter remained a complete mystery. Like how he supposedly ran a gambling ring in high school behind the gymnasium and once made five hundred dollars during a single lunch period. Yeah, as if students are walking around with that amount of cash. Not at her high school. Or how his dad supposedly used to be friends with Arnold Schwarzenegger and would occasionally have dinner with him when he was the governor of California. Was he testing her gullibility? He conveniently had no photographic evidence and, when it came to Boone, she stuck with the "pics or didn't happen" rule. Or how he ran in a knife gang when he was a kid, even though he had too pretty of a face to pull off this level of toughness. Plus, wouldn't there be scars of some kind? The skin of his she'd been exposed to— granted, it hadn't been very much—had proven to be blemish free. Either he'd been very good with a knife or there hadn't been a knife. She chose to believe the latter.

Also, she just didn't like the cocky son of a bitch. He annoyed the hell out of her. Despite this, whatever his answer to her question regarding enjoying the view would be, it would at least be interesting. Aggravating but interesting, which was better than boring.

She lifted her gaze to meet his, trying not to show how much his eyes continued to make her stomach flip uneasily. Naomi casually pulled a Mexican chili-covered dried strawberry from a Ziploc package, this morning's snack, and ate it. Her cool reaction was ruined when a mischievous glint in his golden eyes caused some extra chili powder to hit the back of her throat, and she couldn't stop the delicate cough erupting from her mouth.

"I was just thinking," Boone started, a lazy finger scraping along his neck as his focus slowly traveled the length of her body, "about the beach and the sun and tropical flowers. I want to take you to an island with a cool breeze and hot sand. I'd lay you out on the beach, brush heaps of that sand over your legs and arms and body until it warms you through to your bones. The sunbeams will make the sweat on your skin and hair glisten like diamonds. And then we'll get up and run directly into the surf, let it wash all our previous sins away, just so we can go out and create new ones together. A small-town girl like you is probably due for that kind of adventure."

"I'd rather sleep with a shark," she replied in a light, faux-friendly voice, a tone she'd perfected for whenever her family was nearby, especially her mother. Although, the thought of being on a tropical island, Boone or no Boone, was a tempting one this chilly May morning as she pulled the zipper on her hoodie upward.

His lips tipped at the ends in amusement. "Now we're getting somewhere. Is that what you're looking for? I can be a shark. I can be anything you want." A dark spark in his eyes told her this might be true.

She shook her head, sighing as if disappointed. "Maybe that's the whole problem with you, Boone. I don't want someone who can be anything. I want someone who I know exactly what they are. That feels like more of a challenge for you."

Naomi had a brief moment of satisfaction as the shine in his expression dimmed briefly before snapping back. He leaned forward, resting his elbows on his knees. "Honey, I don't think even you've figured out who *you* are yet." A confident smile slid into place, his drawl growing country as he leaned back and interlaced his fingers behind his head. "But when you do, I have a feeling we'll all have to watch out. I bet you're going to glitter like a jewel."

See? Their conversations were always a perfect blend of intriguing and aggravating. She busied herself by eating another strawberry as if she wasn't affected by his words, as if they weren't needling their way into her skin.

It wasn't because of his teasing or the invention of silly imagined scenarios featuring tropical beaches. She was used to these. If anything, it was impressive how he could skirt the line of an inappropriate proposition without ever going over it. Regardless of his tone and gaze, she wasn't going to fall for it. She was certain it was all a game to him, something he did to keep the boredom away.

Rather, it was his thought of her as a small-town girl who hadn't come into her own, like an underdone souffle. That bothered her. While it was one of the most straightforward things to ever come from Boone's mouth, she didn't want to be seen in this light. It made her feel boring, stuck, and, well, small. While Naomi had no intention of ever moving away and living in a big city, she didn't like being reduced to this. She wanted to be loud, to be seen, for there to be nothing small about her. Naomi considered snapping that he didn't know her, so how the hell could he know anything?

Too bad it was true. She wasn't any of the things she wanted to be. Day in and day out, she sat in this field with him, on the ground, not even in the open sky like Selah, and then she'd visit with her mother for a time, run some errands, do her Pilates class, watch something on Netflix, and do it all over again. Everything he thought about her was right. She *was* boring. Even her hairstyle was boring.

Suddenly, she despised a life of work and life tasks, of choosing to be subdued instead of sparkling. She stewed, silently eating her chili-peppered strawberry snack. Naomi used to have dreams, dreams about running wedding events at the farm. But she got tired of telling them to her father, and to Selah, neither one of them really listening to her, and she just stopped. She gave up.

Naomi slid into a bad mood, and it was all Boone's fault. She slumped in her chair, crossing her arms.

"Like what you see?" It was his turn to catch her staring as he scrolled through his phone looking at some social media page or dating app—she didn't give a shit—as she glared at him.

"Not really." Naomi couldn't be bothered to invent flowery, fake situations like him, not unless it involved them running into the sea, and him getting bitten by a shark. Not anything big or life-threatening—she wasn't that mean—but a nibble from a baby shark would be enough to wipe that smug expression off his face.

In a continued act of rebellion against her thoughts, he released a smooth, arrogant smile, shaking his head as he continued doing whatever on his phone.

Why wasn't *he* boring? He was stuck in this field, same as her. Is that why he told her those fantastical stories? Did it make his life feel bigger? Perhaps this was the trick, and it made her curious. "What do you do afterward?"

"After our secluded beach time on a tropical island?

Well, Naomi, I'm glad you asked. I'd take you to dinner, where you could order all the spicy foods your half-demon self wanted, and then—"

"No, you bonehead, what do you do after this? After work?" She hoped it was a whole lot of nothing, and she could feel better about her own life.

"Today or any day? If you're that interested, you can join me. Not today, but maybe tomorrow. We can go down into one of the lava tubes, explore the unchartered corners of some dark caverns, and then explore each—"

"Ugh. Just forget the whole thing. I'm sorry I asked." As usual, he never answered questions directly, and she wasn't in the mood to play.

"I climb."

"You what?"

With two fingers, he pantomimed walking upwards. "Climb. You know, scaling the cliffs at Smith Rock or wherever."

"Why?" Naomi hadn't put much thought into the sport, even if it was popular in the area. She always considered it one of those activities done by people who were superhuman and had a death wish. His massive arms, which frequently tested the fiber strength of his sleeves, suddenly made a lot more sense. She tried not to eye them with appreciation, an incredible feat, reminding herself they belonged to someone unlikable.

"I had no idea you were so interested in me." This was said with that tone of amusement she hated.

"This is more of a dark psychological interest, like why rats enjoy swimming." Naomi leaned back in her chair, trying to appear confident in her unknown expertise about rats and their swimming abilities. "Why not today?"

"What?"

"Why can't I *hang* with you today?"

"You want to go rock climbing with me?" He seemed genuinely surprised at this, his eyes lighting up.

"No, of course not. I don't want to be with you any more than necessary. I was just curious about what was so special about today."

His attention shifted to off in the distance. "I have to . . . take care of my cat today."

She snorted in disbelief at this excuse, mainly because she couldn't imagine Boone taking care of anything. He was a lone wolf, not-to-be-nailed-down type of guy, if she'd ever met one. "You don't have a cat."

"I don't?"

"What's the cat's name?"

There was a brief pause as he scratched the beginning makings of a beard on his jawline before he answered, "Cat."

She raised an eyebrow. "A cat named Cat? How original. What kind is it?"

"Orange. I didn't plan on taking the thing in, but I was tricked. I'm telling you, this cat is a bona fide swindler."

Naomi gave him an odd look, wondering how nothing in his life could just be normal. No, this possibly imaginary cat couldn't just be ordinary, but was somehow more fantastic than that. Swindler cat, her foot. She rolled her eyes and chalked it up to one more story he was telling her for his own entertainment.

The two-way radio in Boone's lap crackled to life, Selah's

voice coming through. "Coming in for the approach. Get ready."

"Got it," Boone responded. He and Naomi jumped to their feet because neither one had been paying attention to Selah's return, which was closer than expected.

As the hot-air balloon approached, the burner popped slightly and Selah released air through the envelope vent. Her older sister tossed a rope off the side with a black weighted anchor attached to the bottom. Boone grabbed it with both hands, walking backward until the rope became taut and his rock-climbing arm muscles strained against the seams of his T-shirt. As he pulled and Selah kept the vent open, the balloon lowered to the ground.

As soon as the basketed gondola was low enough, Naomi climbed onto the side, stepping into the footholds and grabbing the metal support struts jutting from the basket's frame. Her weight lowered it more. The balloon shifted, dragging them across the ground as it was prone to do as they tried to land it, but, since accidentally tipping over the gondola the previous year, they'd perfected the system and had gotten better.

"Hi," she said, smiling at the four passengers more cheerfully than she felt at the moment. "Welcome back. We'll put out a small stepladder, but please be careful when climbing from the basket. We want everyone to leave here safely."

By this time, Elena had arrived with the company van. Boone tethered the balloon to Naomi's truck nearby. He then climbed onto the other side of the basket, opposite Naomi, grinning like he loved everything about this. With the basket heavy and secure enough to be stable, the happy passengers disembarked, a few of them slipping Selah monetary tips. Elena excitedly greeted them.

"Hello! Welcome! Wasn't that a wonderful flight? Isn't Selah such a great pilot? She's really the best," her mother said to the crowd as she ushered them to the van to return to the farm, where their vehicles were parked.

Naomi loved her sister, loved how happy flying the balloon made her, and loved how her passengers always applauded her upon landing. Selah earned it, and Naomi was proud of her. Regardless, she also couldn't help being somewhat jealous, especially today when she was feeling insignificant.

"Have a good flight?" she asked her sister.

Selah disengaged the burners and together they tipped the basket onto its side to begin the process of breaking everything down to stow away until the next flight.

"Yeah, it was great. Although there was a moment I thought I'd have to radio in to tell you we were going to land just west of the farm because, on the return, some rogue wind took us in a slightly different direction than I had expected. But then I was able to course correct and, look, right on target. I can't wait to talk to Dex because we had some turkey vulture that seemed to be following us this morning, and I want to know if that's normal." Dex was Selah's fiancé, a state park ranger at Smith Rock, and was their resident expert on local birds.

"So, remember when I mentioned to you a while ago that it might be a good idea if we offered specialized tour packages . . . like weddings and stuff? And you didn't want to talk about it because you thought you were leaving? Well, how about we talk about it again? I do have some really good ideas on what we can—"

"Oh, god. This again?" Selah interrupted while taking ahold of the deflating envelope and stretching it out across the ground with Naomi and Boone's help.

"Come on, Se. I'm trying to be serious about this. Weddings are big business, and we could definitely use some of that. We can offer people a unique experience—"

"Were you not listening when I said that I almost landed in the wrong spot?"

"Okay, but maybe—"

"No, I'm not doing it. I don't know why this is so hard to understand. I'm a pilot. That's what I'm good at. I don't want to be responsible for someone's big day, and then I ruin everything because the wind tips over the basket and dumps the bride out, and now she's suing me for damaging her million-dollar dress. Why would I want to take that kind of risk with our business when it's just beginning to do okay?"

"Alright, but all you would have to do is the piloting, and I'll take care of the rest."

Selah released a frustrated groan while continuing with the task at hand.

"When do *I* get to do something I'm good at? I'm not asking you to do anything more than to let me try. That's all I want. Just to try. I'm here to support you on the ground for as long as you need me, but when are you going to support me?" Naomi wanted to be as strong and determined as her oldest sister, but the emotional parts of her words were hitting her in the gut. Did people not have faith in her? Were her ideas not good?

While this moment of self-doubt had worked on her in the past—enough for her to stop bugging her sister about this topic for at least a year—this time, Naomi was determined. Enough was enough. Naomi was going to push her sister until Boone's opinions about her boring life came back to bite him in the ass. She lifted her chin and stared unflinchingly at Selah.

Her sister studied her, seeming to listen this time, her lips scrunching in thought. "Alright," she finally said.

Naomi's heart lifted with a bubble of unexpected joy. "Really? You'll do it."

"No, no, I didn't say that. You can at least look into it. If you put this project on your shoulders, work out the practicalities, and find someone who actually would pay for a hot-air balloon-themed wedding on our farm, then you might have something."

"Okay, well, I already know a couple getting mar—"

"I don't want to work at my own wedding. Dex and I want to do something small and simple. You need to find someone else. If you want it bad enough, figure it out."

Throwing a huge event was one thing. Finding wedding clients out of thin air was something else entirely. She wasn't sure how she'd pull it off. Either way, she had to because Naomi needed to turn over a new rock in her life with this opportunity.

Despite what Boone thought of her, she wasn't going to live quietly anymore.

Chapter Two

T HE WORD "CON" in con man stood for confidence.

Boone Reyes never had much of a stomach for the actual swindling part of conning people. But the confidence? Yeah, he liked that part. He wasn't a con man, as much as he was a people person with a plan. He enjoyed having people's confidence. And if it got him what he wanted, even better. At least, that was how it used to be.

These days, he was all about trying to get what he considered to be a normal life, one where he didn't have to worry about people finding out about him and cutting him off when they did. He wanted to settle, live, and have people who actually cared about him. Who knew getting this would be harder than obtaining someone's credit card number?

Even more ironic, the person's confidence he wanted the most proved to be as difficult as breaking into Fort Knox. Naomi Moreno. Her soft voice had a husky edge, like something belonging inside a smokey jazz club. It fit with the rest of her, like the sultry toned curves of her body and the smile that turned her eyes into bright crescent moons. Who knew she'd also be the hardest nut to crack? He wanted to—no, he *needed* to—break through. He needed to crack Naomi's shell so hard and so good she wouldn't be able to see a nutcracker without thinking of him. It drove him a little wild, to the point of obsession.

Except this wasn't what he was supposed to be contemplating as he sat on a bench, waiting for his father to emerge from the Deer Ridge Correctional Institute. He shouldn't be thinking about Naomi or how much she burned hot in her apparent despisement for him. He also burned, but not in the same way. He didn't despise her, but, instead, was endlessly frustrated. He hadn't ever broken through. Nothing was believed. Boone could tell her anything, even the truth, which he almost always did, and she never accepted any of it. People believed him more when he'd been lying than she did when he was truthful. Somewhere along the way, he must have lost his touch.

"Boone! My boy!" his father exclaimed, as though he were returning from a long cruise instead of serving time for crimes. With his thick salt-and-pepper hair, he wasn't as tall and broad as Boone, but they shared a confident gait. His light gray-green eyes were perceptive and sharp like a hawk.

Boone stood from the bench, giving the only person who'd ever look out for him a tight smile. "Hey, Dad. Glad you're out again."

Hank swept him into a bear hug, landing a few solid pats on his shoulder. "The Reyes men are back together. You really filled out, didn't you, son? This, and taking all the handsome genes from your old man, we're going to be back on top in no time. You should shave. You know clean-shaven is the path to people's trust." His father rubbed a hand against the smooth plane of his own squared jawline. "What's this I hear about the booming real estate around here? Sounds like some fertile ground for a growing money orchard, am I right?"

A people-person with a plan didn't come from nowhere. Hank was prepared to walk out of prison and directly into some new, exciting scheme. This sometimes got him into trouble, but considering how long he'd been in the game, it was impressive he got away with as much as he had.

The first stint on his record was for embezzling at a high-profile Medford real estate company, costing about six years in prison. After being released, he grabbed Boone from his current sticky situation, and they made a beeline to Central Oregon. Prison internet research gave Hank a new idea of generating money, supporting them for a short time before Hank was arrested again and sent to prison for a few more years.

He wasn't surprised his dad already had new ideas. The difference, this time, was Boone had changed. These last few years, he'd learned to live a small, simple life without having to look over his shoulder or be worried he'd follow his father into prison. "How about we take it easy, old man? No reason to rush into anything." He led his father toward the parking lot.

In society's eyes, there were probably things wrong with Hank, but they might see things wrong with Boone as well. Maybe Naomi saw these things, and this was why she hated him. Even so, he'd always been a man who lived on hope. People gave up way too easily these days, except for him and his dad.

His mother gave up when he was six years old. Lisa and Hank had never been married. Their relationship had been a volatile off-and-on thing, until it was permanently off. Lisa left Boone with Hank and was never heard from again. He only thought of her when there was the smell of stale cigarettes in the air. Hank had never once abandoned Boone, at least not of his own choice. Because of this, Boone had always felt an obligation toward the man, whether trouble was brewing or not.

"What the hell is this?" his father said when they arrived at Boone's old blue hatchback in the parking lot. "I know you said you were laying low, but am I expected to go from Tina to whatever *this* is? Does this thing even have leather seats?" He leaned into the passenger door, shading his eyes to peer through the window like he was shopping at the world's worst used car lot. Tina had been Hank's most beloved possession, a cherry-red Ferrari F355. Seeing Tina seized by authorities had been the only time he'd known his dad to be truly upset, more so than with anything that had happened to Boone.

"Sorry. The limo for your grand reentrance into society is currently in the shop." He tried not to show annoyance, or bring up the fact that because Hank had secretly used Boone's identity to open up several credit lines in the past, his shit credit got him shit items in the present. "If it's too embarrassing, you can stay here." He felt guilty when a small part of him wished this was a real option.

Hank's grimace flipped to an easy smirk. "Ha, funny. You don't know how much I missed my favorite sidekick. I'm even willing to ride in a piece of junk like this."

Getting on the road, his dad chatted about one great idea after another. He also voiced concerns about whether Boone drove too fast because it'd been so long since he'd last ridden in a vehicle, he'd lost the ability to judge speed. As his father spoke, a growing sense of concern filled Boone's gut. What exactly was he supposed to do now? And, more importantly, what was his father going to do? While he didn't mind his dad crashing at his place, as small as it was, Hank would have to fit himself into the lifestyle Boone had become accustomed to, which was inexpensive in its minimalism. Except, the older man had never settled for that kind of life. Hank didn't do normal when he considered himself entitled to more.

"Have you heard anything about Sophie?" his dad asked, to Boone's surprise.

"You know Freya doesn't want either of us to have anything to do with her anymore." Going to prison and paying fines weren't the only consequences of Hank's crimes, including emptying Freya's bank account. Sophie was Boone's much younger half sister from Hank's relationship with her mother. The girl had to be at least sixteen now. It was difficult to imagine her when his brain continued seeing her as a giggly six-year-old with sparkly brown eyes and ears that adorably stuck out. When Boone missed being a big brother, like this morning, he'd sometimes do searches for her on his phone. Unfortunately, Sophie Miller was too common of a name in Oregon. He also had no idea if she was even in the same state anymore, resulting in more hits than he knew what to do with.

What made Hank think about her? Was he finally experiencing regrets? It was different than his normal frame of mind. In Boone's opinion, Hank should be looking to make some kind of financial restitution for all the years she might have gone without due to his greed. Boone had been wanting to do it himself, to make things up to the kid and give her a better shot because she still had potential. If only he could find her.

"So, I take it, based on the car, you're still doing farm-work?" Hank asked.

"I work on a farm, but I'm not doing farmwork."

"That's not what your hands say."

Boone hadn't noticed the state of his hands, giving them a quick inspection. They were tanned, veins crisscrossing over the top, and were calloused and rough. He preferred them when they were covered in white chalk because it meant he was climbing. "I told you I'm part of a chase crew for the hot-air balloon company."

"Oh, that's right. What's the name again? Mondego?"

"Moreno. It's High Desert Tours."

"Oh, yeah. Seems like a cute little business."

Boone slid a glance toward his father, regretting his big mouth revealing anything. He could be a locked safe of information to anyone else, but somehow, his father had the only key to pry him open. When Boone had mentioned his job previously, his father had been in prison, and he didn't think there'd be any harm. His mistake was forgetting there'd be a time when his father would be free. Boone gritted his jaw together to prevent himself from saying any more.

"You know, businesses these days really give you a lot of information on their websites. It's not like the old days when you had to find a company in the Yellow Pages, and do your own research with nothing but a phone number and address. Now you get all that plus pretty pictures, rates, special packages, and all about how their dad died, and now it's the daughters trying to continue their father's legacy. It's all very sweet. Good to know kids care about things like legacy. I'd like to think you feel the same way."

"What legacy?" The irritation seeped from his words because his father's chatter was never as innocent as it seemed. Even though the Moreno women weren't his family, they had—minus Naomi—welcomed and accepted him. Especially Elena, who was warm, loving, and generous to a fault. She was the opposite of Boone's parents. Instead of cigarettes, she smelled of spices and food and a real home. She gave hugs and wanted to take care of him from the beginning, without knowing anything about him. At the time, he'd thought it was foolish, but soon grew protective, wanting to make sure none of the bad parts of life could touch her any more than it already had. Instead of taking advantage, Boone strived to be as good as she imagined him to be.

Hank laughed bitterly. "Come on, son. I taught you resilience and how to make it in this world. You survived, didn't you? There's no reason we need to be like the suckers who scrimp and scrape and work their fingers to the bones. You know who keeps it that way? It's the rich. It's a rigged system. We're just evening the playing field. Nobody makes their way to the top playing nice."

The modern-day Robin Hood sentiment had been repeated often enough, it might as well have been printed and bound in the Reyes's family bible, if such a thing had ever existed. The one thing his dad never lacked was justifications for doing anything.

"Maybe someday I can come out with you. I've never seen a hot-air balloon launch. Perhaps I can meet the family. I already feel like an honorary member, like I know them myself and—What the fuck, Boone?" His father clutched the *oh shit* handle on the passenger side door as Boone took the turn on the next road too fast, stopping short on the dirt lane and sending a plume of dust wafting around them.

Any easiness from Boone's features slipped away as he turned to his father. "You can live with me. You can live your life how you want. But I don't want you on that farm. I don't want the Morenos to know anything about you." In his twenty-eight years, this was the closest Boone had ever gotten to setting a boundary with his dad. He wasn't sure where it had come from, except it was a sudden scared gut instinct telling him that Hank infiltrating his carefully constructed life could ruin everything.

"So, you're embarrassed by the old man?" He held his hands aloft as though this was an innocent misunderstanding. "Relax. I wasn't going to do anything. I can't take an interest in my own kid?"

"Yeah, sure, right." He wasn't surprised his father was playing the poor, misunderstood victim. "Stay away from that farm. I'm serious. Especially with Naomi—"

"*Especially* Naomi?" His father's brow rose, those hawk-like eyes sparking with interest. "And who is this? One of the pretty little daughters?"

God dammit. Boone had set out to make his dad less curious and had failed. "It doesn't matter because she'd sniff you out so fast, you'd probably break parole violations moving to another state, just to escape her scrutiny. She hates me, which should tell you everything you need to know."

His father's lips quirked at this. "Okay, okay, got it. Although, I'm intrigued." Hank's gaze changed directions toward the window, escaping Boone's hard glare. "Doesn't matter. I have my own plans anyway." Boone wasn't about to inquire what those were because the less he knew, the more he could claim ignorance and innocence. Whoever was desperate enough to get into business with Hank wasn't Boone's problem. "But If I ever need a getaway driver, I'll be sure to cut you in because, goddamn, you can take a corner like a professional wheelman." Hank chuckled, as though the whole thing was a joke.

Boone continued to home, pulling alongside an older, single-wide trailer behind a large, decrepit barn on the Crockett farm. At the sound of the vehicle, an orange feline, now named Cat, stretched his rear legs after crawling from beneath the trailer.

As he had told Naomi earlier, he'd had no intention of owning a cat, but this one had appeared out of nowhere, chirping pitifully and limping. Feeling bad and assuming it may have been hit by a passing car, Boone let the animal into his trailer, fed it a can of tuna, and suddenly the limp disappeared as the cat strolled to his recliner, jumping on it and claiming a new nap spot. Boone couldn't believe he'd been bamboozled by a cat, but he couldn't be mad. Game recognized game. They belonged together.

Hank stepped from the passenger side of the car, interlocking his fingers behind his head while squinting toward the run-down trailer with clear judgment passing over his features. "You have got to be joking."

THE FOLLOWING MORNING, Boone stretched kinks from his back. His dad had talked him into giving up the only bedroom, relegating him to the couch for the night. There were no balloon tours today, and Boone went to Smith Rock to climb his stress away. Climbing required his complete focus and attention. Everything else fell away.

After grabbing his black climbing bag from the trunk, he hiked the snaking river trail along the base of the giant, jagged orange rocks that made Smith Rock spectacular. It had been a popular place for sport climbing since its birth in the early 1980s.

"Hey, Boone, how's it going?" Alan, a local instructor and climbing regular, was at the base of a rock known as Morning Glory Wall. It wasn't a surprise the instructor was here, as it was a popular one to start beginners with. Boone planned to climb the rock beside it for a warm-up. It was challenging but not as dangerous as some of the other climbs since Boone preferred going free solo, both in climbing and in life. While it could be reckless not using all the climbing equipment or a partner, he preferred not to depend on someone else, nor have anyone relying upon him.

Alan, a big white guy with shaggy, dirty-blond hair, had large arms covered in tattoos, the artwork inspired by different climbing locations. It was as if he was using his body as a canvas for old travel stickers rather than a steamer trunk. He acted as belayer to a rock-climbing student, a man with a shiny black helmet, who panted hard while scaling the Morning Glory Wall without much confidence.

"I'm doing okay. Eager to get on a rock. You know how it is." Boone put on his own scratched-up helmet, securing it. It wouldn't necessarily save him if the worst happened, like experiencing a long fall known as a screamer, but he did take a few precautions.

"Still going at it alone?"

"That's how I like to travel." Boone gave Alan a confident thumbs-up.

The guy shook his head in disapproval, not a surprising response from the most "safety first" person out of all the instructors working for Central Oregon Cliff Climbs. "You doing okay there, buddy?" Alan shouted to the student struggling on the rock.

The man huffed some heavy breaths. "I don't know how to do this next part."

"Just relax. Think about when we did the route reading on the ground. You're right at the crux now. Remember where we talked about doing a slight heel hook?"

"I don't think I can do that."

"Sure you can. You just have to fully commit. I got you, if you can't. No worries."

Boone finished putting on his climbing shoes and patted his hands with white chalk until they were dry enough to grip well. He'd done this enough times for climbing to be second nature to him, giving him the outlet he needed when nothing else made sense. Boone understood the rock. It was straightforward. Easy. This one climb, in particular, felt intuitive. He was able to scale at a faster pace than most because he didn't have to worry about the rope or clipping into bolts. By the time he'd reached the top, the student hadn't gotten much farther. Boone marked his accomplishment in his head before making the trek down.

"Where you headed next?" Alan asked once Boone was on the ground again.

"Might see if Cinnamon Slab is open."

"Nice. My younger sister loves that one." Katie was a few years younger than Alan. She also worked for Cliff Climbs and was as good of a climber as any of them.

"I don't suppose you know of anyone leaving and another instructor position opening at your company, do you?" He'd heard *no* enough when he first looked into them for employment not to get his hopes up, but it had been a while since the last time he inquired.

"Haven't heard anyone's leaving," Alan replied before stopping. "Well, actually . . ." He tipped his head, as though in thought, as he increased the rope's tension.

"Alan?" Boone was impatient for the rest of the sentence.

"Oh, nothing, except we just got bought out by a larger nationwide company that focuses on outdoor excursions and experiences. My boss will still be managing things, and we're not changing our name, at least not yet. He did say they were looking to expand, and he's going to be doing more of the business stuff and not instructing anymore. So, yeah, maybe we might need someone else soon."

"Great. Think you could put in a good word for me?" Boone's mind was already buzzing. If he could do High Desert Tours early morning and climbs afterward, it would provide some extra cash while doing what he liked. It also made his idea of helping Sophie, if he ever found her, more of a possibility. He wanted this more than anything.

Alan cut him a look. "Are you serious?"

"I know these rocks just as well as anyone." Boone wasn't sure Alan was a friend, but what they had was close enough. He hoped the man liked him enough to help, and was kicking himself for not building the confidence between them sooner.

"Well, yeah, I'm not saying you don't, but—"

"You know I can do it. I'm out here all the time—"

"It's not that. It's not just about the rocks. It's about being a good instructor. You know my boss is a real stickler about the company's reputation for being the best and getting high marks for safety. It's why this other company fought so hard for us."

"Come on, Alan. I can teach. I can be encouraging." Boone cupped one hand alongside his mouth to amplify his voice before shouting, "You're doing really great up there, pal. Keep going," demonstrating his skill as a rock-climbing cheerleader.

This resulted in a glare from Alan, probably because he didn't appreciate his whole job being boiled down to yelling encouraging words at people. This was a mistake on Boone's part, as he knew there was a lot more to it than that, but this was his biggest shot, and he didn't want to blow it. Alan had a lot of sway with the boss.

"You rarely climb with anyone. You're a free solo guy. This job is about building trust. It's not just them trusting you, but *you* have to trust them as well. It's the trust, the communication. The student should know you're looking out for them and won't let them plunge to their death."

"Wait. What was that?" the student asked between breaths, sounding concerned.

"Nothing. You're doing great, man. You're almost to that next bolt," Alan yelled.

"I've done lead climbing before, and I'm a certified belayer. Can I just try out or something? Give me a chance here." This was the closest to begging Boone did.

Alan took in the rope's slack, locking in a new position for his climber. "I'll tell you what, if I see you working with someone out here, teaching some newb how to climb, showing that you're not just some reckless loner, I'll talk to Will about it."

There was joy at knowing it was at least something. "I can do that. I'll bet my student will be able to climb faster than y—"

"Nope. This isn't a competition. Everyone is going to do it the safe way."

"Yeah. Okay." Boone left with his bag slung over his shoulder, his brain racing as he hiked his way to the parking lot. He was slightly annoyed he wasn't able to charm his way into this job as easily as he'd done at High Desert Tours. He'd actually have to fight for it, but it was also an intriguing challenge. Who was going to be his student? He didn't know anyone besides other climbers. He could ask Hank, but getting his dad's help in landing a job would never come without a price. He was notorious for depositing favors today with the expectation that similar ones with interest would be withdrawn later. Boone couldn't get trapped into anything.

Then it hit him.

The thing about being an ex-confidence man was there were things Boone was great at. Two of these things were listening and observing. Hang around someone long enough, and they will reveal all kinds of things about themselves. He never planned on using the information, but he hoarded everything away like diamonds because he couldn't help it. It was in his nature, and one just never knew.

Naomi Moreno was a romantic. All those old movies and books, where people danced in a great hall and drank tea and spoke about love matches—she was a sucker for them. Maybe it was why, when she talked about weddings and events, her eyes glittered with excitement. She wanted, more than anything, for Selah to take her ideas seriously.

Boone, like Selah, thought all this fancy-pants wedding stuff was frivolous. He didn't care about any of it because he doubted it would ever pertain to his life. But regardless of his personal opinion on weddings, he also realized there was a lot of money in it. Boone couldn't help but see potential. In this respect, he was on Naomi's side completely.

How hard could it be to find a couple of lovey-dovey marks to commit to a hot-air balloon wedding? It shouldn't be difficult at all for someone with his particular talent, a person who had sold people on all kinds of useless ideas. It was no different from hatching any other plot, but better because, ethically, he wasn't ultimately cheating anyone, and everyone would have a happy ending. His dad wasn't the only one who was inspired by a new idea.

His brain turned things over on how he could use what he knew to not only help Naomi, but help his situation as well. Boone told himself this was all that it was—a friendly negotiation of favors and nothing to do with cracking her shell.

Chapter Three

"ARE YOU JUST going to keep staring at me?" Naomi asked before realizing she wasn't sure she wanted an answer from him today.

"I'm sorry. Did you *not* want me to look? If that was the case, maybe you shouldn't have come in looking like a sparkly stick of dynamite."

This morning, Boone could have been looking at her for all kinds of reasons. Maybe he'd forgotten his phone, and being buggy was his single source of entertainment. Perhaps he stared out of habit because he always did on tour days.

Or it could have been the bright raspberry-pink hair.

Yeah, that was probably it.

This morning's new hair was the result of inviting her best friend, Amber, over for tacos, wine, and a *Pride and Prejudice* movie re-watch after co-teaching their Pilates for Seniors class. This led to Naomi crying about how she wasn't a feisty heroine, like an Elizabeth Bennet, but was instead a quiet sidekick, like Charlotte Lucas. The evidence being her whole life, but in particular, her hair being the same since high school.

Amber, being a loving and supportive friend—even more after a few glasses of wine—helped Naomi rectify the problem, or at least the most fixable one. It felt like a sign when they found the hair color packaging Naomi had purchased several months ago on a whim but hadn't fully committed to trying.

Hence, waking with a head full of bright-pink strands and being compared to sparkly dynamite. She was invisible no more.

Surprisingly, the only thing Naomi regretted was the slight headache this morning. The hair, though? She fell in love straight away, the best decision-made-under-alcohol she'd ever had. Maybe she was meant to be a pink-haired girl all along, and had chosen an outfit to match the new Naomi Moreno—cowboy boots, distressed denim shorts she'd never been brave enough to wear because of the short length, and a white, cropped tank top.

Unfortunately, sexy didn't keep one warm, and wardrobe decisions quickly became her second regret, until Boone arrived. His double take was the closest she'd ever witnessed to him looking like he fell on his ass, making her want to guffaw in his cocky face. A satisfied Naomi ate her spicy dried strawberries and flicked her pink hair while flipping through a Deschutes Parks and Rec class catalog that had arrived in the mail the day before. It had to be another sign to show she was a new, confident woman looking to discover herself further.

"I don't care what you think about anything," she answered him, turning to a new page.

"You sure about that?"

"How about this for a hint?" Without looking at him, Naomi raised her middle finger to casually brush an eyebrow and flip him off at the same time. This was something she'd never done before, and she was shocked at how much gall the pink-haired version of herself had. It was as if she'd unlocked a superpower and she loved it.

He chuckled with delight. "I think I'm really going to like this."

She wished this comment didn't set off a parade of butterflies in her stomach. That wasn't supposed to be the point of new Naomi. "Whatever. All I know is that there's nothing boring and small town about this."

His lack of response made her wish she hadn't said that. Despite the truth, he must be thinking she'd done all this for him, which was the last thing she needed. She was surprised when he didn't chime in with arrogance, but instead said softly, "I didn't mean for you to take it that way. Is that what this is about?"

"No. Like I said, I don't care what you think. I just wanted a change. Not everything is about you, Boone. Some of us strive to improve ourselves." She displayed the catalog in her hands as evidence of this.

His eyes sparked with interest. "Come on, you don't want to take one of those overpriced classes from some amateur. How about I offer you something even better?"

She threw him a flat look. Naomi flipped through the pages, folding the catalog over and tossing it onto his lap. "Apparently, I'm one of those overpriced *amateurs*."

Boone picked up the catalog. After a few moments of scanning the page, his eyes widened. "Pilates for Seniors? I didn't know you did that."

"Yeah, because you don't know everything about me. I

have a life outside of this, and it's none of your business."

A grin slid into place. "Actually, I think that's great. I'm sure you're really good at it. Probably better than most of the other teachers in this catalog."

She rolled her eyes at his attempt to turn his original dismissal around. Naomi got the impression he was buttering her up for something, and, as usual, she didn't trust it. He'd probably create some story about how he traveled to Tibet and had been a student of the Dalai Lama to impress her or show her how much cooler he was compared to her.

Except he surprised her with, "Maybe I can get some tips from you on being an instructor. I'm looking into being one for Cliff Climbs. I could really use some of your brilliant insight."

"Here's a tip. Maybe don't call other instructors amateurs." Naomi had no idea what Cliff Climbs was, but assumed it was some rock-climbing thing.

He handed her back the catalog, clearing his throat. "I don't suppose, in your world of self-improvement, you might consider trying climbing. Take a lesson or two for the fair price of free."

She barked a laugh and returned to flipping through the catalog. "With you? I don't think so."

"I'm just trying to help, Pinky. You want to break out? Do something fun and a little risky? Show people that you're not this sweet, nice girl, but someone who wants to push herself both mentally and physically? Come out with me. Let's do it. It's going to be way more exciting than anything else you'll find in that catalog."

"Pinky?" She wasn't sure she liked the nickname, or hated it because it was given by *him*. Either way, spending more time in his presence was a recipe for disaster, and this was before scaling a death cliff was taken into consideration. "I don't think—"

"How about this? You take lessons with me, and I'll help you land your first wedding client. I can be . . . useful for getting people on board with your ideas. And you can finally show Selah that this plan of yours is a good one."

She paused, not only because she wasn't sure what he meant by *useful*, but she was shocked he believed in her plan more than her own sister. "You think a hot-air balloon wedding is a good idea?"

"Yeah, of course. I think most of the ideas you come up with for the company are good." His brow lifted in apparent sincerity. If it was anyone else, she would have felt encouraged.

Something inside her wanted to believe him. On the other hand, it also made her suspicious. "If my ideas are so great, why would I need your help?"

"I'm not saying you need my help as much as I could make things easier for you because I have certain abilities."

What, in the Liam Neeson hell, did that mean? Naomi crossed her arms. "And how is that?"

His cat-like gaze washed over her, and she tried to ignore how it made her skin buzz. "Let's just say I'm pretty resourceful at getting what I want and convincing people."

She scoffed with disbelief. "And, yet, somehow *I'm* not convinced."

He casually crossed his hands behind his head, which accentuated his biceps. She struggled to maintain eye contact. "Well, Pinky, you'll always be my greatest challenge. I'm trying to go about things the right way for once. We can both benefit here."

Did that mean he'd gone about things the wrong way before? And what did that entail? Naomi found herself intrigued by the mystery he was. Although, not enough to agree to anything. Pink-haired Naomi wasn't reckless enough to jump to the dark side already. "Let's cut the bullshit, Boone. What exactly are you trying to do here?"

"Nothing. Just a friendly you-help-me-and-I'll-help-you type of situation."

"Okay, but helping me isn't going to require you to put your life in my hands, and the same can't be said the other way around. Look at who you are. You're some carefree, arrogant lone wolf." She threw a hand in his direction. "You really think I'm going to feel comfortable risking my life with you?"

The confident expression vanished from his face, and Naomi felt bad for her harsh remarks. His focus drifted away, not saying anything. There was something deeper, maybe darker, and also sad here. Regardless of his comments about her being small town or not knowing who she was, they weren't as mean as her own words.

Old Naomi swallowed the bubble of guilt in her throat, returning to her catalog and attempting to concentrate. She'd always told Boone what was on her mind without any censorship. Naomi didn't have this with anyone else, not even Amber or her family. She could say whatever she wanted to Boone. He'd take all her words, even the ones meant to strike him, as though he secured a piece of Teflon to his chest before getting dressed in the morning. But this time, his quietness bothered her. She hadn't realized there'd been a line, that he'd been trying to do something for her, and she'd bulldozed over it.

She glanced at him while sweeping her hair to one side. "How's Cat?"

"Who?"

Her temporary bout with sympathy died at knowing he'd lied to her again. "You already forgetting about your imaginary pet?"

"Oh. No. He's fine."

"A name and a sex? He clearly must be real then."

Boone suddenly scooted his seat closer until it was practically butted to hers. "What the hell are you doing?" She tried to move her chair back, to reclaim her five feet of space again, but the bottom of the chair legs sunk stubbornly into the dirt.

"Okay, look." He leaned forward with those tanned, strong forearms of his resting on his thighs. This put him in her direct line of sight, his golden-brown eyes demanding her attention. "It was a stray cat that I offered some tuna, and now he won't leave. So, I'm doing things like buying a bag of actual cat food and making a little *pss-pss* noise to get him to come to me. And you're right that I didn't have an actual real name for him because I just think of him as *the cat*. So when you asked me, that was the only name I could think of."

"Oh." Why was he telling her, and why did any of this matter? For whatever reason, this one insignificant detail of his whole enigmatic life seemed important enough for her to know. And it felt . . . well, ordinary and personal, as if he was a regular person instead of some mysterious scoundrel. Perhaps this was the whole point. He finally gave her something of substance.

"That was sweet of you to take him in. What kind of cat did you say he was?"

"Orange with darker stripes and light-green eyes. He likes to be held—like a baby. And he sits by his bowl at exactly four o'clock, like he can tell the goddamn time."

The picture this created in her head warmed her soul. "When I was a kid, we had a dog named Sweetpaws that seemed to be able to tell time too."

A slow smile eased across his face, his posture relaxing. "Sweetpaws?"

"Don't even start. I named him when I was six, and I thought it was cute—"

"I'm not saying it's not." His gaze swept across her face.

"It's better than Cat."

"I'm really liking the pink. It suits you, like an unexpected swell in a symphony." He took a long, wavy strand, rubbing the hair between a finger and thumb as though fascinated by it, before lifting his head to catch her eyes. A breeze tousled his hair, sending his soap's scent floating in her direction. It was something spicy, like cloves mixed with cedar. Even with his facial hair, his lips were visible, and they were usually clever and expressive, but at the moment, they were soft, inviting.

"Stop trying to charm me." This helped anchor herself to reality before things got carried away. Old Naomi wasn't letting go easily.

He frowned, releasing her hair. "Why are you so resistant to nice words? It doesn't have to be this way."

"I'm not resistant to them, only to you."

He rubbed his temple as though fighting off a headache. "What exactly do you want from me?"

"It's easy. Stop making it seem like you're trying to sell me on something, and talk to me like a normal person."

He released a grumble tinged with bitterness. "I'm not sure what normal is coming from me. This *is* normal. This is who I am."

"Then just give me the truth. Why do you want to teach me? Why is it important?"

"I've been trying to get this instructor's job for a while, and this time it feels like a real possibility, but, like you, they don't see my qualifications or skills. I'm just some untested guy who's a bit reckless. They don't trust me with the company's reputation. But Alan said if I could show that I could teach someone, maybe it'll be enough."

"Would you be leaving High Desert Tours, then?" As much as she was eager not to work with him anymore, it would put their company in a bind. She wasn't sure she wanted to explain this to Selah, especially if she helped him get it.

"The hours here are early. I should be able to manage both." He leaned forward again. "So, what do you think?"

She wasn't sure. Her? Rock climbing? When she perused the catalog, she'd considered taking a class on foraging or cake decorating. Climbing was on a different level. Yeah, she was in good shape as she hiked and exercised regularly, but— Could she do it? Naomi wasn't as brave as her new hair color made it seem. What if she was bad at it? What if her failure meant he didn't get the job? What if it was too scary?

"I don't know. I'm not sure if I'm ready for something like that." She didn't want to commit, not to him. Plus, in this deal, she was doing him a favor more than he was doing one for her. She didn't need him. And didn't want to need him.

He reached toward her, palm side up. "Let me see your hand."

"Why?" Unless it was accidental, she and Boone didn't touch often. The logical side of her brain wasn't sure why this made her heart anxious, as though some of his charismatic energy could pass through her, putting her under a spell through skin-to-skin contact. It was better to not take the risk.

"I'm not going to hurt you. You can put the claws away." She wondered if he'd said something similar to Cat in an effort to befriend the stray feline. It was childish of her to be more scared of him than an animal. And there was no way she wanted to be held like a baby in those muscled arms. Not much anyway.

She clucked her tongue in annoyance, as if giving into his demands didn't affect her one way or the other, placing one of her hands in the space between them. He took her hand gently between his large ones. He began to massage it, and while his skin was rough and calloused, every muscle on every finger was strong. This small massage felt better than some of the full-body ones she'd received in her life. It was tempting to relax in her chair, giving over with a groan, but she didn't dare. The man had to be excellent at climbing because the control and strength in his fingers alone were impressive.

After a moment, he returned his attention to her face. "I know we've never gotten along. Although we both know it's been entirely one-sided, since I haven't really done anything to inspire your intense dislike." Naomi didn't need accusations, regardless of the truth. She pulled away, but he gripped enough to trap her hand within his hold.

His voice turned low and soft, like heavy fog rolling through the hillside. "Now, now, relax, honey. I just want you to listen. As I said, we've never gotten along. Maybe I did do something to piss you off, or you just don't like my face. I don't know, and that's okay. But let me tell you what I've noticed about you. Besides being incredibly stubborn, you're not what people expect. People underestimate you. You're able to slide under the radar because maybe they look at you, and all they see is a sweet, pretty girl, and think that's all there is—that there's nothing else to discover."

"Gee, thanks," Naomi said with sarcasm. She didn't appreciate the hand massage turning into a palm reading. Worse, she didn't like how true everything felt. Not anything specific, but close enough to be uncomfortable, like he somehow could see into her life too well. What he saw wasn't flattering, and it annoyed her.

Boone continued, "And while you are pretty and can be very sweet, at least to other people, you also have this intense flame burning inside of you, wanting to get out, to be seen. This is why you decided to color your hair on a whim. Yes, on a whim. You may fool a lot of people, but you can't fool me, Naomi Moreno, just like I can't fool you. Maybe someday we'll talk about it, but not today. But this flame makes you capable of doing a lot more than you think. You *can* do it. You can scale mountains if you want to. And I can give you the tools to do it. The only thing holding you back right now is fear, and you don't need to be afraid of it or me."

Well, shit.

Naomi was dumbfounded. She'd made a mistake in assuming the unserious, breezy Boone from the last couple of years was his final form. He hadn't even been fully flexing his charisma muscles. He was right. *That* was him trying to be normal. But this? This was something else, something that could get her to believe him. It would be easy to fall under a spell and let him smooth-talk her into anything. Or, worse, fall in love, because no one else on Earth understood her as much as Boone had at this moment.

"Will you at least think about it?" he asked, his tone gentle, his fingers stroking along the individual tendons of her hand, giving her the same heady effect she had after drinking the wine that led to her raspberry-pink dye job.

"Okay. I'll think about it." Her lips saying words opposite of her brain must prove he also had abilities in hypnosis. She shouldn't be held accountable for whatever she did or said in such a moment or why she yearned for him to touch her more.

His eyes grew heavy and soft, as though he was falling into a trance himself. One of his hands gently slid along her wrist to the outside of her forearm. Her own drifted across the inside of his arm, her nails lightly scratching the surface of his skin. She should have brought a jacket because a shiver passed through her. He was the definition of warmth, like a mug of hot cider—

"Hey, I think the landing is going to overshoot our original spot about fifty yards or so," came Selah's voice, crackling over the two-way radio.

The hot-air balloon's arrival catching them off guard was turning into a bad habit. Naomi leaped from her chair, nearly knocking Boone over, breaking the spell.

"Shit," he said as he scrambled for the radio. She dropped the paper catalog on the ground, its pages fluttering in the wind. "Yeah, okay. We got it," Boone replied into the radio.

Naomi's heart raced as though she'd been caught at something. They were moments away from Elena appearing with the van, and her mother would have seen her doing . . . what? She hadn't been doing anything. Even so. It was better if Boone kept his chair at a sensible distance away, so whatever it was, it wouldn't happen again.

They grabbed their chairs without folding them, tossing them in the bed of her truck. In the driver's seat, she turned the ignition as Boone got in. The chasing part of the chase crew was on. "You see what direction they're headed?"

"Looking." He leaned out the passenger window, studying the sky.

"My mom is on the way." Her rearview mirror showed the white van approaching.

"Okay, start driving that way toward Smith." He did a shrill whistle from the window to catch Elena's attention and pointed to where they were moving the operation.

The balloon descended quickly, a giant shadow falling

across them as they drove, blocking out the sun with the giant envelope. After parking, they jumped into action as they helped guide and secure the balloon's landing.

"Welcome back, everyone," Naomi said with extra cheer as she climbed onto the outside edge of the basket to steady it. "Did we make any good memories today?"

Selah threw her an odd look. Naomi hoped it was because she acted more chipper than usual, and not because her sister figured out what had been happening on the ground between her and Boone—which, again, wasn't anything. The rest of the passengers whooped excitedly as one of the women presented a bejeweled hand, featuring a sparkling rock on her third finger.

"I'm getting married!" she screamed, setting off cheers from the rest of the group.

"Congratulations. It's beautiful." Naomi smiled, trying to act naturally instead of an invader at the party. "Have you ever thought about having a hot-air balloon wedding—"

"I'm getting married! Look at my ring!" the woman shouted at Boone, who'd climbed onto the other side of the basket, grounding it further.

"Aww. So, there's no hope for the two of us? Now you're just breaking my heart," he replied, a grin snapping into place.

The bride shrieked in laughter at this, drunk on the attention, as she clamped an arm around the future groom before being struck by inspiration. "Oh my god! We have to start planning the bachelorette party! Girls, we need to go to Vegas!" This created more excitement within the group, so much so, Naomi couldn't get another word in before they all climbed from the basket, with the bride showing off her ring to Elena.

Naomi hung on the basket with Boone on the other side. A crabbiness draped across her mood. It didn't help that his expression was his usual confident one. His eyebrows pumped in a flirty manner. "Come on, Pinky. You know you want to."

She sucked in a breath, not sure what she was getting herself into and going for it anyway. "Alright, fine," she replied. "You have a deal."

Her fate with the devilish Boone was sealed. Heaven help her.

Chapter Four

BOONE WAS ALL too happy to escape the trailer these days. His home was small enough with him alone, but with another grown adult, it was suffocating. Especially when his dad complained about feeling locked away again and getting cabin fever. Boredom was always a precursor to trouble for the elder Reyes.

"Then go get a job, like the rest of us," Boone responded, tired of hearing about it.

He might have followed this advice because, the following day, his father was counting a wad of small bills in the kitchen, asking if Boone needed anything when he went out.

"Where'd you get that money?" He tried not to sound suspicious.

"Will you relax? I didn't do anything wrong. Just did a couple of favors out there, like a good citizen."

This wasn't reassuring, considering his father's idea of "good" didn't line up with the rest of society's. Regardless, Boone didn't dig into the particulars. It wasn't his business.

Besides, he had better things to do, like meeting Naomi at a climbing gym. While Boone was eager to jump in and start her off climbing at Smith Rock, her reluctance over the past week was enough to worry she'd change her mind. He conceded they could start in a more controlled indoor setting, such as at Bend Rock Gym.

The excitement shooting through his veins was from a good plan coming together. Obviously, the goal was to show Alan he'd be a great addition to the team and not at all anything to do with Naomi in particular. While Boone had been able to convince himself of a great many things, he failed to do so here.

For one thing, the old version of Naomi already had him absentmindedly scratching his chest, experiencing things a lone wolf shouldn't feel for anyone, wondering if he needed the use of his heart after all. It was like Superman discovering he had other vulnerabilities besides Kryptonite. But the new her, the one who wanted to show the world she wasn't quiet, with her colorful hair and take-no-shit attitude, set his blood afire. Even climbing wasn't enough to clear his mind anymore.

When he arrived at Bend Rock Gym, he didn't see her truck in the parking lot, and went inside to wait. While he preferred climbing outdoors, this gym wasn't a bad place to start. It was a huge open warehouse type of space with a variety of different wall challenges covered in various colored rubber hand and footholds. Beneath all the climbing walls were blue safety fall pads. As he waited, Boone chatted with Tom, an overly friendly employee behind the counter.

"I hit 'More Sandy Than Kevin' this last week," Tom said, brushing his wild, wavy hair from his forehead. "Got my line tangled, switching to the next pitch, and had to redo the sequence three times. It was a real bitch, but I got it done eventually." While Boone didn't climb with the rope often, he'd done it enough to understand the frustration of having to move from one rock route to another one, especially when the location made it tricky.

"What's the grade?" Boone leaned casually against the counter, keeping most of his attention on the door.

"It's 5.11a. Been a while since I did one at that level, but sometimes you have to challenge yourself. Let yourself feel alive, you know."

"Yeah, I know exactly what you m—"

Naomi pushed through the door like a burst of spring sunshine, her bright-pink hair pulled into a high ponytail. She wore workout clothes of a baby-blue tank top and light gray joggers and held a pale-peach water canister. Her glorious figure was on full display, looking like a lollipop on legs. He wanted to lick her everywhere. When her gaze met his, his brain disconnected.

"Damn," Tom said beside him. "That's a grade I'd like to climb."

Boone resisted the temptation to send a death glare toward the man. An unexpected kick of possessiveness took hold. His soul transformed into a bull hoofing at the ground in frustration, grunting hot breaths of steam, like he was a goddamn Looney Toons cartoon.

"Hi," Naomi said as she approached, her keys jangling in one hand nervously.

"Oh, shit, you know her?" the Bend Rock Gym employee asked. "Hey there. I'm Boone's friend, Thomas . . . Tom. Welcome." Boone didn't know where the guy got off with that claim because they were definitely not friends—at least, not today.

She gave him one of her sweet smiles, one reserved for people who weren't Boone. "I'm Naomi. I'm—"

"*My* student," he interrupted. The words emerged more growl-like than intended, and she threw a confused look in his direction. His brain must have gone into panic mode because he continued with, "If you're here to learn how to climb, you need to come on time. We're not here to social-ize."

Who *the hell* had he become? Boone had never been a stickler for time, having a casual relationship with a clock for most of his life. It was only in the last few years he'd made an effort to keep an alarm in order to show up at the Moreno farm in time for launches.

As expected, Naomi's soft expression melted away, re-placed with the standard scowl he was well familiar with. It made things more normal. Good. It better stay this way for his sake. She flicked her wrist to check the time on her smartwatch. "I'm, what, two minutes late?"

"Five." He was being ridiculous, but he couldn't switch his attitude over. He was as annoyed with himself as much as he was with everyone else.

She rolled her eyes. "Oh no. Has my tardiness thrown off your whole day of loafing?"

He almost cracked a smile. Boone liked when Naomi gave him shit because it felt like a tease, a prelude to some-thing else—something better. But he kept his stern expression in place.

"Day pass." His grumpiness made it impossible to use full sentences.

"Oh, did you need a day pass?" Tom snapped into work

mode. She paid and filled out the safety release form, being sugary nice to the employee while sneaking glares at Boone.

When Tom awkwardly complimented Naomi on her penmanship, he grew impatient again. "Come on, man, just finish up and let us go. You don't need to flirt with her."

Except Naomi then leaned on the counter, smiling at Tom as she reached for her water canister on the counter. "So, if this lesson thing doesn't work out with him, are there other instructors I can talk w—"

Boone had enough, grabbing one of her arms and pulling her away from the counter. She wrenched from his grip. "What the hell is wrong with you?"

"Look, I'm not here to fool around. I need you to take this seriously." No, really. *Who had he become?* He was as baffled as her.

"I'm surprised you have a serious bone in your body. If you're going to snap at me, manhandle me, or just be grouchy, then we can forget the whole thing. I'm doing you a favor here, remember? I don't need this."

She was right. If she walked out the door, there wouldn't have been anyone to blame but himself—and a little bit of Tom . . . but mostly himself. He'd find himself in the same situation of having to find a new student. Boone forced a calming breath through his lungs. "Okay. I'm sorry. I'm"— he didn't know how to finish the sentence as he wasn't sure what he was—"nervous." This had to be nerves, right?

She crossed her arms, not appearing sympathetic to his confession. "I don't believe you've ever had a nervous moment in your life."

He sighed, tired of being seen through a negative lens,

but pushed forward. "Can we start over, please?"

She mulled over his request before her brow raised in a manner that said *fine*.

Boone stepped nearer into her space, her face one of defiance as she maintained eye contact. "Thank you for coming and letting me give you a lesson. It's not going to be easy, but I like climbing, and I hope it'll be the same for you."

She appeared not sure what to make of this before softening, dropping her arms to her side. "I'm already sweating from nerves."

"I find that hard to believe. I don't think a girl with pink hair gets nervous." He gave her a small smile.

"Except the pink hair is new."

"I think the pink hair has always been there, just waiting to come out."

Those full lips parted in surprise as an attractive blush spread across her cheeks. A sense of pride popped inside his chest. Naomi may think she was resistant to his charms, but she wasn't as much as she thought. It was shocking how much this gave him such a positive, warm feeling as well. Especially since he meant the words and didn't have to lie.

"Come on," he said, breaking the moment because he knew it would be too easy to get distracted by her, and this wasn't why they were here. "Let's get started."

He led her to one of the beginner walls, away from the other climbers. As her gaze rose, her eyes grew large, as though they were standing before Everest.

"So, obviously, the goal is to make it to the top. These handholds are in different colors. Each specific color goes together for a certain route. But the important part is to stand back and read the route before you start. This way, you can see where your path is and know what sequence of movements you'll need to take to get to the top."

"Okay, but . . ." She looked toward people on the other side of the gym who were doing top rope climbs. "Am I not going to be wearing equipment like everyone else?"

He secured a helmet on her head. "Not yet. You're gonna climb this wall to start—"

"I've never done this in my life, and you're just going to toss me into a free solo climb."

"It's not free solo. This is just bouldering."

"There's a difference?"

"Well, yeah, the height. This isn't even that tall."

"Not that tall?" Her chest moved with increased breaths as she wiped her palms across her legs.

He took a step behind her, speaking low in her ear as he took her wrist and placed her hand on an easy-to-reach hold. "Breathe. It's just one movement at a time. How about we just go as high as you're comfortable with?"

"You're going to do this with me?"

"Mm-hmm," he said. Obviously, he would be climbing next to her—not pressed against her, even if he wanted to. It would be impossible. Regardless, he couldn't stop thinking about how soft the skin on the back of her neck looked. How much she invaded his senses with the scent of sweet berries. He had an urge to slide his other arm around her middle to pull her even closer and breathe her into his lungs, to calm the impatient bull inside his soul.

"Okay, one movement at a time," she said.

Reluctantly, he stepped back, watching as she placed one

foot on a hold, then the other, before reaching to grab the next handhold. He could see the strength of her shoulder muscles working as she pulled herself upward, mesmerized by it. Was this how some ladies felt by watching a muscled man doing physical labor? Because, yeah, he got it now. Her flexibility and intentional control in choosing her movements, although slow, had to be the result of the Pilates she did. His imagination wandered toward what it would be like to have her as a regular climbing partner. He liked the idea.

"I thought you were going to climb with me," she hollered, her voice straining.

He took the route beside hers, ascending until they were even, about halfway up the wall. Tiny dots of perspiration were scattered along her hairline and upper chest.

"Are you a spider?" She acted offended, instead of impressed with his skills. "I feel like if I just breathe funny, I'm going to fall. I'm terrified."

"This is a beginner wall." He probably shouldn't have told her this, but he wanted to impress her somewhat. He was at ease on the wall, as if he could spend hours here.

"Shut up. You know where I could be right now? At the farm, eating a giant stack of pancakes. My mom is upset because I turned down coming over for breakfast because I'm helping you. And here I am, feeling like I'm about to slide off this wall at any moment and break my neck, all while you're telling me how easy it is."

"You know what your problem is right now? And it's not me, even though I know that's exactly what you were going to say."

Her opened mouth shut quickly, as though it had been

her planned response.

"You're thinking too much. It's just supposed to be you and the wall. That's all you need to focus on. Shut off everything else in your brain."

"That's probably easier for some of us more than others," she grumbled between clenched teeth. "I don't know if I can go any higher because I feel like I'm going to slip. Like seriously, what are you supposed to do when your fingers get all sweaty?"

It was then Boone realized he'd been so distracted by Naomi, he'd made a huge mistake, one that would not get him the instructor position if anyone at Cliff Climbs ever found out. "Oh. Well, actually, we probably should have gone over chalking."

"What do you m—" A horrified expression passed over Naomi's face as her hands slipped from their grip. Her arms did a small windmill before she free-fell to the safety mats underneath, landing on her back with a cushioned smack.

"Shit." Even while knowing the climbing gym was safe, his heart leaped into his throat. The last time he experienced a similar sensation, he'd been lead climbing with Alan and missed a hold he'd jumped for. He received the worst whipper of his life as his helmeted head smacked against the rock wall after falling a short distance. But that was him getting injured due to his own mistake. Him overlooking something big, and being the reason Naomi got hurt, was infinitely worse.

He jumped to the mat, falling to his knees hard but not caring as he scampered to her. "Are you okay? Are you hurt?"

Boone was thankful when she propped on her elbows

with a hard stare before lightly smacking one of his biceps. "What the hell, Boone?"

He rubbed his arm, knowing he deserved it. Although, it didn't stop him from inspecting her arms and legs to assure himself she wasn't seriously injured, no matter how much she tried to shoo him away.

"Oh, god, are you okay?" Tom asked, rushing over.

Boone couldn't stop worrying about what could have happened if he'd had his way and they started at Smith Rock, where there were no safety mats, unless he brought some in. He, suddenly, was losing years off his life at the thought. Cliff Climbs had been right about him. He wasn't a good instructor and possibly a dangerous one.

Naomi pulled herself away from Boone's hands, standing and putting some distance between them. "I'm fine."

"She's fine," Boone reiterated to Tom, trying to reassure himself while also attempting to get rid of the guy who kept popping up like a bad penny.

"By the way, you forgot your chalk on the counter," the gym employee said, handing the small-belted pouch to him. He claimed it with a great deal of guilt.

At this point, Boone's desires regarding his career were secondary. He was sure Naomi was done with him, not only today, but probably the whole deal. His imaginative dream of having a regular climbing partner was also in the dumpster. This was why he climbed solo. Alan was right. This hobby was all about trust, and he never had it. History proved he was successful only when he cared about results that benefited him and no one else. He'd never felt lower in Naomi's eyes.

Tom returned to his section of the gym, leaving Boone and Naomi alone again. He prepared himself for whatever she was about to deservedly unleash on him.

She leaned against the wall, staring at him. "You were saying something about chalking."

"Yeah. Anyway." He made a half-hearted motion to the pouch in his hand. "You can put chalk on your hands to keep them dry and make gripping the holds easier."

"Yeah, I can see why that might be helpful," she replied.

"I'm really sorry. I'm guessing this is probably the end of our lessons."

Her hazel eyes studied him, but they were no longer shooting daggers. "If we were to continue, can I at least do the one with the rope?" She pointed in the direction of the other climbers.

He couldn't believe she wasn't walking away. "Sure. We can do that if you want. Let's get the equipment."

Boone didn't know if it was the fall, but Naomi's nervousness vanished. She showed an eagerness to get on the wall again. He, on the other hand, turned into an anxious mother, using his teaching as a cover to triple-check everything. He told her about top rope climbing and what he'd be doing on the ground as the belayer, keeping rope tension, assuring her there wouldn't be any more accidents like before.

"The fall actually wasn't that bad," she said, her brow pressing together in annoyance as he again checked to make sure her helmet was strapped in, the harness around her waist was secured and correct, and her hands were properly chalked. Only through touching all these things could he be assured she was safe.

"Okay. Are you ready?" Or maybe he should check everything once more.

"Good night, yes! Stop fussing over me. Can I please climb now?"

"Have you done the route reading yet? Do you know what path to take?"

She released an impatient breath. "Yes, I did that while you were checking everything for the hundredth time. I'm going with yellow."

"Okay."

With this, she climbed as if she'd been doing it for years. She wasn't fast, but her movements were more confident, transforming her into a woman who was becoming aware of the power her body held. She even, at one point, held with one hand while reaching to her back hip and dipping her fingers into the chalk bag. It was amazing.

"You got me?" she'd asked.

"Yeah, I got you, honey." He brought his hand over and under to take up the rope slack, locking it into place with his belayer equipment. "You're doing great. About five more feet until you reach the top. You got this."

Boone never imagined he could have such a sense of pride for someone else's accomplishments, but his chest expanded all the same when Naomi reached the top.

She shot him the most electric smile he'd ever witnessed, more beautiful than the sweet ones she gave to everyone else. This was better. "Oh my god! I did it!"

Some nearby people clapped at her declaration, including Tom. One couldn't help noticing Naomi, especially when she was lit up and confident, like a sparkler. Her excitement didn't dissipate as he gradually fed her rope, helping her to the ground. She leaped the final few feet to the mat, launching herself at him. "Boone, I did it!"

He had a split second to prepare himself, turning his hips so she didn't impale herself on the belayer equipment at his waist. He wrapped his arms around her shoulders and pressed his face into the gentle crook of her neck, inhaling the salty scent of perspiration mixed with sugary floral perfume. "You did really great, Pinky."

"My fingers are sore."

"You'll get used to it." He wanted to press his lips to each fingertip, to soothe the ache. Instead, he helped remove her headgear, relishing the attention as her focus remained on him, eyes glittering like jewels. Some fine baby hairs had been pulled loose from her previously neat ponytail, and they curled adorably, framing her face. He brushed them back with care.

"I get a feeling I might be creating a climbing monster. A cute monster, but a monster all the same," he said, his hand stroking along her temple.

Her giddiness melted away when he, almost unconsciously, dipped his head closer to hers. It would be easy to celebrate her win with something more delectable. He wondered how she'd taste, already knowing her lips would be perfect, being both sweet and a little sassy. Boone was tempted to find out—

"Great job," came Tom's voice behind him. "You seem to be a natural. Not sure you even need Boone."

This guy was a menace. Why couldn't he take a goddamn hint, stay behind the counter, and leave the climbers alone? Before he could be tempted to whip around and hiss at the man like Gollum from *Lord of the Rings*, Naomi stepped away, her cheeks tingeing with pink. "Thanks, Thomas. It felt amazing."

Boone wanted to give her something else to feel amazing about.

Then it hit him.

This wasn't about simply charming her. Boone wanted her—and not just for a climbing partner. The revelation was heart-stopping, and also unwelcome, because it wasn't part of his plan. But like the rope in his belayer equipment, he was already locked in.

What the hell was he supposed to do now?

Chapter Five

"NAOMI! TELL ME! I want to hear all about the reactions." Curly-haired Amber Martinez stretched in the corner of the rec room where they co-taught the Pilates for Seniors class. Her fellow Latina friend was a chronically early arrival person, beating everyone to class, including Naomi.

They'd been good friends through high school. After graduation, her friend got into fitness and was a personal trainer at a local Redmond gym. They'd been doing Pilates together for years. When Amber was invited to teach this class and needed a partner to help, she brought Naomi along, who could always use the extra money, saving as much as she could in case of a rainy day or something happened to High Desert Tours. Because of her dad's mistake, Naomi no longer trusted putting all her eggs in one basket.

"My mother was a little shocked, but my sisters loved my hair. Even Hailey said it looked hot."

Amber gave her a funny look. "Come on. You think I'm asking what your family thinks?"

Naomi crossed her legs at the ankle and leaned forward until her palms pressed against the floor as she stretched her hamstrings. "I don't know what you mean. I don't really see anyone else but them, you, and this class."

Amber snorted. "The faux ignorance is astounding. Fine. You want to play this game? What did Boone say?"

It was fortunate Naomi's head was tipped down to her legs. She could hide any sudden redness from Amber's observant eyes . . . or, at the very least, she could blame it on blood flow rushing to her head due to hanging upside down. "You know I don't care what he thinks. That's not why I did it."

"Not much. You just talk about how much he annoys you *all* the time."

Naomi lifted her head to glare. "I thought you and I were venting besties. And he gives me a lot to be annoyed about. He makes me want to scratch my eyes out."

She didn't want to think about Boone because she didn't know what to think. Their climbing session had been . . . confusing. He hadn't been his normal self and, therefore, she hadn't been either. This could have been why she'd gotten befuddled and felt something of a spark between them. He'd given her a glimpse of himself, one who sometimes experienced self-doubt, and it had been like looking under the hood of a fancy car and discovering it was still a car. Boone was human, who was vulnerable and made mistakes and worried about things. She saw all of this, especially after her fall.

Naomi didn't know what to make of Boone but, even more, she didn't know what to make of her own reactions. She'd lain in bed at night, going over everything. Climbing day had her feeling all the emotions, from exhilaration to something suspiciously like yearning. She was questioning everything she knew about herself and of him.

But at work, a few days later, it had been as if nothing had happened at all. He hadn't mentioned their climb, hadn't acted as if they'd touched. He'd returned to regular, breezy Boone, making up some ridiculous imagined scenario about how he wanted to take her on a rocket into space to watch her hair swirl about her head in zero-gravity and fling strawberries into her mouth. Whatever. Apparently, nothing mattered, at least not to Boone.

"Okay, I'm sorry for breaking the venting code," Amber said. "You know you can vent to me anytime, and I'll try not to use it against you." This ended with a sly smile, which wasn't much of a commitment from her friend.

"Ugh, okay, I took a rock-climbing lesson." Naomi plopped into a sitting position on the ground.

"Wait. What? First the hair and now climbing. That's so dope. Where are you doing it? Is it Cliff Climbs? We could have signed up together."

"No, it's not anything like that. It's more casual private lessons . . . from Boone."

"Shut up. *Boone* Boone. That Boone? The one you just said made you want to scratch your eyes out?"

"How many Boones do you think there are?" She wasn't sure she could handle more than one.

She briefly considered if it would be possible to swap places. Amber could take lessons with Boone, letting Naomi off the hook. He might prefer it because he'd get a student, and wouldn't have to uphold his end of the bargain of helping her on her quest to find some couple to have a hot-air balloon wedding.

When Amber had seen a news story from the previous year, one featuring their hot-air balloon business and Selah's love affair with Dex, there had been a brief glimpse of Boone in one of the shots. At the time, Amber had texted her, *that's who ur hatin on??? I'd let that boy hate on me all nite long. Yum.* No explanation from Naomi had been enough to convince her friend that a pretty face didn't make him any less annoying.

So, sure, she could make the suggestion that her best friend take lessons with Boone. Maybe he'd like it better because Amber would be nicer to him than Naomi had ever been. She was fun, adventurous, and a true Sagittarius if she'd ever known one. Not like Naomi, who'd always been quieter and softer and balanced her friend out because she didn't mind drifting into the shadows.

Except the thought of them having climbing lessons without her unexpectedly irritated her heart. She didn't like the idea at all. Boone wasn't Naomi's, but she'd be damned if she didn't feel some ownership in their relationship. Either way, she didn't want to explore it too deeply, and seniors were trickling into class.

"Hey, Maggie. How's the arm feeling this week?" she asked the outspoken lady with the silver pixie-cut hair.

"Good as it can be. Enjoy your youth while you can, princess. Loving the pink."

Amber smacked her arm. "Stop trying to get out of this. You didn't answer."

"Ow. What? It's not a big deal. It's just a few lessons. I'm doing him a favor."

"I bet. I knew all the pent-up annoyance was foreplay. Good for you."

"What? No. I'm—It's not like that at all. He's still the most aggravating man on Earth. But he's trying to get an instructor job at Cliff Climbs. I'm basically the guinea pig, so they see he can do it. That's all."

Amber waved at one of the regulars walking through the door. "Think you're being sly, don't you, Miss Guinea Pig? Or maybe he's the sly one."

Naomi couldn't help it . . . she laughed. "Stop. We're sharing favors. I'll be his student, and he'll help me find someone willing to pay to have a hot-air balloon wedding with a company that has no experience or event reputation."

"Oh my god. You finally convinced Selah? That's great."

"Yeah. So, how are you and Aaron doing? Are you guys talking about getting married yet?" It was worth a shot.

Her friend's lips stretched into a flat line. "Are you kidding? I'm about to commit myself to singlehood. Four months in, and he already doesn't want to do anything or go anywhere. If he can't appreciate all this, I'm breaking up with him for real."

"Oh no. Really?" It was disappointing for her plans, but also bad for her friend, who had the worst dating luck. Not that Naomi was doing much better. Personal experience taught her it was slim pickings in the dating world.

"No one is crying or having a funeral for this relationship. Least of all me. I know my prince is out there." Amber never stayed single for long. She was a hot commodity and deservedly so because her friend was amazing—too amazing, which was why she needed to stay away from Boone. He didn't deserve someone like Amber.

"But one of my cousins is getting married."

"Oh?" Maybe she didn't need Boone helping her if Amber's family came through.

"But it's next month."

Naomi's face fell. "I suppose she's already set up with everything."

"Yeah, I'm sure. I know they put down a huge deposit. They're doing it at McMenamin's Crystal Ballroom. But if I hear any engagement rumors, I'll see what I can do. You know the Martinez family is huge, so there's always something going on. Oh, I know my cousin went to that huge wedding expo in Portland. I think it's always held in June, and that's where she checked out a lot of vendors. You should go, start putting the business out there. It's already May, so it might be too late for this year, but maybe you'll get people booking things for next year."

Amber then stood, clapping her hands together as she addressed the class. "Hey, everyone. Great to see you. Are you ready to get in a good workout?"

After class, Naomi couldn't stop thinking about this possible wedding convention, researching it as soon as she got home. Her friend was correct. It was being held the first weekend of June, which only gave her a week to make plans and look into it.

She could attend as long as there weren't any hot-air balloon flights on the books. It was too late to get a booth, but she wasn't prepared, wanting to go all out when she was ready. At least it gave her time to convince Selah, since they remained on a tight budget, especially when it came to marketing. Regardless, it would be fun to attend this year and see what it was like.

The following morning, while she sat in her usual folda-ble camping chair in the field with Boone, Naomi sent a text to Hailey, the keeper of the High Desert Tours schedule. *Do we have any tours this weekend? Thinking of taking a trip to Portland.*

Boone cleared his throat. "So, what do you think about doing another lesson this coming weekend? We can do one of the easier climbs at Smith Rock if you want to try some-thing outside. Get in some real-world sports climbing. I think you'll really like it."

"Oh, um." She'd momentarily forgotten about that commitment. While she was excited about trying a real climb at Smith Rock—and also nervous because . . . was she ready to do something like that? It felt a bit like removing the training wheels. What if she just embarrassed herself in front of the other climbers and disappoint—

"Stop getting in your head. You can do this," Boone said.

His X-ray vision into her mind was astounding. She pushed her hair behind her ears in an attempt to appear casual. "It's not that. It's just I might be busy."

His brows unexpectedly pressed together in irritation. Rude. She was allowed to have a life outside of—

"Are you going out with Tom?"

"Who?" He may as well ask if she was meeting up with royalty for how surprised she was by the question.

"From Bend Rock Gym."

She scrunched her face in thought, trying to place the information and remember the face. She now recalled the white guy with the scruffy hair, but hadn't given him a second thought since leaving the gym. "What makes you think I'm going out with him? And even if I was, why does it matter? I can do whatever I want. Is that the reason you want to throw me on a climb at Smith Rock? Do you have something against this Tom guy?"

The annoyance didn't leave his face. "No. That's not why. I just saw him talking to you in the parking lot after our lesson."

"Is that why you were just sitting in your car? Are you actually afraid that I'm going to switch to another instructor? I was just joking about that. I don't have plans to take lessons from anyone else, but if you're going to be weird about it, maybe I don't want to take them from you either." What was wrong with him? It was confusing how he could switch from silly, flirty scenarios to whatever this was.

Her phone buzzed with an incoming text message from Hailey.

You're going to Portland without me?! Don't you want me to come with you, hermana? You know it'll be so much fun! We can get into trouble 🦉 🦉 🦉 Don't tell Selah. My friend told me about this one bar that she said was jammed packed with 🔥 🔥 🔥 guys!!!!

As much as she enjoyed her sister's company, and would prefer not to go alone, she needed to shut this down. Naomi wasn't going for a fun, wild weekend, and she needed to treat this project with importance. *Not going for fun or men. I want to go to a wedding con for research.*

Ugh! What?! Why tho????? Who wants to drive all that way for that? Now I want to go out! Naooooommmmmmiiii! Think I can get Selah to go out?! Why won't she let me plan her bachelorette party? You know I'd be good at it. I was talking to our cuz and she suggested we do a brewery and river float. Isn't that a great idea?!

Can u talk to her plzzzzz?

Naomi didn't want to get dragged into this, especially since Selah hadn't picked a wedding date, nor was she the type of person who enjoyed the same type of activities as Hailey. As far as sisters were concerned, no two were more different than Selah and Hailey. Naomi had always been the bridge between them.

Deciding to ignore Hailey's request, she texted, *So are there tours this weekend or not? I just want to know if I can go.*

It took a few moments before a reply came in. *One Saturday AM but nothing on Sunday unless we get a last-minute booking. We're getting a lot of requests for next month, so get your weekend in now while you can.* 🐵 *te quierooooo.*

The wedding convention was happening all weekend. She could leave after the tour on Saturday morning, walk around the city, try some new food carts, and then rest up and attend the convention on Sunday. She didn't have to go on both days. It sounded kind of fun now, like a mini-vacation, and she was getting excited about it. She'd never done a solo trip before, but if she could conquer a climbing wall and rock pink hair, maybe she could do anything.

"Alright. I'm sorry," Boone said.

She'd completely forgotten about him and their previous conversation. She glanced at him, and he sat slouched in his camping chair. His features were pulled into a grumpy expression. She'd never seen him this way before. It was odd.

"You're free to go out with whoever you want," he conceded in a grumble.

She gave a short laugh. "Great. Like I've been sitting around waiting for your permission on going out with people." This might have been poking the grumpy Boone bear because his eyes grew dark, but she didn't care.

Naomi put her phone down and sighed. "Not that it matters or is any of your business, but I haven't been asked out, nor am I going on a date. I accidentally left my water bottle on a bench after our session and he ran out to give it to me. That's all." She wasn't about to add Thomas had been awkward enough in their short exchange that she'd been suspicious he'd been working up the nerve to ask her out. Even if he had, she would have said no. She wasn't ready to go on a date with someone who purposely picked a goatee as their facial hair of choice these days.

"Oh." His crabbiness melted away.

It was curious. Had Boone wanted to kiss her at the climbing gym? There'd been something in his look then. The way it sparked and heated. The possibility sent a swirl of butterflies fluttering around her chest. Their relationship had rarely been friendly, and, yes, she'd admit it was almost entirely because of her. How might things have been between them if she hadn't come out of the gate already prejudiced against him?

"But you still don't want to go climbing this weekend?" he asked.

"It's not that I don't want to go climbing. It's that I might be doing something else. I'm thinking about going to Portland to check out a wedding convention. I was just talking to Hailey about the schedule."

He leaned forward. "Well, now, that's interesting."

"Yeah, interesting for me. Not sure why it would be interesting to you." She inspected her nails, pondering if she should treat herself to a manicure before her trip.

"According to our deal, I should go with you."

Her focus snapped to him. If her gut told her going to Portland with Hailey was a bad idea, it was for sure telling her it would be dangerous going with Boone. Not that he was dangerous in the typical sense, but . . . Well, her and him, spending a lot of time together, especially after that climb? It had the potential to make things more awkward. The car ride alone was at least three hours one way. What would they even talk about?

"That's okay. I'm sure you'll find it boring," she replied, using Hailey's reasoning. "I really don't mind going by myself. I was just planning on checking it out and wandering around. It's too late to get a booth, anyway, but maybe we'll do something next year."

"Why do you think I'll be bored?"

"Because it's wedding stuff. Most people find that boring unless it's their own."

"Yeah, but it's important to you. And it's not boring when I see it as a challenge."

She wasn't sure how to respond to this. He took his side of the bargain more seriously than she'd expected. Truth be told, she'd be fine taking a few lessons, helping the guy out, and calling it a day. Especially since she had no idea what his help entailed, and why he kept making it sound like a game to be won. "It's fine. I don't expect you to travel all the way to Portland. I'm okay with just getting help with local things."

Local help, in her mind, was doing some of the grunt work, such as setting up the balloon or tables or whatever.

The part she stressed about the most was finding a couple who'd be interested in getting married in the middle of a field turning dry and brown due to the High Desert heat. This was before considering the possibility of wild brush or forest fire that turned the whole sky grayish brown. She didn't want to saddle Boone with extra pressure when no amount of charm on his side could do anything about it.

Her father had never been so nervous about things financially one summer season because nonstop smoke prevented him from flying the balloon at all. It may have been why Robert had so much time to watch YouTube videos and was desperate enough to take a huge gamble. It was after this he'd made all those investments. He was making big plans for the following year to make up for a lost summer of no tours. Naomi now understood some of the pressure he faced.

Boone didn't respond, and she told herself this was a good thing and was happy to let the matter drop. Naomi didn't know what she was doing, anyway, and this trip wasn't anything more than to check things out, to see if it was worth talking to Selah about.

Regardless, Naomi moved on with her day and didn't think anything more about Boone or their deal.

Chapter Six

"HOW LONG ARE you going to be gone for?" Hank asked Boone as he threw some essentials into his travel bag Friday night, packing some of the nicer clothes he hadn't utilized in a while. If a con man had a motto, it was to always dress for the results you wanted, and Boone took this seriously.

"Not long. Only a couple of days."

"And you're going to a wedding? Do you get a plus-one? I do like going to weddings. You know that's sometimes the best place to find opportunities." His father's eyes took on a mischievous glitter.

Boone raked a frustrated hand through his hair. "I'm not going to a wedding. It's just some convention. I'm helping out a friend. Do you think you can feed the cat and give him treats while I'm gone?" He worried the animal would miss him without his daily attention, and would search for a better home if he thought he'd been abandoned.

"The damn cat will be fine. He knows how to survive. He was doing it long before you started giving him that fancy cat food we can't afford."

Boone rubbed the back of his neck, trying not to appear annoyed. He had only asked his dad once to buy a couple of cans, and two for a dollar was far from fancy. Even if it was more, Boone believed the purring, sweetheart of a cat was worth it.

"And what am I supposed to do?" his dad asked. "It sounds like you're working some plan and not cutting me in."

"There's hardly anything to cut in," he answered absentmindedly while zipping his bag closed. What exactly did Hank want from him? He gave his dad a safe place to crash. He didn't think he'd also have to entertain the man. "Just do whatever you've been doing. You're a grown man. I think you can figure it out. If you want to eat the leftovers in the fridge, go right ahead."

"Is that more food from that Moreno woman?" His dad's eyes lit up.

Elena had always been generous in feeding Boone, which was one reason he'd stuck around doing the chase crew thing for High Desert Tours. Not only was her cooking the best he'd ever had, but she offered it frequently enough to keep him well-fed and save money on groceries. Sometimes, he wondered if he was returning to his old leeching habits, but one look at his bank account was enough to justify free food. Besides, even if he declined, Elena would find a way to spoil him. Boone had found himself endeared to the older woman because of her kindness.

And the other reason he stuck around? Well, he wasn't ready to dive into that yet.

The following morning, there was an early morning tour. Boone and Naomi didn't talk much, as their conversations had grown weird. It was his fault. He'd been kicking himself ever since his jealousy of Tom had reared its ugly head. Boone had always been careful about keeping his true feelings hidden. It made one vulnerable, and the information could be used against him at some point. As hard as he tried, he seemed to fail at this whenever she was around.

"And you're leaving directly after this?" Selah asked Naomi. They were in the barn and using the truck lift to lower the gondola from the bed to the ground to unload it after the tour had finished for the day.

"Yeah, but I'll be back Monday afternoon, depending on how things go."

"Remember, don't commit to any booths or tables. Yeah, this season looks good, but we don't know how it's really going to end up. If we get a wildfire or a lot of cancellations . . ." Selah shrugged. "I just don't want us to get locked into something, and then money is tight, and we're screwed again."

"I know," Naomi said. "I'm just going to get information, and maybe I'll hand out a few business cards."

"Nothing fancy," her sister reiterated because she was a practical type of person. It wasn't certain she believed the old adage, *One had to spend money to make money.* "Oh, and if you see anything sparkly or cool on the ground, bring it home for a souvenir for Harper. I'm sure there's lots of good trash at those sorts of events."

"I'm not going on a trip just so I can scavenge garbage for a crow," Naomi replied with a groan.

Her older sister chuckled because *she* was willing to look for sparkly garbage for her fiancé's pet bird. Maybe that's what love did to a person. It made them willing to put up with trash. Boone couldn't imagine.

Speaking of which, the man in question appeared with a cup of coffee for Selah, wearing his park ranger uniform and, thankfully, without his creepy pet crow.

"Hey, handsome." Selah took the coffee as she leaned into Dex, wrapping an arm around him in a quick hug. "I was just thinking about you. Are you on your way to work?"

After handing over the drink, he helped Boone muscle the basket into the center of the barn. "Yeah. Wanted to treat you and see if you're up for a date tonight."

From Boone's observation, Selah was in a prime position to take everything Dex owned, because the guy gazed at her with unabashed adoration. Luckily, Dex fell for a Moreno woman who was too nice for cruddy schemes, like ones that used love as a weapon to clean a person out.

"Yeah, sure, I'd love that," Selah replied, walking away with Dex, all mashed together, side by side, before she stopped to turn to Naomi again. "Just be careful. I don't like the idea of you going all the way to Portland by yourself."

Naomi huffed, appearing frustrated at being mothered by her older sister. "I'm twenty-six now. You used to do it all the time."

"That was different. That was for work."

"And this is for work too!"

"She's not going alone because I'm going with her," Boone said, jumping into the conversation. All gazes swung to him at the interruption.

"You're going with her?" Selah sounded skeptical.

"Yeah, we'd talked about it the other day. I volunteered to help."

THE WEDDING CON

"Help? You guys can barely stand being around each other for the few hours we have a tour. Now you're going to spend the whole weekend together?" Both Selah and Dex raised their eyebrows, but the former crossed her arms while asking the question.

When Selah put it like that, it did sound odd, but she was the one in search of crow party favors, so he took it with a grain of salt.

"We're doing okay these days. Right, Pinky?"

Her staring at him wide-eyed and playing with the ends of her hair didn't do a great job of making a convincing argument. He gave Selah an easy smile. "It's part of being in the chase crew. She looks out for me, and I look out for her. It's like a pilot and co-pilot thing. You get it, right?"

Some of Selah's skepticism faded as Boone tapped into something he knew she'd understand. He'd heard stories from Elena about how close Selah had been with their dad, her adopting a mostly co-piloting role to him. He understood, as he used to have a similar relationship with his own father. Although Boone was sure Robert had been a better man than Hank. This was why the Moreno woman turned out better than him.

"Yeah, I guess," was Selah's response. "Well, I hope you both have fun. Don't spend too much time fighting, and try not to spend any extra money."

"Boone! What do you think you're doing?" Naomi whispered harshly as soon as her older sister was out of earshot. He got back in the truck with her as she drove the short distance from the barn to a spot next to his car. "You're not going with me, and I don't need your help."

"I happen to disagree with you on both of those things."

"You're *not* going," she said, getting out after parking and slamming the door.

He got out as well. "I *am* going. I already got someone to watch my cat. I can't just show up again after all the fuss I made when saying goodbye to the little guy. He'll never take my goodbyes seriously ever again."

She threw her hands in the air. "What? That doesn't even make any sense, and it doesn't matter because you're not going."

"It's only because you haven't met my cat yet. If you had, you would care a lot. He looked like this." Boone switched his expression to the saddest, most pitiful one he could do. "And I was only able to bear leaving him because I knew you needed me."

Naomi opened her mouth to answer before noticing Elena walking toward them, smiling. "Oh, Boone, Selah said that you're going to Portland too. I made you both sandwiches and brought some water to take on the road. I'm so glad you're going with her. You'll take care of my baby. You know how dangerous the city can be."

Naomi dropped her head backward in apparent frustration. "I've been to Portland before. I think I can handle it. I don't need to be taken care of."

"I know, but it's just because I love you and I don't want anything to happen to you. Maybe someday we can take a trip together. I'd love to get out too and we need to hang out more. I miss that," Elena said.

He took the sandwiches and the chilled bottled waters from the older woman before she hugged them both and left them alone. "Do you still need to grab your stuff or something?" he asked Naomi.

She grumbled under her breath as she stomped toward her mom's farmhouse.

"Okay," he replied after her. "I'll just wait for you here, and then we can go." He sat on the hood of his car as he waited, eating a sandwich since he was hungry.

Ten minutes later, Naomi reemerged with a travel bag and purse slung across her shoulder. She narrowed her eyes when she noticed he was still around. "I'm serious, Boone. I appreciate the offer, and I know we had a deal, but this isn't necessary. Just go home to your sad cat or go climb a rock or something."

He decided to change tactics, pressing his brow upward. "I'm a little hurt that you're trying so hard to get rid of me. Do you think I'm not dependable enough to keep my end of the bargain? All the trust I thought we built during our climbing lesson seemed to be for nothing. I'm actually trying to be someone you can count on."

Her lips pulled into a frown, appearing to think this over. "Alright, fine. But I want to take my time and look around while I'm there. I don't want to hear anything about how boring it is or—Where the hell is my sandwich?"

"I might have eaten it," he replied sheepishly. He honestly didn't remember, but he wasn't paying attention while he ate, and only a ball of wrapping remained in his hands as evidence of his crime.

"*Both* of them? And you want me to trust you when you've already eaten my food? This is unbelievable."

"Do you want to go grab another one?"

"No. It's fine. Let's just go."

He climbed off the hood, pulling his keys from his pocket and unlocking his car.

"What are you doing? We're going to take my truck?"

"Come on, Naomi, are you really going to fight me on everything? My car has better gas mileage and is smaller for city parking than that behemoth."

"This truck was my dad's. How about we just go separately?"

"What sense does that make? Get in the car."

She took a stubborn stance with hands on her hips. They were off to a great start. How could he take pride in winning any kind of victory when every interaction was like wrangling a cougar? Strong-arming her wasn't going to work. "If you get in the car, I'll give you exactly what you want this weekend."

Those words gave her pause, her cheeks tingeing with a slight blush he found intriguing. Either way, she maintained defiance by keeping her features set. "Since you don't know what I want, I find that a little hard to believe."

He focused intently in her direction, wishing for once he was an actual mind reader instead of using his usual ways to figure people out. What did she want? And was it similar to what he wanted? His hand rubbed absently at his bottom lip as he thought about all the things he could do to make her blush harder. "So you admit that there is something that you want from me."

"No." Her tone was light and not in any way convincing.

He closed the gap between them, stepping near enough for his lungs to take their fill of the delightful scent of her shampoo. "Naomi." He softened his tone, fighting the urge to touch her. "Just because you don't like it doesn't mean it's not true. I do know what you want and I'm willing to give it to you this weekend. How is this not a win-win situation for you? If you want it, take it." He stroked the soft skin along the inside of her wrist with one of his index fingers. A slight shiver passed through her, making him feel both powerful and weak. He couldn't cross the chasm between them without getting stuck in the trap himself.

Those eyes, like two gorgeous, earth-tone crystals, met him head-on. "Okay, then. What do I want?"

As much as he wanted to answer with his own desires, he stuck with his original plan, the safer one. "I'll answer whatever questions you have and tell you whatever you want to know about me. That's what you've always wanted, right? Pieces of me, things I don't like to share with anyone. I'll give it to you on this trip. Only the truth."

She cocked her head, and a small smile tipped the corners of her lips. He'd hooked her. Sure, the bait was something precious, something he didn't like to offer without a ton of stipulations, but he knew it would work. He wondered if this had been the issue from the start, why he'd been so disagreeable to her. Naomi was the type who didn't trust someone unless the person was genuine, and he'd never been willing to show all his cards before—until now. "Ah, see. I guess I do know you, after all."

"You say that now, but just you wait." Her smile turned coy, and her eyes glittered. Her response was too beautiful to be upset about bargaining bits of himself.

"Will you get in the car now? Can we finally leave?"

"Fine," she responded, getting into the passenger side. "But don't think I'm going to forget about you eating my sandwich." Naomi didn't waste any minutes into their car ride before jumping right into a hard question with, "We're not going to trick people, are we?"

"I . . . what? Trick who?" Maybe it was ignorance on his part, but he thought having an honest conversation was going to be easier. She'd already stumped him.

Naomi turned in her seat toward him, studying him intensely. "When you say that you have special abilities to help me get someone to . . . you know, have a wedding with us . . . you're not talking about tricking people are you?"

She made his talents sound like a bad thing. "Do you think I'm in the habit of tricking people?"

"I think you're in the habit of being very convincing, using your"—she roughly waved a hand over his general person—"charisma to get what you want."

He waggled his eyebrows. "So you admit I have . . . *charisma*."

"God. Don't ever think you can pull off humble because you can't." She rolled her eyes, but there was a slight smile playing on her lips.

"I don't think it's something you can get mad about, considering you have this quality yourself. You're a very charismatic person."

She always kept him guessing, because instead of being pleased with his comment, her mouth stretched downward. "You do not think that."

"I don't?"

"I've never been called charismatic in my life. I've been

sweet, nice, cute." She ticked off each quality on her fingers. "But never charismatic."

"So, let me get this straight. Just because I'm the first person to tell you that you're so charismatic I can hardly pay attention to anything else when you're around—"

Naomi snorted her disbelief.

"*I'm* the wrong one?" he continued. "I hate to break this to you, but . . . you're charismatic as fuck, honey."

Those beautiful, plush lips of hers parted in surprise, but her attention quickly flicked to the window again. She nibbled on the edge of a nail. Here she was trying to find a bride, and he had the rogue thought she would make the prettiest one.

"Why weddings? Why is that something you want to take on?" Sure, he gave her permission to dig into his brain, but it didn't mean he wasn't going to do the same.

"I just love big events, and there's usually nothing bigger than weddings. They're something special, something you don't forget. My parents just did the courthouse thing when they married. They really loved each other. It was sometimes embarrassing, but also sweet. My dad kept talking about them having a special vow renewal, using the hot-air balloon, but he died before it could happen. I adore that idea and want to make it a reality for our business. It makes me feel like I'm contributing something important to this dream he started. And that's why I don't want to trick people into it. I want them to truly believe that we're going to make their day special—that they can trust me with that."

Naomi may think she and Boone were completely different, but they both wanted the same thing. They both wanted people's confidence. In the end, the only difference between Naomi and the old Boone was how they went about trying to get it and what they did with it afterwards.

He cleared his throat. "I think I overstated my abilities a bit. I can't force someone into doing something they really don't want to do. I'm not a Jedi. But, usually, people are just looking for permission to do something they already wanted to do in the first place. Sometimes talking to them, giving them the encouragement they're seeking, will give you both the results you want."

She scrunched her face. "That sounds like something a con artist would say."

He covered his discomfort at her observation with a smile. "There's no denying there's artistry in it."

Naomi leaned against the passenger door, propping her head on a bent elbow. "The problem with you is that you think you're oh so clever, so smooth. You've been that way since the first moment I met you. I bet you have this thought in your head that whatever your perception is, is exactly what's happening—as if there isn't any other possibility than whatever you want to see."

"Oh, you figured that out since our first meeting at the interview?"

"I know that you lied."

He choked on the water he'd been sipping from a bottle. "What? I didn't lie. Is this why you've hated me this whole time?" This revelation from her was truly surprising.

"I don't hate you. But you also don't give off the most trustworthy vibes, and that's really important to me."

He took a few moments to think about which part of

himself she'd found distrustful, all of this confirming he'd never had her confidence, hadn't a chance, right from the beginning. He racked his brain to discover where he'd slipped up, but no easy explanation came. Had she been holding a grudge for over two years because of this? He didn't even remember answering a lot of questions during that interview. Selah had done most of the talking, and he'd been more than happy to let her because the less he had to say about himself, the better.

"You're going to have to give me a hint, honey. I remember some particular things about that day, but lying wasn't one of them." Back then, she'd spent most of the interview leaning in the doorframe's shadow in her mother's kitchen, as though she hadn't wanted to be noticed. She didn't have Selah's calm strength or Hailey's bubbling charm. He shouldn't have noticed Naomi, but she'd been there, arms crossed, studying him. He'd felt it down to his bones.

"You told my mom that you grew up in Medford, but on the pre-interview call, you said you were from Bakersfield. Whether you lied to me or my mom, I don't like it."

"Are you kidding me?" He laughed at how absurd it was, even while knowing she took it seriously. It wasn't surprising because she was protective of the family.

"Yeah, nice, laugh it up. I don't find it funny."

"This is what you've been holding against me the whole time. Even if it was a lie—"

"Which it most definitely was," she said with a full amount of righteous tone.

"You're acting like you're the CIA agent who caught her

first spy when this is an insignificant detail at best."

"If you lie about something small and insignificant, then you probably have no problems lying about something bigger."

Fair enough, and her instinct, at least in this particular instance—meaning him—was about as good as he'd always suspected. He couldn't be mad when he was impressed. "Sure, you're probably right about that, if I *had* lied. But I didn't."

"Both things can't be true, though!"

"That's because these are different questions. Where are you from and where did you grow up are not the same. Therefore, they can have two different answers."

Her mouth popped open to dispute this, but nothing came out. It was clear her brain was turning this information over to make some kind of sense of it.

Except, this wasn't a riddle, it was his life. "I moved around a lot. I don't really belong anywhere. I was born in Bakersfield, but only lived there until I was six. It's technically my hometown, where I'm from, and what I tell people because I have to pick somewhere. But most of my memories growing up are from a chunk of time I lived in Medford."

"Oh," was all Naomi said, a response tinged with sadness. He wasn't sure if it reflected her feeling sorry for him or regretting her accusation. He didn't want the former because he didn't think his life had been that bad. True, he didn't have the lovely type of upbringing he imagined in the Moreno household, but he didn't deserve sympathy, either. He was fine, or at least Boone didn't know any different.

"So, we agree then that I didn't lie, and I've finally been

vindicated in your mind?" He said this with good humor as if the whole thing was a joke. But, in truth, the distinction and how she saw him was important.

"I guess I can see your reasoning in this particular situation."

"Is there another situation where you think I lied? I'm open to getting this all out."

"What about the whole story about you running a gambling ring in high school? You're telling me that wasn't a lie?"

"One hundred percent bona fide truth." Maybe doing Two Truths and a Lie would have been a fun game to play, but he had never done it with her.

She threw him a skeptical look. "Come on."

"There was a short period of time where I attended a private school with a bunch of rich kids. Trust me. No one was crying about any of the money they lost because they just had more of it."

"But why would you do it in the first place?"

Boone shrugged. "I don't know. I guess I just wanted to see if I could." This had been his reasoning for a lot of mistakes in his life. It was only until now when he realized how messed up it must have sounded to her. He regretted ever having the thought in the first place.

"Okay, but in my defense, you're not the easiest person to read. Again, untrustworthy vibes. Sometimes I don't know what to believe."

The first part was true, but it was on purpose. While Naomi always wanted to be seen, Boone had never wanted too much scrutiny. It didn't serve him to be studied. The last part of her statement, though, was depressing, because maybe she'd never trust him, never believe he was authentic. "I get it. You don't trust easily, and maybe I'm the same way. It's always been easier to keep everything to myself. But I like sharing things with you and—I don't know—maybe it's silly, but I tell you a lot of these things because…I was trying to impress you."

"You know what impresses me? When you tell me about how you rescued a cat and how he has you completely wrapped around his little paw. Those are the stories I actually like."

Boone laughed. "Did I tell you he doesn't really meow? Instead, he chirps like he's part bird. I feel like he's really trying to talk to me when all he wants are pets."

"You've been completely suckered in."

"I know, and I'm not even mad about it. Maybe he just loves me for the food, but his attachment feels real, and sometimes that's enough." In fact, he was already missing the little guy. He hoped his dad would actually take care of Cat. Perhaps, when they get to Portland, he should send a text to his dad to make sure. Even when lost in thought, he could feel her gaze on him. "You're staring at me again."

"I'm sorry if things haven't always been easy for you, with all the moving around. And I'm sorry if I've been kind of tough on you," she said.

His jaw worked together, and he wondered if he pre-ferred her contempt to what sounded like sympathy. This uneasiness of being vulnerable wasn't as easy to sit with as he thought it would be. It was showing her some of the things under his skin, things he protected for years. "I'm okay.

Better than okay. I don't know if you heard, but I work with this absolutely charismatic woman at a hot-air balloon business." He flashed a grin, hoping she wouldn't see anything deeper.

Naomi shook her head. "Is it your friends in Medford who gave you the name Boone?"

"Uh, no. That was from my parents. Apparently, I was a rambunctious kid who had a thing for explosives."

"What does that mean?" Her eyes grew wide.

"Obviously, not real explosives, but my dad said, as a toddler, I used to run around and yell out *Boom! Boom!* while making my toys explode into a mess, but I mispronounced it. I kept saying *boon* instead, and then it just stuck. At least this is the story my dad has always told."

To be honest, Boone wasn't sure if the story was true, or some folksy thing Hank enjoyed telling people to make them feel at ease. His father changing his name on a whim didn't seem outside the realm of possibility. The history of their family or his name weren't things he'd ever bothered to investigate to see how much was actual truth. As his dad used to say, they could be anyone or anything they wanted. But he'd only felt like a Boone. The only one who'd ever called him Jonathan had been Monica, the older woman he'd been involved with after his father had been arrested.

"That's the story? You really played it up like it was going to be something bigger." She made an impression of what he could only imagine was supposed to be him. "*Maybe someday, honey, I'll tell you.*" She shook her head. "So, the whole name thing isn't because you're a criminal or something?"

His heart froze at this remark. "Wow, you really did think the worst of me. No, I've never been to prison." Boone told himself he wasn't breaking their agreement because it was technically the truth and they weren't talking about Hank.

He quickly moved on. "So you see, Naomi Moreno, there was nothing sinister about how we met. I was only a guy who wanted a job. If I talked my way into getting one— well, maybe it was because your family really needed to hire someone. All I did was give your family the permission it needed that it was okay to hire me. Just like I know you wanted me to go on this trip with you, to help you with this wedding thing. Just as I know that it's only a matter of time before people are lining up to get married in a hot-air balloon."

She nibbled on her bottom lip. "You think so?"

He took his focus off the road for a second to look at her. "I know so. And I hope, in your gut, you know this too. I think together, with our charisma, we'll be unstoppable."

She was quiet a few moments before pointing a finger in his direction. "Okay, but whenever we do decide to do this—and not just, you know, walk around a convention, but do it for real—there's still no tricking. We're trying to sell people on the idea, not pull a wedding con or anything."

He gave an amused chuckle, thinking her idea of a con job had to be more elaborate and glamorous than most real operations. Besides, in his mind, selling someone on an idea versus getting a mark to fall for a con was essentially the same picture. But he'd let it slide since they may have turned a corner in their trust issues. "I don't know. Maybe old Naomi would be against that kind of excitement. But Pinky? Yeah, I think Pinky would be really good at pulling off a wedding con, so maybe you shouldn't knock it."

She burst out a shocked laugh before shaking her head. "Boone, I mean it—"

"Okay, Naomi, I promise I won't *trick* any of your potential clients. Besides, I don't think I'll need to. That's how much I believe in your idea."

She bit her bottom lip, as though trying to control the grin wanting to break out, her eyes creasing into cute crescent moons, warming him through to his soul. "Thank you," she replied lightly.

All he could do was smile to himself because she had no idea what kind of things he had planned for their Portland weekend—what he'd be willing to do to keep her grins shining in his direction.

Chapter Seven

NAOMI HAD TO admit that traveling with Boone hadn't been what she expected. He was more complicated than she had pegged him, and not like anyone she'd ever known. Boone intrigued her enough that old barriers around her heart began to crumble. It made her nervous because when she wasn't pushing him away, she wanted to draw him nearer, and she wasn't sure she was prepared for this. It would be too easy to let him give her enough justifications to permit herself to let go completely.

He answered whatever questions she threw at him. He let her pick what music they listened to. He didn't even tease her when the first place she wanted to go, once they arrived in the city, was Powell's Books to buy a few romance novels. He was easy to be with, to laugh with, and she wasn't sure if he had changed or she had.

After they left the bookstore, they trekked a few blocks to a lot filled with a variety of food truck options. Naomi was starving, and Boone offered to pay for the meal since he'd eaten her sandwich. She chose a spicy lamb vindaloo while he got a vegetarian curry from an Indian food stand.

"Phew!" she said after a few bites. She had purposely chosen the spicy option on the menu. The heat and burn in her mouth and gullet were delicious, but her skin had to be the same color as her hair at this point. She was sweating. Naomi loved heat, the spicier the better, but this was testing her capacity.

"Let me try," Boone said. They sat on the concrete ledge beneath a huge oak tree. It was, surprisingly, a bright, sunny day in Portland, and the blue skies and soft breeze put her in a great mood, one that made her enjoy having him for company.

If she could barely handle the heat, she wasn't sure how Boone would do it, but she liked he had an adventurous soul and was willing to try anything. She broke off a piece of her naan, scooped some of the spiced meat on it, and offered it to him. Naomi couldn't help but laugh when he opened his mouth, expecting her to feed him. Her fingers shoved the mouthful of food inside, not allowing him to back out.

"Oh, god! Demon woman!" he said around a giant mouthful of food, coughing hard while covering it with a hand. This caused Naomi to break into the biggest giggle fit until she couldn't breathe while Boone collapsed to the side as if he were dead.

"Here! Water. Here's some water." She hurried to set down her food and open a bottle of water. In her rush, she fumbled the bottle, dousing half of it onto his shirt and lap, while he shouted about his mouth being on fire. It had been the most hilarious, favorite moment of her life in a long time.

"My eyes are still watering. Does it look like I'm crying?" He used a paper napkin to wipe his mouth and the tears from his cheek. "I mean, look at you. You're eating this incredibly spicy food like it was a bowl of ice cream. You must be a woman made of straight up iron."

She fell into snickering again, leaning into him while holding onto his T-shirt sleeve to keep herself upright. It all felt natural—and also weird how she could go from never touching him to acting as though they touched all the time.

"I like seeing you laugh." Boone's eyes crinkled as he swept a finger across her jawline to brush away some of her hair. The gesture was gentle . . . and something else. She couldn't put her finger on this thing sparking between them like a flickering firefly.

The pink-haired version of Naomi wanted to press her lips against his, to see where it took her, hoping it led to a place where her heart raced and set her blood on fire, and not just because of the spicy lamb vindaloo. It shocked her, and also not, because—

He released another cough, breaking the moment. "Sorry. There's a fireball or something stuck in my throat."

Afterward they walked around the city for a while, before she directed him to the no-frills motel where she'd booked her room, but came to the awkward realization they'd never discussed the overnight situation. Mainly because she'd assumed she was doing this trip by herself and made one reservation.

"So . . ." she said, after getting her key card and he continued following her to the room. Did he expect to share her room with her? It was a bit presumptuous, and she wasn't sure she was ready for that, even if her feelings had switched from pure contempt to curiosity about what his lips were like. "Did you book your room somewhere else or . . .?"

Naomi wasn't sure how to approach this.

"It's fine. You don't have to worry."

Well, now she had to worry about it. "What do you mean? We should coordinate something since we're going to the convention together tomorrow."

"Yeah, I get that." He rubbed the back of his neck. "Can I just hang out with you until you go to bed? I just planned on sleeping in the car."

"What?" Naomi wasn't sure she heard him right, stopping on the motel stairs.

"It's not a big deal. I've done it before."

She wasn't sure why he had slept in a car, but she didn't like imagining him doing it tonight. "I don't care if you've done it a hundred times. You're not sleeping in your car." Naomi unlocked her room, a blast of cool air greeting them as they entered.

"That's very sweet of you to offer, but I don't think it's a good idea for us to share a room." He leaned against the entry wall as casually as could be.

She sent an odd look in his direction as she dropped her bag on one of the two queen-sized beds. Why would his mind go there when she hadn't offered the option? Nor did she intend to. Even so, she was curious as to why he didn't think it was a good idea . . . and was it for the same reason running through her mind? "There has to be a solution between bunking together, and you sleeping in a car for a couple of nights. I'll just ask the front desk to book another room. This is kind of a business expense, so I'll put it on the company card. It's not a big deal."

"What about Selah? She won't be happy if it's three

hundred bucks a night?"

"Huh? What hotels are you staying at? This is a discount motel, not a Ritz Carlton." She wasn't sure if a person could stay at a luxury hotel for only three hundred dollars. Her family had been staying at discount places her whole life. "It's ninety-five bucks, and if Selah has a problem, then I'll deal with it. Yeah, she likes sticking to a budget, but she wouldn't expect you to sleep in your car."

"Reception," said the young woman answering the phone.

"Hi, I wanted to see about booking another room." She held the phone between her ear and shoulder as she dug into her bag for the company credit card.

"Is there something wrong with your room?"

"No, it's fine. I just want to get another room for someone else."

"For tonight?" Keyboard clacking came over the line.

"That's right."

"I'm afraid we actually don't have any more rooms—"

"What do you mean?" Naomi didn't know how this was possible, especially in a big city like Portland. But there was the fancy garden across the street, so maybe there was a big wedding or event nearby.

"It means that we're currently booked up," the woman said carefully, as if she was explaining this to a toddler. "I can check with one of the other hotels in the area. We do have some vacancy on Sunday, though."

"Oh."

"Do you want me to do a booking for Sunday evening?"

Naomi made a quick decision with a passing glance at

Boone. "No, that's okay. Thanks, anyway."

She returned the phone to the receiver and tugged on an ear as she took some time to think. "You promised me that you'd answer any of my questions this weekend and tell me the absolute truth, right?"

"Yeah," he answered.

"You didn't plan this, did you?"

His brow furrowed. "Are you asking if I somehow knew which motel you were booked at and then made sure all the other rooms were taken, just on the off chance you'd feel sorry for me and let me stay in the same room as you? Especially when history has shown that you've never felt sorry for me once in your life?"

"When you put it like that, I guess it does sound ridiculous." Except the idea had run through her mind, regardless.

"I'm offended that you think I would need to stoop to those kinds of tricks to get an invitation into someone's room."

Another good point. She would bet he'd talked his way into all kinds of rooms without breaking a sweat.

His eyes glinted. "It's fine, Naomi. I get that you don't want to share your bathroom. I'll just squeeze myself into my car for the night while you spread out on those two really nice beds. I'll be okay."

"Oh, for the love of—Fine. You can have the other bed. You better not breathe a word of this to my mom . . . or Hailey . . . or Selah."

He slipped his shoes off, dropped his bag on the floor, and stretched out on the other bed with his arms crossed under his head, as if it was a moment of true luxury, and he sighed happily. Was he used to sleeping on a fold-out or something? It's not as if these beds were any better than what one would find at a discount motel.

"Are you afraid your reputation will be ruined? We'll be forced to get married, like in one of your stories?" he asked.

"No, I just don't want them to get any weird ideas, just because I'm a nice person and didn't want you to sleep in a car." She dug into her bag for her pajamas.

"Answer another question for me, and I'll reveal something else about myself."

"I'm going into the bathroom to change. I'll think about it."

"I didn't bring any pajamas, by the way."

"Is *this* what you were going to reveal about yourself?" The question sounded more panicked than she'd intended. Gah, because what was she supposed to do with that information? Was she finally going to see a bit more of him? Not that she planned on gawking while he stripped . . . at least not much.

"Naomi."

"What?" The question burst from her, much too loud for a tiny room.

"Is it okay?"

"Is what okay?" She had no idea what he was referring to, but it must be something relating to him potentially being naked in the next bed over.

"Since I didn't bring any pajamas, because I thought I'd be sleeping in my car, I'll sleep in my clothes, but I at least want to take off my jeans. Is that okay?"

"Oh. Yeah. Fine." She swept her hair across a shoulder,

trying to display an unbothered air. "I'm going to change now," she announced for no reason.

She washed her face, splashing it with cold water to bring her temperature down before putting on her pajamas and brushing her teeth. Gathering her street clothes into a pile, she took a breath before emerging from the bathroom. She kept her eyes averted, afraid he'd be mostly naked, wearing something absurd, like a red man thong, and she wouldn't be able to not react.

"Those are really cute," he said from his bed.

She snuck a glance at him. He remained fully dressed, on top of the covers, but laid on his side with his head supported by a bent elbow.

"Mom gift. I think all moms have an instinct to buy their kids pajamas for the holidays." Her cotton pajamas were covered in tiny cats wearing sunglasses. She slipped her hair behind her ears nervously.

He frowned, his eyes dulling. "I wouldn't know."

His response caught her off guard. Besides knowing the guy moved around a lot, she didn't know anything about his family, if he even had one. Was he an orphan? Was that why he moved around a lot? She found herself with a bucketful of questions but no courage to ask them, even if he'd given her permission to do so.

"Did you decide?" he asked.

She zipped her bag, putting it on the floor before crawling under the blankets on her bed. "Okay. You can ask me a question." Naomi turned on her side as well, facing him.

"What did I do to cause you to hate me? It couldn't have just been the *where I was from* bit. Nobody is going to hold a grudge just for that."

They were staring into one another's eyes from a few feet apart, her in one bed and he on the other, and she could see it bothered him. With her evolving opinion about him changing, she was beginning to feel bad about her initial prejudice, especially if he hadn't deserved it. Naomi swallowed hard, deciding to tell the truth.

"My dad was a great guy. Besides showing us that you can get your dreams if you just stick with them, he was also kind, funny, smart. My mom couldn't have picked a better husband, and we couldn't have had a better dad. After he died, it was really hard. We'd lost our anchor, the person we'd all leaned against." Naomi paused because talking about it continued putting a lump in her throat. She wasn't ready to be *that* vulnerable. She'd rather let him sleep in his car before letting him see her cry.

"Anyway, it wasn't until after he died that we realized how much of what he did for the business put himself in a bad money hole. I'm not sure my mom even knew the true extent of it. Even now, she refuses to believe that my dad was anything less than perfect. I get it. I do. You don't want to see the bad side of a person you love, especially when they're no longer around.

"But I can't forget because I saw what happened. I was there. I knew my dad was making bad financial decisions before he died. I could have told everyone. But I wasn't as close to him as he was with Selah. We didn't have that same bond. And I wanted to try to have something, so I'd hang out with him and read my books while he was watching YouTube videos and . . ."

She reminded herself this wasn't anything to be ashamed of. Except, even though Boone had never met Robert, and didn't know much about him other than what her family told him, she loved her dad, still thought the world of him, and didn't want Boone or anyone else to think badly of him.

"And?" he asked lightly when she didn't finish the sentence.

"He'd . . . he'd started to watch a lot of videos on how to quickly make your business a success. I don't know if he was addicted or he just got sucked into some kind of algorithm, so these types of videos were the only ones he'd get. But looking at his financials after he died, he was giving these money gurus hundreds and thousands of dollars to take online courses and virtual seminars. Like our tiny hot-air balloon business was suddenly going to be a giant multi-million-dollar company or something. And when he did invest, he used their *special* financing programs because he trusted them, which probably screwed things up even more. And I remember one time, I couldn't focus on reading because of this video, so I sat and watched a little bit over his shoulder, and I said, 'Why are you listening to this guy? Just because someone is on YouTube doesn't make someone an expert.' But Dad blew me off. He said he was watching for tips because they were successful and doing something right."

"And you were correct." It was more of a statement than a question.

Naomi pulled the blanket closer to her body. "I don't blame him. He still very much saw me as a kid. What did I know? I think, at the end of the day, it was a combination of wanting to believe he could make his dream bigger, and being confident enough to think he was too smart to get caught in a predatory trap."

"He should have listened to you, Naomi."

"I didn't try very hard. I didn't know that much at the time. It was just my gut. But when you're used to not being heard and seen, you stop trying at some point."

She took another deep breath, readying herself to confess all. "At your interview, Selah was talking about the pay rate. We were all embarrassed it wasn't at the rate my dad had with his old chase crew, but we were back to being a bare-bones operation and didn't have a choice. You were right. We needed to hire you. Except when she mentioned the rate, you told her it was okay because you were investing in yourself right now, and maybe the money trees would grow later, which I know doesn't mean much—But it struck me because that money guy said something similar at the beginning of all his videos. 'Invest in yourself and the money trees will grow.' So here you were, some smooth-talking guy, using a phrase from my nightmare, and . . . I know it wasn't you, and it's silly, but I was scared. If my dad could get trapped, what chance did the rest of us have?"

Boone's brow squeezed together. He didn't appear mad, but rather perplexed. "And you still hired me?"

She huffed a sheepish laugh. "Don't thank me. I was outvoted, the only one against it."

The room was silent after this. Naomi didn't have anything else to say. She realized she'd been unfair. Boone hadn't anything to do with her father's bad financial decisions. She could look back and realize that Robert's passing made her overly paranoid. Either way, she couldn't apologize. She'd done it for a reason and didn't want to be weak, which was exactly what she worried he was going to make her feel.

Naomi shut off the lamp on the nightstand between them. In the dark, his words drifted to her before sleep could find them. "Your family isn't anything I've ever experienced before. You don't know what it's like to have the type of family you can trust, to have what you and your sisters have. I wouldn't do anything to ruin that. I like there are people like the Morenos in the world. You're better than the rest of us."

Naomi wasn't sure how to respond. Despite her bad experience with predatory internet opportunities, she still wanted to believe scammers to be a small percentage of the population. Most people were simply trying to live well. Boone's experience seemed to be different. She was glad he had the chance to be with people who genuinely wanted the best for him and nothing more.

"Hmm. Maybe," she said lightly. "But then my family aren't close, personal friends with the Schwarzeneggers."

He laughed. "I never said that! I said that my dad knew him. He'd gone to a few political fundraising dinners for Arnold."

"Stop. I doubt they were even at the same table. Knew him, my ass!" But she couldn't help giggling in response.

"You're impossible to impress, do you know that?"

"Yeah, and I kind of like being that way. But I'll give you another shot because you promised earlier to reveal some deep, dark secret of yours if I answered your question. Well,

I answered, so whaddya got?"

"Oh, yeah." Boone rolled onto his back. Several more minutes ticked by with nothing before he spoke again. "So, when I was . . . My dad . . ." Boone cleared his throat before trying again, his voice more upbeat this time. "Anyway, uh, several months ago, I was bored and decided to stream one of those prissy historical shows you love because I thought maybe it might be easier to find something to tease you about if I actually watched one."

"Oh? And why is that something to tease me about?" Some of the old annoyance returned. Why would he tell her this when they were finally getting along?

"You can relax, Pinky. Did I tease you about it? No. And you want to know why?"

"I haven't the foggiest idea, and I don't care because I'm not going to feel embarrassed for liking that kind of stuff—"

"Yeah, I liked it too."

"What?"

"You heard me. I, um, kind of got addicted and binged all three seasons and even watched the spin-off series."

"Wait, did you like it, or did you *love* it?" She couldn't help grinning in the dark, reveling in glee at knowing this secret, especially when he groaned in irritation.

"Come on, Naomi. This is hard enough already."

"Ahhhh, you loooooovvvvveeed it!" She hugged the extra pillow on her bed.

"Alright. Are you happy now?"

"Yessssss. Oh! Maybe when the new season comes out, we can have a watch party together! Neither my family nor Amber want to see it, so it'll be fun to have a watch buddy. I can make us themed snacks and everything." When he didn't answer, she wondered if she took the whole thing too far. "What?" she asked, expecting a rejection.

"Nothing. You're just so . . . extra. You can't just watch the season. You need to have a party with snacks. I don't know. It's something else. I'm also having trouble processing this because this morning you didn't even want to share a car with me, and now you want to watch a show together."

"If you would have told me this before, we could have spent the whole three-hour trip talking about it."

He chuckled lightly. The reaction sent warm bubbles popping inside her chest. She liked having this wholesome moment between them.

"We can talk about it now," he said.

"Nope. We gotta get up early tomorrow because I want to eat my free continental waffle breakfast and get to the convention right when they open."

"A woman with an agenda."

"Yup. Now go to sleep and stop bugging me." She threw her extra pillow, hitting him in the head, but she continued smiling until falling asleep.

WHEN SHE WOKE in the morning, it took a moment to orient herself. Boone's bed was unoccupied. Oh god! Did she snore last night and he decided the car was a better option? But the bathroom fan was on, and there was a slight buzzing sound within.

She stretched, doing her best to untangle her hair with

her fingers. She didn't care if Boone saw her sans makeup and messy hair, but she ran a finger along the bottom of her eyes in case there was any evidence of sleep.

Naomi jumped when the door opened, steam slipping from the bathroom along with a shirtless, sockless Boone wearing a pair of slim tan-colored pants. She had to keep her eyes from bugging because—*What?* No, really . . . what?! Someone who did rock climbing was going to be in good shape, but she wasn't prepared for this. Good god in heaven, his body had all those ridges like a cloud, only solid and muscled. If anyone could pull off a red man thong, it would be him. It took a lot of effort to move her gaze to his face, and then she was shocked for another reason.

"What the hell did you do to your face?" she shouted, without thinking. After she'd grown used to seeing him with a healthy amount of facial hair, Naomi had almost forgotten what a beardless version of him looked like, reminding her more of the guy who showed up to the interview and set her completely off-balance.

He ran a hand against his newly sheared jawline. It wasn't bare, more of a stubble. "What? You can do a drastic color change, but I can't shave?"

"No, it's not that, it's just . . ." She was at a loss because it was hard to breathe at the moment. His appearance did all kinds of things to her insides and she wasn't ready to face it. "Mustache."

His finger swiped across his upper lip where the hair was thicker and more noticeable, giving him the slight impression of a mustache. "You don't like it?"

"I . . ." Normally, Naomi would say no. Tom at Bend

Rock Gym had an awful goatee, putting him in her nope pile. This made her rethink everything. Was she a mustache girl? She swallowed hard. "I don't know. What happened to your shirt?"

He raised the pale-blue garment in his left hand. "I wanted to iron it. And I thought you wanted to get breakfast and get a move on everything this morning."

Naomi grabbed her bag from the floor as she slid from the bed. She held her breath as she squeezed past him. If he smelled good on top of how he looked, she'd swear to god her mind would vacate her skull, freeing her body to throw herself at him.

She quickly got ready, putting on a light summer dress with large, pale-yellow and peach flowers on a dark-blue background. The dress was short but flowy, gathered at the waist with a stretchy neckline she set off her shoulders. She wasn't going to come out va-va-voom like him, but it was cute enough. She left the bathroom while trying to slip on her sandals. He stood before the sheer-curtained window with his back to her, his hands in the pockets of his pants.

"Ready?" she asked.

He turned, their eyes connecting from across the room. Boone was fully dressed at this point. The pale-blue button-down shirt was neatly tucked into his pants, with a navy jacket worn over it. With this and the mustache, she was willing to admit to being completely on board with his appearance. And this was before he slid on a pair of glasses as though to see her better.

"Since when do you wear glasses?" Her question was more breathless than she'd intended. The Boone she'd always known, the one who was a bit of a scoundrel and a little rough around the edges, had transformed into some Mister Professor. His lips pulled into one of his smooth, charming smiles, his gaze drifting across her body with some appreciation. Discombobulation was sweeping its way in her direction again.

He approached closer, sliding a strand of hair from her shoulder. "Since I decided to give my eyes a break and not wear contacts. Miss Moreno, aren't you the pretty picture of an Oregon sunrise? I want to take you on a picnic to the greenest, lushest hill and pluck flower petals, weaving them into your hair until you look like a forest queen."

She was unable to stop the heat from spreading across her skin, sucking in a breath to hold it along with any obvious swooning. "As usual, you're being ridiculous. I'd rather you take me to the waffle station. I'm starving."

They departed the room, walking side by side. She fought the urge to let her hand brush against his, to take it within hers, because they weren't together. Maybe it was the exciting prospect of the day with waffles, or being in Portland during beautiful summer weather, or the fact that the man had blown her mind by making the mustache sexy as hell. Either way, she wasn't able to shake the feeling.

After breakfast, they stood in line, waiting for the convention to open. She felt somewhat awkward, standing beside the most handsome man there. His glasses transitioned into sunglasses, making him look like a European traveler on vacation. Naomi almost couldn't take it and distracted herself by texting with Amber.

She was reminded they'd have to buy him a ticket to enter because she'd only gotten one for herself. Tickets had been free but only if done in advance. She turned, finding him staring in the distance toward the other end of the convention center.

Before she could say anything, he said, "I'll be right back. I'll meet you inside." He strolled away before she could ask any further follow-up questions. What the hell was he doing? He briefly turned to look over his shoulder at her with a grin, but this led to him bumping into another man. Boone appeared to apologize and then possibly asked the older gentleman some questions. Or directions? There was a lot of pointing. Weird.

A text from Amber buzzed on her phone. *I need a pic of this mustache! Also, you're sharing a room? What?! Are things finally happening between you???*

Nothing happened. He stayed in his bed. I stayed in mine. And now he just walked off. I have no idea what's happening.

This is better than streaming.

"The line is moving," the woman behind her said.

"Oh, sorry." Naomi pulled her digital ticket up on her phone and showed it to the attendant. She entered the large convention building filled with rows upon rows of booths, ranging from specific wedding services, like floral arrangements, to catering to honeymoon options and everything in between. It was somewhat overwhelming.

He just disappeared. Do you think he left me and drove away???

Maybe an emergency diarrhea situation. It happens.

Naomie burst out laughing. *Stop. I feel silly waiting around for him.*

Standing off to the side of the entrance, she scrolled

through her phone's contact list. He remained listed in her phonebook as *Wickham*. She should probably change that. She hit edit, typing the name *Boone* before calling him.

He answered on the fourth ring, his tone low and smooth as a radio DJ. "Has anyone ever told you how beautiful you are?"

"Excuse me?" Was he talking to her or some other person on his end of the phone line? She swore if he left her to go flirt with someone, she'd not only kick him from her room, but she'd call a tow truck in the middle of the night and cackle from the window while he and his car got towed away together. Good riddance. "What the hell are you doing? If you didn't want to come, you should have just—"

"You have no idea how much I want to sweep that gorgeous hair of yours aside, and press my mouth to that smooth bare skin at your shoulder. How agonizing it is to look at you and not run my hand up your leg to your thighs. I want to push all your buttons, and I mean *all* of them, because I've never met anyone who needed them pressed more than you. I'd do it with my mouth and my hands and, well, everything until you're a wet, sopping mess and can't decide whether you should beg me to stop or keep going."

Her mouth grew dry. She wasn't sure if he was going to overheat her phone talking this way, but something was getting hot. His way with words. That voice. The man must be fantastic at phone sex because she felt faint, with barely enough strength to keep the device pressed to her ear. He had to be talking to someone else because his fantastical scenarios never went this far before.

She was about ready to disconnect with the infuriating

man when he finished with, "When I'm done with you, you're going to reflect your nickname in more ways than one, Pinky." This was said not only through the phone but directly behind her as if he'd been inside the building the whole time, waiting for her. Naomi released a surprised squeak, almost jumping out of her skin from finding him so close.

"What the hell?! Where'd you come from? I've been watching the entrance the whole time."

He leaned forward, those golden-brown eyes glinting. "You don't know all my secrets yet." He slipped a blue lanyard over her head, the same ones being worn by those working the convention.

She glanced at it and the identical one around his neck, being thrown for a loop. "Wait . . . what's happening?"

"It's your wedding con, honey. Now, let's go find your booth."

Chapter Eight

"MY WHAT?" NAOMI stopped walking, her brow knitting in confusion. Boone expected this reaction, but he didn't want to have this conversation in front of nearby security guards, who appeared bored enough to welcome small-time trouble.

"Let's keep moving." He took her by the elbow, pulling her farther into the space.

She inspected the badge hanging from the lanyard, flipping it to reveal its original owner, an older woman named Treasure with unnaturally blonde, spikey hair and big red lips. "Boone, what exactly is going on?"

"Okay, quick version. I wanted to surprise you and get a booth like you wanted. Surprise." Boone wondered if she originally didn't want him to come because she didn't believe he had much to offer. Perhaps she was right in the traditional sense. On the other hand, he could help in his own unique way, something he wanted to do very much.

"A booth? Wait a minute. Will you just wait a minute?" She stopped again. "How am I getting a booth last minute? And with what money? I'm not even prepared for that."

"Don't worry about it. I took care of it. That's what the lanyards are for."

"Stop." She held up a finger as she tried to put the information together before leaning closer, her eyes widened in shock. "Did you *steal* these? I told you I didn't want to trick anyone."

It hurt that her opinion of him could drop straight to the bottom, but Boone shouldn't be surprised. Most people had some aversion to stealing, and, clearly, she did as well.

He raised his hands as though to defend himself against the accusations. "I promised I wouldn't trick potential clients. And we're not. You're going to sell them on your idea like I know you can. I'm just helping you get the opportunity to do it. And don't look at me like that. No one is getting thrown in jail over a few lanyards. Besides, these aren't stolen because I paid for them." It was close enough to the truth.

Boone never wanted to lie to Naomi, especially after how much she revealed the night before. It had happened. He'd gained her confidence. The only thing he wanted to do was keep it, to hold her confidence to his chest like a money sack. Continuing to help her reach her goals had to be the best way to keep her happy.

She lifted the badge to demonstrate how much the photo wasn't a resemblance to herself, especially since she scowled and the real Treasure did not. "You paid for this? How much?"

"Twenty dollars."

She squinted skeptically. "Twenty dollars?"

"Yup, I swear to you. I paid twenty dollars. A little steep, but you're worth it." If it had been him alone, he'd have paid zero. But if throwing out a few bills for borrowed lanyards made her feel better, he'd do it. Of course, the owners of the lanyards didn't know they'd been part of the transaction, but the extra cash wouldn't hurt.

The first one came from an older gentleman outside of the building. The blue lanyard had been shoved haphazardly into the man's pocket, half of the neck strap blowing on a breeze. It was careless. The man would have probably lost it at some point anyway. When Boone accidentally-on-purpose bumped into him, he used his old skills to smoothly swap the lanyard for a twenty-dollar bill. With this lanyard in his possession, he had no trouble getting through the vendor entrance, security not even glancing at the badge because Boone was too well groomed to be anyone but another wedding vendor. This wasn't like breaking into the Capitol building. No one here cared.

Before Naomi called him, he'd already been on his way to her before spotting Treasure. She'd also been careless, her badge on the edge of a table. She'd been organizing products, appearing frantic as if running behind schedule. As he passed, he'd let another twenty-dollar bill drop on the ground near her.

"Sorry to bother you," Boone had said to Treasure.

"Yeah?" Her impatient tone and manner changed once her eyes connected with him. He flashed a smile, and she returned it, smoothing her outfit with a flustered hand. "Yes. Can I help you?"

He pointed to the twenty-dollar bill on the ground beside her table. "I wasn't sure if you dropped that, but wanted to let you know. Nothing can make your day worse than losing money.

I really love that shade of lipstick, very eighties punk rocker. It fits you."

The woman flushed, her eyes lighting before noticing the money. "Oh." She made an effort to pat the pockets of her too-tight, white pants as if this was sufficient to check if anything had vanished. "I am missing money. Aren't you sweet? Thank you." When she leaned to retrieve it, he palmed her lanyard, slipping it into his jacket pocket.

"Glad to help. You have a nice day now."

So, yeah, a part of the old Boone had come out to play, a part he swore he'd never resurrect again, except to give Naomi a tiny taste of her dream. In his mind, he owed her. He hadn't known his one innocent comment at that interview would have had such an effect on Naomi's psyche, but he'd caused it all the same. And while he hadn't known which specific YouTubers had cheated Robert out of his money, he knew that world, had been connected to it in a small way, because of Hank. His dad had probably run similar seminars but, back in the day, it was from hotel conference rooms and not streaming sites. He'd dragged Boone along to help, to learn, and the phrase he'd uttered was something he'd heard a hundred times before. Within his father's many disciples, it had become a familiar motto.

It took away any shiny remnant of Hank's reputation as any type of Robin Hood. Robert and the rest of the Moreno family weren't people who deserved their fate. He was a man who made a poor decision based on hope and desperation.

Boone hadn't always been on the up-and-up, either, but he could make it right for the people who were decent. What he was willing to do for Naomi was his way of tilting the table in a direction where some good could come out of it. Of course, he wasn't ready to tell Naomi this. She might not be ready to accept him, including parts of himself found on the gray part of the spectrum.

She stood before him with a frown stretched on her face. "Boone, I didn't bring anything but a couple business cards. I was going to have hot-air balloon stickers made. I don't have any stickers. I don't have any pamphlets or a website. I'm not ready for this. I can't do it."

This was the least of his worries because he was used to winging it. "I think you're more prepared than you realize. This has been on your mind for a while now. You got this, and I'm going to help you get it. I just need you to trust me." He gently took her hand, holding it to his chest.

"I just . . . Why are you doing this?"

How could she not know? How could she not see? While everything about himself was used to being stored inside a lockbox, one single aspect of his feelings must have been bright enough to shine through the keyhole. He didn't know when those silly imaginary scenarios he told her went from something he did to annoy her to him meaning every word.

True, a guy like him didn't belong with a decent person like her, but somewhere between their rock-climbing lesson and seeing her this morning in the motel room, he'd thought, *fuck it*. The old Boone had never been afraid of going for any opportunity available. He wasn't going to avoid it now.

So when the gaze of her big hazel eyes lifted to him, he tossed any remaining care aside. He slid his hands along her jawline to the nape of her neck. "This is why."

Tilting her chin, he ducked his head, pressing his mouth to hers. Her body stiffened with a sharp intake of breath. He was about to regret everything for thinking she'd welcome any of this, but then she softened. His selfishness turned into delight at discovering his kisses wouldn't be repelled. It emboldened him as he took what was originally a press of his lips, turning it into a real kiss. It was like going to a concert hall expecting the orchestra to play a soft symphony to lull one to sleep before a drum solo hit, and the whole thing turned into jazz. This kiss was simply an inspiration to something bigger, more exciting.

If he had known how perfect her lips would feel against his, how her lush mouth could make him forget about everything, he wouldn't have wasted two-and-a-half years not making amends and getting on Naomi's good side sooner. He was so used to sweeping other people away for his own ends, he'd fooled himself into thinking he was immune from getting swept away himself. The moment her lips parted with a sigh and her tongue slid against his, he was lost, taken, no better than any other foolish mark. Even worse, he no longer cared.

There was a "Woooo" and shrill whistles, which snapped his brain from whatever cloud they'd ascended to and returned him to Earth. They were at a wedding convention. Public kissing in the aisle wouldn't be frowned upon here, but they had work to do. He reluctantly pulled away from Naomi, her face one of surprise as she raised her delicate fingers to touch her mouth.

"Um." She flushed, releasing a short laugh while bringing her hand to her forehead, appearing flustered and unsure of herself. It wasn't clear if she would finish her thought, but she answered, "Okay, I trust you."

With his heart beating brightly, he took her hand, leading her to the end of an aisle. The last booth was occupied by florists with a banner reading, *The Floral Chaise*. A purple velvet fainting couch was nearby, with several flower garlands draped across the back. Two beautiful Black women worked the spot, one of them petite with short bouncy curls and the other more shapely and taller, with braided hair pulled into an elaborate updo decorated with flowers and wearing long eyelash extensions.

A black backdrop ran the length of the row, extending past the half-wall barrier of the florist booth by about four feet and leaving a half-sized booth area containing a couple of gray trash cans. This might work out perfectly. "Here, hold this," he said to Naomi, handing her the leather satchel which he'd brought with him. Grabbing both trash cans, he dragged them out of the way.

The woman with the work-of-art hairstyle flicked those long eyelashes in his direction. "Um, hello. Excuse me. What do you think you're doing?"

"Hey there." He approached with an easy smile, switching to an Australian accent. "Looks like we're going to be booth neighbors, ladies."

"I'm sorry?" The woman said, "No, no, no. You weren't here yesterday. Believe me, I would've remembered you." She gave him a long, assessing look.

"We don't know you, and that's not even a real booth," her friend added.

"Yeah, see, we only paid for today, and there seemed to be a bit of a mix-up. They double-booked our original booth. Since we traveled all this way, they gave us this one as a concession. But, no bother, we're used to making do with what we can. Isn't that right, Treasure?" He directed his question in Naomi's direction, who had the wide-eyed gaze of someone who wasn't sure what she was supposed to be doing.

The shorter woman pushed herself in front of her friend, her smile less suspicious and more flirty. "Where are you from? Are you from one of those English countries?"

The other woman scoffed at this. "Honey, this man is an Aussie."

"Ooh, I just love accents. Is that where those Hemsworth boys sprouted from?"

"I met one at a party once. Not one of the more well-known brothers, but the other one. Maybe later I'll tell you about it," he said with a wink and a grin before reaching out a hand. "I'm Charlie."

"Trisha," the taller woman said, taking a good grip on his hand, as her gaze ran the length of his arm. "Aren't you a strong one?"

"My name is Sadie." The shorter woman with the curls smiled at him with an appreciative look.

Uh-oh. Perhaps he was playing too loose with the charm. He needed to shut it down because his alter ego didn't need this kind of action. Unlike Boone, Charlie was normal, well-adjusted, and happy with Treasure. "This here is Treasure"—he yanked Naomi to him—"and she absolutely is too. Love of my life, this one." Boone put a hand to his chest as though his heart beat only for her. Charlie was one lucky bastard.

"I'm sorry. Did he say your name was Treasure?"

At this point, Naomi hadn't said anything. He hoped he didn't throw her too much into the wilderness, and she'd play along. He could see the wheels moving behind her eyes, probably wondering if she was expected to do an accent as well. Oh god, what if she tried and it was horrible or she talked like a Jane Austen character? But then she smiled brightly.

"You can blame my parents for that one. They're horrible at coming up with names. I have a brother named Barney . . . short for Barnacle." Boone almost snorted at this, surprised Naomi was capable of making up a story on the spot.

"Barnacle? And you're not from Australia?" Sadie asked.

"No. Central Oregon. I met Charlie when I rescued him from a coyote on a hike."

Naomi didn't choose to elaborate on this story. Sadie and Trisha turned their focus to Boone, as if expecting he'd pick up where she left off. Point one to Naomi/Treasure for throwing him out on a limb, and based on her expression, she did it on purpose. How was he supposed to explain how an Aussie, like himself, could grow up in a land with giant spiders, dingoes, aggressive kangaroos, crocodiles, and sharks and be afraid of a skittish coyote?

He laughed as if it was a joke before saying, "Yeah, well, that's why I fell head over heels for her and moved to Oregon. I always say when you find yourself a good, strong woman who's willing to rescue you from a coyote, grab her while you can." He slipped his arm around her, pulling her close. "Isn't that right, Treasure?"

Her eyes sparkled with humor. "You're definitely a very lucky man."

Charlie *was* a lucky man. In fact, Charlie probably got lucky every night, and slept in a real bed with a beautiful, spirited woman and not in his car or the couch, where he had to listen to his ex-con dad snore. Boone tried not to feel jealous of the imaginary man's life and instead leaned into it by tipping his head to press a gentle kiss to her temple. "That I am, Treasure."

This small display of affection did the trick. Sadie and Trisha switched to being booth friends, and they were incredibly funny and kind. For the first time in his life, he felt bad lying, wondering if it had been necessary. What if there were other people out there who would do something nice for a person, not because they were tricked into it, but because they were good people? Maybe the Morenos weren't a fluke.

"Your hair is absolutely on point," Sadie said to Naomi. "That color is gorgeous on you."

Naomi blushed prettily, leaning into Boone as though bashful at the attention. He found it funny she wanted to be seen by people and, yet, was not quite sure what to do with it once she was perceived. "Thank you."

"Would you mind doing us a favor?" Sadie continued. "Can we take a picture of you for one of our social media posts with some of our flower designs?"

Naomi looked surprised before she smiled, a new sense of confidence glowing from her. "Yeah, sure. Whatever you need. We're booth neighbors, after all."

She joined their side of the booth, which was fine because Boone had work to do. He dug into his leather satchel and removed a cardboard tube he'd brought. Inside was a simple, inexpensive banner he'd had printed at a local print shop a few days prior, when this whole plan had taken shape in his mind. Except he'd forgotten to bring anything to attach the banner to their backdrop. Luckily, The Floral Chaise ladies came through, and Trisha provided some pearl florist pins to attach the banner to the fabric. It was a bit odd, but then their whole booth situation was different.

Naomi re-emerged to their side of the booth, this time wearing a beautiful floral wreath crown on her head. The flowers were large and in different shades of purple. Sadie had been right. Naomi was gorgeous. She was glowing and took his damn breath away. He wanted to kiss her again, to never stop.

She touched a hand to the flowers on her head. "Isn't it pretty? They said I could keep it if I push people toward their booth if anyone asks about it."

The florists were kind but also business savvy. Naomi caught his eyes and also passersby. "I love your hair," someone shouted.

"Thank you," she replied, beaming. When they asked about the flower wreath, she directed them to Sadie and Trisha, as promised.

It wasn't until Naomi turned did she notice the banner, her hand going to her mouth with a gasp. Sure, it wasn't a hundred percent professional, and the photos of hot-air balloons photoshopped into wedding scenes were not legit, but he thought it looked well enough. Overlaid across the images was *High Desert Sky: Wedding Events*. "Oh my god, B—uh, Charlie. Where did that come from? You planned this?"

A sense of pride at her happiness seeped into his chest, but he responded while adjusting his glasses. "It's not much of a plan, more like covert convention-boothing. If you act legit, people will think you are. Simple."

She smiled at him. "We need a name for ourselves if we're really pulling off a"—she switched to a whisper—"wedding con. Otherwise, it doesn't feel official."

He leaned into her. "We already have a name, honey. We're The Chase Crew."

Boone put his Charlie game face back on, switching to an affable grin and his Australian accent when he noticed a couple eyeing the hot-air balloon banner. "Are you still looking for a wedding venue?" As he approached, he slipped his hands into his pockets, doing his best to take on a friendly, non-aggressive posture.

A petite woman wearing a vintage bombshell-style dress and sexy librarian glasses adjusted the tote bag on her shoulder. It read, *There's no place like home . . . because that's where all my books are* with an image of a Scottish terrier and ruby slippers on a stack of books. Her expression sparked with interest while the man with her was more closed off.

"We're just looking around," the man said.

"But you are looking for a venue, right? I can see it. Let me tell you a little secret." He lowered his voice, forcing them to lean closer. "We're not entirely out yet, still trying to gauge if people would be interested in our unique setup.

Because of this, we're priced below what you can get from any other venue, a lot lower." He directed this last part at the man, whose brow lifted in interest.

The man tried to fake aloofness. "Yeah, sure. We're just looking, thanks."

Boone pointed to the banner. "You've probably been trying to figure out how you can afford a venue when they're charging seven to ten thousand for the bare minimum. Ours is four grand, and it's next to Smith Rock. Plus, there's the hot-air balloon. Gives you that real vintage, somewhere-over-the-rainbow type of wedding your lady deserves." Boone and Naomi had never discussed pricing, but he'd researched, knowing it was temptingly cheap while also offering High Desert Tours a nice payday.

The woman clutched the man's arm, buzzing with excitement at the prospect. An easy sell. "Oh, that sounds amazing. How does the hot-air balloon part work?"

Naomi took a spot by Boone's side, her enthusiasm matching the woman's, sparkling at an eleven. "We do what is called tethering the balloon, so it'll be tied to the ground, and the ceremony will take place in front of it. You can bring your own officiant to do the ceremony, or we can include one, if you wish, done by the captain of the hot-air balloon. At the end of the ceremony, you and the groom get onto the balloon, it'll lift you up, and after you kiss, you can release rose petals to the ground. Your photographer can take pictures on the ground or go with you up in the balloon. You'll get the best view of your guests and Smith Rock."

"For four thousand dollars?" The man was skeptical, but now there was a spark of interest from him. He wanted to believe this deal was on the level. Boone could see it in his eyes.

"Yup," replied Naomi. "This would be for the venue, seating, and the balloon services. We don't provide catering but can offer local suggestions. If you're looking for flowers, you should talk to The Floral Chaise in the booth next door. Sadie and Trisha's designs are works of art. In fact, I noticed that they even offer custom floral arrangements using aged book pages if you want to combine your love of books into your wedding design. Our balloon business is family-owned, and we have a lot of experience with tours, but we're just dipping our toe into the wedding part of it. Since this is a new venture for us, we're willing to work with you."

God damn. Naomi was selling this thing, and quick on her feet. Turned out, she didn't need much of his help at all. She could sell it as well as anyone.

The couple exchanged glances, appearing to have a silent conversation.

"When were you planning on having your wedding?" Naomi asked.

"Next year. May," the woman replied.

Naomi tilted her head for a moment before she was all smiles. "That would be perfect. We should be able to do it, no problem. What was your name?"

"Madeline. This is Scott."

"Have you guys ever visited the High Desert before?" Naomi asked.

"We've been to Bend during ski season," Madeline said.

"We're in Terrebonne, right next to Smith. Let me give you my business card." Naomi searched in her purse before turning to Boone so she could write on a business card, using his back as a table. He wanted to laugh. Here he was, thinking he was going to charm someone into getting married at the Moreno farm, and impress Naomi enough she might let him kiss her some more. Instead, he was reduced to being nothing more than a solid surface for her to write on.

"I'm writing my name and email address. Contact me if you decide to take a trip to the area, and we can set up a tour of the place. You can even meet with our pilot and take a small ride. It's still a little cool during that time of the year, so May's a good month, not too hot. We get about three hundred days of sunshine a year, which is really nice if you want a beautiful outdoor ceremony. I know Portland can be a little more undependable that way." She handed the business card to Madeline.

The woman took it with a smile. "How long are you in town for?"

"Just today," Boone answered. "Since we're getting started, we're only offering a few openings of this service. Summer tends to be the busiest months, with tourists and all, so right now, we're being very exclusive."

Scott took the business card from Madeline, inspecting both sides, pondering the whole thing over. "Okay, we're interested, but we still want to think it over. Most of our family is in this area, but we've talked about possibly doing a wedding that wasn't necessarily local because of the cost of the city and still wanting something unique. We're just not sure yet."

"Yeah, of course, I understand," Naomi replied. "If you have any questions about the business or the area, I'll be happy to answer and help you out the best I can."

The couple left soon after, chatting between themselves. Boone could have analyzed what he might have done differently to land the mark, how to get them back and seal the deal. Except . . . this wasn't about him. All he focused on was the shining beacon of happiness and confidence coming from the woman beside him, looking like a person who'd already won. That was good enough for him. She'd never been more attractive to him, someone he wanted to capture and claim like a gift.

She took his forearm, squeezing it in excitement. "Oh my god. I think I can do this! Can you believe it?"

"I've always known you could. And the whole tethering idea? Brilliant. Was that your plan the whole time?"

"No. I don't even know where that came from. It just suddenly came together in my mind at the perfect moment. That's never happened to me before."

The next couple of hours went by quickly. They talked to a few more couples. Naomi took the lead because she was on fire, improving her tactics all the time. His instinct told him no one was as good of a get as that first couple of the day. He kept his eyes peeled, hoping Madeline and Scott would pass by again, decide to pull the trigger, and make a deposit or something.

Sweeping a quick assessment of the area, he noticed a security guard leaning against a wall. The man tried to be casual but wasn't doing a good job at it as he kept sliding a look in their direction, talking into a walkie-talkie. It got Boone's senses on alert.

He shoved his hands into his pockets, ambling over to

Naomi. In a low voice, he said, "Don't look, but we might have been made. There's an emergency exit about twenty feet to our left. If I can't talk us out of this, take it and get to my car. Understand?" Boone had been able to talk himself out of worse situations. He wasn't worried. This was a wedding convention, after all. The worst that could happen was they'd be asked to leave.

Naomi didn't react except for a single nod of her head. Good girl.

As Boone suspected, something was up because two more security guards joined the first, along with a man who looked suspiciously like the one he'd bumped into outside the venue. Charlie. "Shit," he said under his breath.

"Sir, can I ask you what exactly you're doing here?"

Boone took on a friendly grin and was about to bullshit about some misunderstanding to the security guard, but before he could get a word out, Naomi bolted like a startled deer. She held a hand to the wreath on her head, kicked up her feet, and raced straight to the emergency exit, leaving him behind.

Boone gave a sheepish shrug, and then took off running after Naomi, following her as she burst through the door and kept running toward the parking lot.

And The Chase Crew's first con came to an end.

Chapter Nine

*O*H GOD! WAS she about to get thrown in jail all because she tried to sneakily sign up a few people to get married? That wasn't a crime, was it? She heard footsteps fast behind her but was afraid to turn around in case there was a whole fleet of officers on her tail ready to tackle her and throw her into the back of a cop car. Despite this, and being completely out of breath, she had the urge to laugh, feeling exhilarated. Nothing like this had ever happened to her before. What would Selah say if she had to bail her out of jail? It made Naomi giggly, thinking about having to explain the whole ludicrous situation.

She didn't stop until Boone's car was reached, breathing hard and finding the courage to peek over her shoulder. Boone was the only one behind her. Naomi should be mad at him for having stolen those badges. She should have known better. Except she wasn't the least bit angry. While she would have preferred to have done everything on the level, everything he had done for her had been unbelievable and amazing. She'd never had this level of support before, and her heart was full of gratitude.

He leaned against the driver's side door, trying to catch his breath and fumbling his car keys. "What the hell, Naomi?

The Chase Crew is supposed to do the chasing, not the other way around. And you just left me." Regardless of his words, he didn't appear mad. His eyes sparkled as though he enjoyed their adventure as much as her.

"You told me to!"

Unlocking the door, they got in. "It's nice to know my partner-in-crime has a self-preservation instinct and will just leave me out to dry. Where's the loyalty?" he asked while starting the car and pulling out of the parking spot.

A giggle burst from her. She had to admit she had fun partnering with him. He made everything feel possible. He let her shine when he could have eclipsed her in his own charismatic shadow. She'd never had that, and she liked it. "Do you think they can find out who we are and come after us? Should I toss this badge out the window when we're on the freeway? Can it be dusted for fingerprints? I'm not used to this kind of life."

"Ah, yes, we're officially on the lam now, trying to out-run the wedding convention division of *Law & Order*. And are you implying that *I'm* used to this kind of life? If anything, you corrupted me. I'm just some poor, innocent country boy caught up in a beautiful enchantress's dreams, willing to do anything for her."

She released a small snort. "Innocent country boy, my ass. But, seriously, can they find us?"

"No. Obviously, they have my banner, but it doesn't have the company's real name or any contact information, and none of the photos are real. When it comes to *crimes*"— and he added air quotes around that word—"in my expert opinion, this is very small potatoes, Naomi. You act like a girl who just got away with shoplifting for the first time."

"I don't think I have the constitution for hard crimes like that. I already feel bad that I took Sadie and Trisha's flower crown. Maybe we should go back, and I can sneak in and give it to them." Sure, they said she could keep it, but she didn't deserve it and they had been very nice to her. They made her feel beautiful. Not that Boone hadn't also made her feel this way, but it was entirely different. He made her feel sexy, those dangerous cat eyes taking her in, his lids heavy as his gaze drifted the length of her. The heat behind it was nearly enough to singe her clothes.

The kiss he had given her at the start of the convention was something she hadn't expected from Boone. She was trying to differentiate between what she'd always believed about him and what he was slowly evolving into as he revealed more about himself and who he truly was.

His kiss this morning seemed significant, like it meant something. It was a kiss she felt everywhere. It dug into her soul, kept pinging back to her like a sonar echo, reminding her of his touch and how he tasted. She could barely breathe, knowing he was right here with her and helping her. He let her shine, gave her exactly what she wanted. She was yearning for him, wanting to recapture the experience.

"Look, I know this wasn't exactly what you had planned, and I'm sorry if I kind of ruined things for you. I just wanted you to have something special." His brow lifted sympathetically as he turned to her after parking at their motel.

"You didn't ruin anything."

"I didn't?"

"Outside of the whole being chased by security guys—"

"They didn't exactly chase us. When you bolted, they looked more confused than anything else."

"Really? God, that's hilarious. Okay, well, outside of that last part, this has been the best day. I never thought I'd be able to do all that. I've never been a badass like my sister. And if we ever tell anyone about this, we were pursued by twenty giant guys and barely escaped by the skin of our teeth. Also, thank you."

"You're thanking me?" He looked around as though she meant to direct her gratitude to someone else. "I didn't do very much. Never forget that you can be a badass when you want to. And let's make it forty men and throw in a few vicious dogs and a honey badger."

She didn't let him say anything more, grabbing his jacket lapel and pulling him in for a kiss. They'd picked up where they'd left off that morning, emotions exploding inside her chest like Pop Rocks. His hand latched to the nape of her neck while his lips parted hers, allowing his tongue to slide inside. The kiss turned heated on a dime.

"Pinky, you're steaming up my glasses," he said between breaths. "You have no idea how much I want to take you to—"

"Don't you dare tell me one of those ridiculous scenarios right now. If you're going to take me anywhere, it better be upstairs." She didn't want to talk when she could have action, the kind of action capable of melting her from the inside out.

A small grin played at the edges of his lips, his expression endearing rather than cocky. "Yeah?"

"Mm-hmm." She gave him a smile of her own, scraping

a finger along the hair above his ear.

They jumped from the car, racing to their room. Naomi was positively giddy as she pulled him along by his hand. It had been a while since she'd been with someone. She thought she'd feel nervous, but she didn't. This was Boone, after all, and she didn't know when she'd started trusting him, but she did. After fumbling with the key card as he pressed against her, dropping kisses along the skin of her neck, the door popped open, and they tumbled inside.

The door slammed shut, bags dropped to the ground, and then he had her in his grasp. Lifting, Boone pushed her against the wall, gripping her thighs. She wrapped her legs around his waist. Naomi gasped as he notched himself against her, his hold on her shifting to one hand as the other pulled the elastic of her neckline lower, his mouth going to the heart of her cleavage, sucking on the delicate skin there. It was overwhelming, happening fast, out of control. Yet, Naomi couldn't get enough, clawing at his clothes, searching for the heat of his skin. His hands were rough, his grip impressive, probably due to his skill as a rock climber. It was hot, and she was sizzling.

"Naomi," he groaned, rocking his hips into her.

She clung to his shoulders, moaning as his mouth trailed kisses from her chest to her neck. "Yes." She panted, becoming desperate to relieve the ache building inside of her.

His hand fit between them, easing under the fabric of her dress and his fingers slipping into her underwear. He rubbed her while kissing her neck and sending her breathing into overdrive. "Oh god," she whimpered, her grip tightening.

He edged her closer until he lifted his head, his eyes dark, filled with desire. "I want to give you a ride."

"What?" What were these words he was saying to her? Why was he talking at all? She released a squeak when he moved from the wall, carrying her to one of the beds and setting her on the edge of it.

"You didn't think I shaved into this mustache for nothing, did you?"

"Oh, you shaved it for me? What made you think I'm a mustache girl?" She watched with interest as the man shrugged off his jacket and then undid one button at a time, teasingly removing his dress shirt.

"I told you I can be pretty convincing." There it was, that arrogant grin again, but this time she had a feeling he was going to earn it. Regardless, she wasn't looking at his face anymore once his shirt was removed because those massive arms and tanned chest were marble sculptures belonging in a museum.

"I don't want any more of your smooth talk, mister."

"That's fine, but you better get used to this mouth because I'm about to use it on you, honey."

Her eyes may have bugged at that moment, her mind going in a direction she wasn't sure it was supposed to go in. Surely he didn't mean *that*. Naomi knew of such things from some of her romance books, but none of her previous boyfriends had ever offered, and she'd never asked.

Naomi almost swallowed her tongue when Boone kneeled in front of her, his hand reaching under her dress to peel her underwear down her legs. "That's okay," she heard herself say. "You don't have to do anything, uh, like that."

"Like what?" Those eyes glittered with mischief.

"Um, anything out of the ordinary."

"Naomi Moreno. Does a sparkler with bright pink hair, who's able to kick ass to make her dreams come true and outrun a hundred security guards on horseback, sound like someone willing to settle for just the ordinary?"

When he put it like that, she reconsidered everything. She looked to the far wall where there was a mirror and could see their reflection—Boone on his knees before her, she wearing her flower crown, and her long, wavy pink hair messy from running and kissing. To seek things a little less ordinary felt a lot like wild, exciting passion.

She met Boone's gaze head-on and offered a coy smile.

"That's the Naomi I know," he said before leaning closer, his breath whispering across the delicate skin on her shoulders. "Just so you know, this ride isn't free. The price of admission is I need to hear you say it. Say you want a mustache ride."

"Really?"

"Yup."

"Do serious people actually call them that?"

His thumb and forefinger smoothed the hairs above his lip. "Only if they want the real thing."

She willed herself not to blush or titter, something easier to accomplish when it wasn't awkward. Boone was right. She was a raspberry-pink-haired badass who deserved something more than the ordinary, and he was more than willing to give it to her. She stared him straight in the eyes. "Boone, I want a mustache ride."

"Good, because I'm dying to give you one."

She expected him to lift her skirts and go to town, but he

stood, removed the glasses she'd become attached to, setting them on the nightstand. He then slipped off her shoes and removed his own before getting on the bed and lying down. "All right, Naomi, come take your ride."

Despite being confident a few moments prior, a nervousness fluttered in her stomach. She reached to remove her flower crown, but he stopped her. "Keep it on."

She crawled across the bed, not sure if she should be attempting to do it in a seductive way, and the thought made her release a nervous laugh. Tentatively, she straddled his hips, continuing to support herself and not put her full weight on him.

He gave her an amused look before using two fingers to beckon her closer. "You need to come higher. A lot higher. I want you right on my face. I won't bite, but I will eat you out."

"Oh gosh," she said with a light breath. Was she really going to do this? Was he? She inched forward until reaching the top of his shoulders.

"Quit teasing me, Pinky. I'm absolutely starving for you." With that, he lifted her himself and moved her exactly where he wanted. When he said he was starving, he must have meant it because he gripped her legs, pulling her down on him, his mouth not wasting any time in finding her under the skirt of her dress.

After the initial shock of his tongue on her, Naomi melted into the heated bliss of the moment. Gripping the headboard for support, she closed her eyes, her head dropping backwards. A long, throaty moan escaped her mouth. His approval vibrated through her in the form of a rumbled growl. "Boone," she sighed, understanding exactly what she'd been missing and appreciating his determination to show her.

She kept climbing, her moans growing more pathetic as she got into the motion of riding his face until she couldn't help but explode, crying out, doing her best not to collapse and suffocate the man. But, good god, her whole world might have changed. Pleasure wrapped itself around her in a glow.

After finding herself again, she crawled off of him, unsure of where to look. Things were changing between them, but this jumped them several levels without a doubt. He sat up with his back against the headboard, wiping a hand across his lips and pulling her to him. "Can I see the rest of you?" he asked, not as shy as her.

The room wasn't bright with the curtains drawn, but it was more daylight than she was used to when undressing for a man. That was the old Naomi. The new one wanted him to see her. She transferred the flower wreath to his head, making them both smile before pulling the dress off. She undid the strapless bra, flinging it aside.

A look of wonder passed across his face as he took in her body. His expression was dazed and enthralled, giving her the upper hand on the guy. She snuggled into him, kissing along his neck and jawline. His free hand went to a breast, encompassing it with his hand, testing the weight and feel of it. She did her own inspection, lightly scraping her fingers over every ridge of his chest, touching as much of his exposed skin as she could.

"Are you looking for something, honey?" he asked with

humor as her exam shifted to the back of his shoulders.

"Yeah, I'm looking for those scars you got from when you were in a knife gang."

A blush swept across his features. "Okay, I might have been exaggerating that time. When I was nine, I and all my friends got pocketknives and we called ourselves a knife gang. But we really didn't do more than scratch out '*Knife gang was here*' into old park benches."

She laughed. "Seriously?"

"Like I said, you're hard to impress, and I might have been feeling pretty desperate that day."

Her touch traveled to the top of his pants. She made quick work of undoing them before sliding inside and gripping the absolute hardness there. Her pride swelled at his response of a sharp intake of breath before swearing.

"Boone," she said while gazing at him, "listen to me. I don't need to be impressed. I just need you to be real with me. Okay?"

He studied her for a moment, his beautiful brown eyes searching and serious. "Okay."

"Hey, I want you."

"You have no idea how much I want to be inside of you. You trust me, right?"

"Yes," she whispered, and she did.

Relief flooded his features. "Let me just—I have a condom in my bag." He pulled away, reaching for his overnight bag on the floor between the two beds.

While she was grateful they could continue, she wasn't beyond giving him a hard time. "Wait, did you purposely decide to bring condoms with you on this trip? What exactly did you think was going to happen?"

"I'm just a mortal man who lives on hope, woman."

"Hmm," was all she could say because she couldn't exactly be mad about it now.

He dug in his bag, retrieving a condom package before resuming his previous position on the bed. Waiting in anticipation, she tracked his hand as it traveled to the open waistband of his pants. "Look, I've never been bashful, but the way your eyes are burning a hole through my pants, it's making me a little self-conscious."

"Now you know how it feels. Stop teasing this out."

His dick was released from its confines, allowing him to roll the condom on. "Satisfied?" he asked, sneaking a peek at her.

"I think we both know that I'm about to be *very* satisfied." She helped him remove his remaining clothes before climbing onto his lap. Her mouth pulled into a smile at how cute he looked, wearing nothing but a floral crown. Their lips found each other easily, his face clasped between her hands as his arms wrapped around her.

He attempted to talk between kisses, between breaths. "Naomi, you have no idea . . . how much I've been . . . you're so beautiful—It's not just a line. I mean it. It's real."

Maybe it was her happy mood, her willingness to be swept away at the moment, but she believed him. "Thank you." She kissed him gently as she lifted and guided his dick into her.

He repeated her name with a sigh, looking at where they were connected before lifting his head to her, his tanned skin flushing, his golden-brown eyes glowing bright. She sensed her power and control over him, sliding up and down, gripping his shoulders as she increased the pace. Boone pressed his face into the crook of her neck, his fingers teasing with soft strokes where she needed it, telling her how good she felt, not noticing when the wreath slid off and fell to the floor as their pace increased.

"Yes," she agreed, her control slipping as she moaned. He surprised her with a burst of energy, grabbing her around the waist and forcing her back until she was underneath him. He drove into her with everything he had. They were the chase crew, after all, chasing each other to an entirely new point of being. She held on as he continued to push her, unable to stop herself from arching beneath him, crying his name when she hit the cliff.

He grunted as his movements became more intense before collapsing on her. Breathing hard, and the dampness of their skin pressed between them, he dragged himself away, but not before dropping kisses along her chest, shoulders, the edge of her hairline, and, finally, her lips. The gesture was sweet and gentle, like he was grateful.

While he was in the bathroom, she rose to look in the mirror, finding herself flushed, with wild, messy hair and smeared makeup, never feeling this sexy before. She reveled in the tingles continuing to travel through her body, flopping back with a satisfied hum.

HER PHONE, SITTING on the nightstand, buzzed with a notification. She and Boone lay together, lazily watching some movie on TV while she cuddled into his chest. When it buzzed again, she pulled away to check it.

"You can tell Tom he's too late. You've been claimed."

A thrill went through her at his words, at the insinuation this thing between them had permanence. "Claimed, huh?"

"I suppose that is a little caveman of me. What if I just claim this spot here beneath your left ear?" He pressed his lips there. "Although, it's really not fair for me not to get the right side in a two-for-one deal." To make his point, he pulled her hair back and kissed this area as well. One of his fingers slid down to the dip at the center of her collarbone. "I should get this spot, too, in a package deal."

Her eyes drifted closed. "Hmm. Someone is getting greedy."

"Honey, I'm just getting started. You have no idea how greedy I can get. So, you might as well tell him to back off."

She laughed lightly, snuggling into him again. "Relax. He doesn't even have my number. It's just my sister."

"Which one?"

"Hailey. She wanted to know how it's going."

"I have a sister."

She stopped scraping her fingers along his forearm at this reveal. The way he said it made it seem like this was something of significance in his life. "You do?"

"Yeah."

While Naomi was dying to know more, she approached the topic carefully. "Do you have any other siblings?"

He shrugged. "Not that I know of."

"What's your sister's name?"

"Sophie. She's . . . a lot younger than me. I was twelve

when she was born."

"Oh," was all Naomi replied, unsure if she should push for more information, if they had the kind of relationship where he trusted her enough to open up. "Well, look at Selah and me. She's six years older. Yeah, sometimes it can feel like having another mom, but she's also really great and always looking out for us."

Boone took her hand in his, running his fingers along her palm. "What would Selah say about this?"

"About this?" She spun her finger in a circle to include the frenzied mess of their motel room. "Or about your sister?"

"The first one."

"I don't know. You know Selah's focus is flying, outside of the family and her relationship with Dex. She's good at minding her business, unlike my mom and Hailey."

"I've always liked Selah. She's pretty straightforward."

"And I'm not straightforward?" she asked in mock offense.

"You are a beautiful puzzle that I've enjoyed trying to figure out."

Even if that was a line, she liked it. "Despite the age difference, are you close with your sister?"

"I haven't seen or talked to her in a really long time. Things didn't end well between my dad and her mom. I'm not sure we'd recognize each other anymore."

His tone was somber. No wonder he'd never wanted to discuss his past. Anytime she'd gotten a hint, it was sad in comparison to her own upbringing. Despite being a physically strong, big guy, there was something fragile beneath the shell, something hidden beneath a cocky grin and bravado. It had to be an exhausting way to live. "Have you ever tried to look her up? How old would she be? She has to be on social media."

"Sixteen, I think. I've done some searches, but I haven't been that successful."

"I don't know if you care if Hailey knew, but I can ask her to look. That snoop can out-detective anyone when it comes to finding someone online. She was able to track down our cousin's ex-boyfriend, who moved out of state with her car. She's like Van Helsing hunting for Dracula once she wants to find someone."

He didn't respond, and Naomi wondered if she pushed too hard. "I won't say anything if you don't want me to. And I, obviously, can't guarantee results."

"Okay, you can tell her. I just want to know that my sister's okay. I don't feel good with how everything was left. This is why I'm trying to get this climbing job, to make a little extra money if she needs it, or is trying to save up for school or something."

Naomi took her phone from the nightstand again, retrieving Hailey's most recent text so they could both see her phone screen. "Okay, what do you want me to tell her?"

Boone gave Naomi the few details he knew about his sister, which she then relayed to Hailey. She wasn't sure if this was going to provide anything for Boone or not, but it felt good to help him after all he'd done for her. For the first time since knowing him, she wanted Boone to have a happy ending, both in regard to his sister and his own life.

If she got to be a part of it, so much the better.

Chapter Ten

B OONE WOKE THE following morning in Naomi's bed. He half expected her to push him out the prior night, but he was glad she didn't. He preferred this. He lay on his side with one arm shoved under her pillow and the other draped over her waist. His left leg tangled with hers. She faced him, sleeping heavily, her hair fanning across a cheek. When he used a finger to gently push it back, his heart squeezed in his chest.

He was a lone wolf, and had been one for a long time, even when sleeping with someone. He could have sex and not feel anything emotionally, something that had been proven to him several times in his life. He wasn't sure he knew what love felt like or if he was capable of it. Shame, though, had been a familiar emotion. Lusting after Naomi could have been one more thing he did to latch onto a person, so he'd get what he wanted, whether it was confidence or something more.

Except whatever he'd felt for her yesterday hadn't gone away. Something remained, digging itself further into his soul. He scratched absently at his chest as though it was something he could peel off. Boone didn't deserve her. He didn't deserve her affection or her smiles or her family or any part of her life. He knew he didn't. Yet, he couldn't pull himself away, couldn't leave her if there was something he could do for her. He wanted to memorize every detail of her features, whether she was grumpy or happy or sad. He wanted it all.

He rubbed harder, the emotion beating stronger than anything he'd ever felt. He couldn't deny its existence. He could see himself in the same vulnerable position as Dex, so taken he'd give her anything she asked for. And if Dex was . . . it must mean he was also . . .

Boone loved Naomi.

He loved her.

Loved. Her.

The more the word played in his mind, the more it solidified everything. He was giving her pieces of himself, telling her about Sophie. He wanted to give her more, until she had enough pieces to fill a room. He'd mistakenly thought he wanted her, but, no, he *needed* her. Turns out, he didn't need her confidence as much as he needed her to take his.

The thing that shocked him the most was he'd always assumed if he was ever taken by a woman, it would have been someone more conniving than him. Instead, she had brought him to his goddamn knees by being nothing more than her delightful self.

When those lovely hazel eyes blinked open, a groggy smile spread across her face as warm as sunshine itself, and he wanted to suck it into his being. She stretched her neck in order to drop delicate kisses on his eyelids in a move that was so tender he wasn't sure how to react. He'd never experienced anything like it. How could he con his way into extending this motel stay and not return to the complicated reality waiting for him in Terrebonne? How could he live in this moment forever?

Instead, he brushed a hand across her arm and said, "Have a good sleep?"

"Mmm, yeah. Slept like a rock. I hope I didn't snore on you."

He smiled in return. "No, but then I slept hard, too, so I don't think I would have noticed."

"We should get up and get ready to go home."

"I'm not ready for that yet." He kissed her softly, not caring about anything but her plush lips pressing against his, his heart lifting when she returned the kiss. He was amazed at how thrilling, exciting, and new this all could be, how their rhythm synched as if they'd been kissing for months. His hands went to the buttons of her pajama top, his fingers flicking each button free as he went down the line, his body tightening in anticipation at the thought of getting to have her again.

She was beautifully sweet and authentic. He found parts of her surprising, such as not being shy in letting him know how much she wanted him, as her hands stroked his dick through his boxer briefs. A strangled growl grumbled in his throat.

"I'm finding these cat pajamas really cute," he said, sliding the fabric over her shoulders so he could pay his respects to her breasts by placing his face between them and teasing a nipple with his mouth.

"Cotton is the sexiest fabric." Naomi laughed, gasping when he must have hit a sensitive spot. He took note of it.

"I know you're joking, but I agree with you. It's just so soft, like the rest of you." His hands slid into the front of her underwear to touch her, feeling how ready she was for him. "The fabric is completely immersed in your scent. You're like a field of berries during summertime."

"Boone," she warned him.

She'd tell him to stop, as though he could never mean the sentiment behind the words because she deemed them to be too much. He did mean them, never meaning them more than this particular morning. He silenced her with a kiss, letting it speak for him instead.

So, yeah, Boone was selfish because, while knowing she deserved someone better than him, it didn't stop him from pushing down his briefs and prepping himself with protection before fitting himself between her legs. Boone couldn't help studying her face as he slid into her slowly, watching her breathe between parted lips, her skin growing dewy and pink as she arched into his movements.

He didn't want the frenzy of the night before, not wanting to rush anything, so he took his time, savoring the moment and how it felt to be with her. There was no way he could go back after this.

"Fuck. I can't get enough of you," he groaned, realizing how much he was teasing himself while holding back. It became harder with each passing second when she responded with satisfied moans as she kissed and scraped her teeth along his jawline.

She adjusted her position, sliding one leg higher, nearly to his shoulder, and lifting her hips. Damn, he knew she was strong and flexible, but this angle changed things. Possibly for her as well, because as he pushed harder, she panted while rocking against him and begging. Cool, always-in-control Boone vanished. In his place was someone feral who had this biological need to race toward completion. His grip tightened. Language and higher thought processing had been replaced with savage sounds and grunts, which only increased when she jerked in his arms with a "God, Boone" repeated several times.

Boone could have free soloed the highest, most difficult-rated rock in the world, and he never would have climbed as high as this. This was an entirely new height. It scared him shitless because he burned with a desire to reveal all, to tell her he loved her. He ached for a life he didn't understand, but wanting it anyway. He couldn't tell her and, therefore, kept his mouth busy by pressing soft, thankful kisses along the delicate skin on her shoulders.

They didn't talk very much afterward as they got ready to leave. He didn't feel like putting in his contacts, wearing his glasses again, debating if he might stick with them. He also did a quick shave with his electric razor. When he exited the bathroom, she looked aghast.

"What the hell did you do to your face?" she asked in a similar indignant tone as she had the previous morning.

He ran a hand across the clean-shaven jawline. "I wasn't planning on keeping the mustache forever." Mainly because he knew his dad would make comments about it.

Her mouth tipped into a frown.

"That repulsive?" He adjusted his glasses, finding her disappointment funny.

She blinked, her expression shifting, a smile gracing her

lips as her gaze flittered away. "Of course not. You always look good. I was just . . . becoming attached to it."

"I wouldn't worry. The rides won't stop, mustache or not." Not if he had any say in the matter. This made her blush harder, which he found adorable enough to tempt another round five minutes before checkout time.

To his great disappointment, they departed, starting the drive home. It was difficult not sneaking peeks at her in the passenger seat, especially when she adjusted the hemline of her skirt or played with her hair. She requested a short pit stop at Joe's Donuts to get some breakfast. The hole-in-the-wall donut place only had a few old-timers inside, but he couldn't resist demonstrating some kind of claim on Naomi by rubbing light circles on her back as they waited in line. It was a ridiculous display. Old Boone would have scoffed at this. Of course, when Naomi leaned into him, gazing up with a lovely smile, he kicked old Boone's attitude to the curb. What did that guy know anyway, except crushing emptiness and life in a trailer with a cat?

After eating their donuts, Naomi stopped in her tracks while they walked to the car. "Oh my god," she said after checking her phone. "I think Hailey has already found Sophie, and maybe even talked to her."

Boone's heart stuttered as he waited for news about his sister, expecting it to be bad. It had been so long, maybe she didn't remember him. Or, worse, didn't want to remember him. His association with Hank and general arrogant assholeness during his teenage years could have been enough to ruin his reputation for good. He tried to swallow, but it became stuck in his throat as Naomi silently read whatever was on her screen, attempting to be patient when all he wanted to do was rip the Band-Aid off.

He wondered if it had been a mistake telling Naomi anything. What if old things were dug up by this and it changed how she saw him? He couldn't even excuse anything. He'd worked hard to overcome everything. Her current impression of him was new and fragile enough it could all break apart over one message, losing her trust for good.

She touched his forearm. "Okay, Hailey found Sophie on social media and DM'd her, asking if she had an older brother named Boone. And Hailey said she immediately got a reply back, saying she did, and she wanted to know if Hailey knew you. She also wanted to know if there was a way she could reach you because she always wondered where you went. Hailey got her email address and sent one of her videos from Loop." Naomi tipped her phone in his direction so they could watch together on the social media app.

His brain knew Sophie was no longer a small child. She was almost the same age Boone had been when he'd been kicked out. She looked young, still very much a kid. It was hard to believe the person in the video was her. Although, he could see the similarity—the large, dark doe eyes now framed behind glasses, and straight brown hair. She still had ears that stuck out in a charming cartoon sort of way. This was his sister, a young, gangly girl with an endearing, nerdy style and an expressive face.

He couldn't focus on what she was saying, something about a book she'd read. He was too busy looking for clues about the kind of person she was. Whether she was happy and if she was okay. What kind of room was she talking from? He didn't recognize it as being from the large, modern dwelling he'd lived in before. It was smaller, not as bright, but neat and unfussy. Was that because it was what Sophie liked, or were she and her mom still struggling because of their run-in with the Reyes men? The video was short, too short, in Boone's opinion. They watched it twice and he didn't realize until Naomi stopped it how much he leaned into her.

He cleared his throat. "Have you read that book before?"

"I've heard of it but haven't read it. I think it's a young adult romance."

"She reads romance books too?" He liked the idea his sister and Naomi might have something in common. It was a weird, fleeting thought because chances were they were never going to meet. He wasn't even sure if *he'd* ever see his sister again, let alone with Naomi, although he could hope.

"You both wear glasses," she observed.

"Hmm," he replied. He tried to see any other similarities, but it was difficult. He felt hard, cynical, and much older compared to Sophie.

"Are you going to send her a message?"

"I don't know." He hadn't thought that far ahead. Part of him wanted to rush into reaching out, to glob up every piece of information he could. The other side of him was scared. Maybe Sophie would be disappointed he hadn't broken free yet, that he remained connected to Hank. "She's a teenager. I don't know what to talk to her about. Maybe she doesn't—"

Naomi stopped him with a look. "Listen to me. This is just a sixteen-year-old girl who's excited about possibly reconnecting with her big brother. Trust me when I tell you that teenage girls don't show obvious excitement over just anything. That's when we start to mute ourselves, afraid of causing too much attention to shine in our direction, to take fewer risks because we don't want to look silly. It's hard to outgrow that. She wants to hear from you. She gave you her email address. So you can tell her that she's been on your mind and you want to know if she's doing well. Then just tell her a little bit about you and your life. That would be enough. That's all anyone wants from you, Boone. It's enough to be who you are."

"Yeah, okay." He didn't have the words to say more. He appreciated Naomi's sentiment. It was good in theory, but she didn't know everything, and maybe if she did, her advice would be different. "I'll have to put some thought into it, I guess. Anyway, we should get going. Can you thank your sister for me?"

The rest of the drive was quiet. Boone was drawn into his own thoughts as he drafted and redrafted variations of emails to his sister in his head. He leaned an elbow against the car door and rubbed his temple. He varied between telling her everything, good and bad. Or telling her a little, but painting a rosy picture so she'd feel good. Or he'd tell her nothing about himself and keep the focus on Sophie.

He was jolted from his thoughts when they drove onto the road to the Moreno farm, and Naomi spoke up. "Let's not mention this to my family . . . you know, about what happened this weekend. They don't need to know every-thing."

Boone was taken aback. He hadn't thought about how it

would go moving forward. Perhaps this was his fault for assuming they'd naturally move into a new phase of togetherness. Her words sent cracks into his newly discovered heart, wondering if he was again falling into being someone's dirty secret. Maybe he was a fool for hoping for something different this time around.

He tried to stamp down the negative emotions triggering within him, the feeling of regret for opening any part of himself up in telling her about Sophie. He was about to tell her he wasn't going to play that game because he didn't want to hide anymore.

"Who the heck is that?" she asked before he could say anything.

His line of sight followed her finger pointing in the direction of the Moreno farmhouse. There were a few old chairs on the large, wraparound, covered porch. They weren't used often, at least not that Boone had noticed. This time, a familiar man sat back in one chair as casually as can be.

Boone squinted through his bug-smeared, dusty windshield to make sure his eyes weren't playing tricks on him.

Shit.

It was Hank. The man who could ruin everything for him.

Chapter Eleven

A VIBE SHIFTED in the air between her and Boone. Naomi didn't quite understand it, but something was off. He'd parked the car in his normal area. Her truck remained in the same spot she'd left it Saturday morning, dustier than before.

The appearance of the mystery man on the porch made her anxious. She was eager to see her mom and Hailey, to make sure everything was okay. While unknown people were common during tour days, it was unusual for people to visit the farmhouse during other periods, unless her mom's side of the family came for a visit.

After parking, Boone didn't remove his grip from the steering wheel, leaning forward and touching his forehead to his hands. His eyes closed as if in a silent prayer. Was he sick? Was something wrong? He'd been quiet on the car ride, but she'd assumed the news about his sister had turned him introspective. He'd driven with a silent intensity.

It was clearly a sensitive topic for him. She didn't want to push if he wasn't ready. Sure, they'd slept together, and she was coming to really like him, but she wasn't in any position to start digging because of it. She wasn't sure if he wanted her in his life like that or if he was a conquer-and-move-on sort of guy. She tried to prepare herself in case she'd been assuming too much, telling herself it was a great weekend regardless of what happened next between them. Either way, it was best not to tell her family about any of the particulars until she knew for sure. Better not to make things awkward if it didn't need to be.

"Is everything okay?" She wasn't sure if she should get out of the car or not, even if she was eager to find out what was going on.

He muttered something, low under his breath, words she couldn't decipher.

"What was that?"

"It's my father," he repeated louder. His words came out a little short. It was the first time she could describe Boone as downright irritated and not simply grumpy because of some laughable jealousy over Thomas.

At least the man on the porch wasn't a total stranger, calming her nerves somewhat. He wasn't her family, but he was Boone's, and she trusted him. She could relax, right? Except Boone didn't appear happy about this appearance.

"Okay. Why would he be here?" She'd been hoping she and Boone could continue to hang out at her place. But if he'd already made plans with family, it squashed her idea.

"I don't know." Again, his words were short. Boone straightened and got out of the car, slamming the door behind him. He trekked across the dirt toward the house. Naomi grabbed her purse and overnight bag, scrambling from the vehicle to follow him. Halfway there, Elena emerged from the house, carrying a drink and a plate filled with food, her smile brightening at seeing them.

"Ah, I'm so glad you arrived home safely. Did you have a good time? I want to hear all about the convention. Are you two hungry?" Elena handed the food and drink to Boone's father as if it were the most normal thing in the world. He set the items on a nearby small end table before standing to greet them as if this was his home too.

What the hell was going on?

"Boone, welcome back. And look at that beautiful, clean-shaven face coming together like a good plan." A model-perfect smile slipped easily into place on the older Reyes's face. He was tall, like Boone, although not as broad. While the man looked about the same age as Naomi's father had been, he'd aged well, the lines on his face not taking away from a general handsomeness. His hair was neatly trimmed and styled as he adjusted what looked like an expensive watch on his tanned forearm. He stood with an ease that reminded her of Boone, as though he was never out of place, fitting himself in any way he could. Everything appeared right, and yet there was something off about the whole situation.

If this was his father, everything about Boone clicked to-gether in perfect sense. Except she didn't see him like that anymore. She knew there was more to him than all of this. It made her doubt herself, because she didn't want to do to Boone's father what she had unfairly done to him. It was weird to have an instant distrust of someone simply because they had a natural ease and charisma.

She forced a smile. "Hello." She was curious about what it would be like with two overly charming men coming together. Would they collide together like a glitter asteroid and dazzle her whole family away? The quiet Moreno farm might not be ready for something like that.

One glance at Boone, and she was surprised to see no glitter in sight. In fact, his brow knitted together in gloom. "What are you doing here, Dad?"

His father's smile faltered for a brief moment before returning. "Come on, son. I just missed you is all. Plus, after hearing so many good things about the people you work with, I thought it might be nice to check it out myself. Got kind of lonely house-sitting for you, and all I got is that damn cat to talk to."

"Great," Boone replied. "You've met them. Now I don't think we need to bother them any further. We should go—"

"I don't mind," Elena said. "I was making lunch anyways, for Hailey and me." There wasn't any sign of Hailey, but her sister spent a lot of time in her bedroom when she was home. She mostly was online, making social media content.

"Yeah, see," Boone's father said, giving them a friendly wink. "I already feel like one of the family, and this food smells so good, I'm surprised everyone isn't showing up to this farm. It looks excellent, by the way, ma'am. I do love some honest-to-god, heart-on-a-plate, home cooking." He spoke with a slight country twang. There was something too folksy about it. But, again, she didn't know if she was being her old suspicious self or if something was off because of Boone's behavior.

Folksy or not, her mother didn't seem to mind. Elena released a giggle in response to his words. She was easily charmed, especially when it came to people appreciating her cooking efforts. When he turned his attention in Naomi's direction, he offered her a soft smile, his eyes the color of a stormy sea, almost unusual in how they captured the light. He focused on her like she became the most important person in his orbit. "Well, hello, darling. Aren't you a bright bit of sunshine in a field of wildflowers? Which one of Elena's beautiful daughters are you? I'm Hank, by the way, Boone's poor, lonely old man."

Naomi resisted the urge to roll her eyes, working to keep her face from revealing any thoughts as she raised a hand in greeting. "Naomi." In normal circumstances, she might have offered a handshake, but Boone positioned himself between Hank and Naomi and her mother, which made the whole thing awkward, so she didn't.

Hank's eyes lit with recognition, his brow raising. "Oh, so you're Naomi. I've heard a lot about you. You've clearly made an impression on my son, and I can see why. We Reyes men are suckers for a pretty face. We lose our hearts to them every time. Isn't that right, Boone?" His gaze flickered over her. "I can see you got those beauty genes from your mother. A cook and a beauty. I don't think a man needs anything else." He laughed heartily at this.

"Yeah," Boone said flatly, stepping more in front of Naomi, resulting in her having to crane her neck to see Hank. "Well, Naomi and I have had a long trip and I'd like to get home. I'm sure Naomi wants the same. We better take off and leave them alone."

"Now, Boone, what's your hurry? I just got my lunch and—"

"Take it to go," he snapped.

Hank didn't seem bothered by his son's attitude, his smile warm when he turned to Elena. "Seems the long ride has made my son a little cranky. I'm sorry to be a bother, but would you mind if I took your delicious food home with me?"

"Of course. Of course," her mother said, taking the plate back from him. "I'll just run in and put it in a Tupperware. I'll put in some extra food for you, too, Boone. I know you're tired, but you might be hungry later."

While Elena went inside, Naomi stayed on the porch, feeling perplexed but also surprised. Before the weekend, she knew nothing about Boone's family, and now she knew about a sister and father. It was a lot to take in.

"I'm sorry we need to cut this visit short. I would have loved to stay longer, but it was real nice to meet you. Ever since Boone talked about the Moreno women, I've been itching to meet y'all. You got yourself a real pretty spot here. Definitely a place where you can breathe and put some pretty color in your cheeks. Not a problem for you, I can see."

"Yeah," Naomi said. "So, do you live here, Hank, or are you just visiting?"

"Just moved to the area. Wanted to be close to my son. He's nice enough to let me crash at his place until I can get set up. I'm amazed at how fast the area is growing. So many new housing developments since the last time . . . I came through. A real housing boom, isn't it? And y'all are sitting right at the heart of it."

"I guess so," she replied.

"Here we go." Elena returned with the food wrapped.

"Maybe we can have both of you over for dinner soon. Wouldn't that be nice? Boone comes all the time, but we have more than enough room for another, and you're more than welcome."

"Thank you, ma'am. That's real nice of you. We'd love that," Hank replied while Boone encouraged his father to walk away by pulling on his elbow.

"You can call me Elena," her mother said. "We'll set something up soon. Boone, I hope you get yourself some rest, and thanks for looking out for my baby this weekend."

Boone didn't give Naomi a second glance, focusing straight ahead as they made their way to his car. She leaned against one of the porch support beams with her arms crossed as she watched them go.

The last thing Hank said was, "Sounds good. In the meantime, we are nothing but mortal men living on hope." The last sentence struck her because Boone had said something similar this weekend. She supposed it could have been one of those things his dad said a lot and something he adopted himself, but it was odd. It tainted her memory as though perhaps there was a chance Boone had been feeding her lines to get her into bed, and he'd succeeded. Had she allowed herself to fall too easily?

Boone reversed his car fast enough to kick a cloud of dust before shifting into forward and driving away. Elena stood beside Naomi, wrapping an arm around her.

"That was weird, right?"

"Was it?" Her mother was not the least bit suspicious, but she'd always been a trusting person. "I thought it was nice. You girls are always off doing your own things these days. It was nice to have someone to visit with."

"How long has Hank been here?"

"Not long. Just walked up and—"

"Walked? From where?"

Elena shrugged. "I guess the Crockett farm. That's where Boone lives, and it's not that far. He said he knew Boone was coming back today and wondered if he could have some company while he waited. Hank is a very nice man and so handsome."

Naomi shot her mother a glance. "Handsome?"

"Of course he's not as handsome as my Robert, but— What? Don't look at me like that, mija. I'm allowed to notice handsome men."

She understood her mother may eventually decide to have another relationship, but it had been some faraway theory, not a nearby possibility. Naomi told herself she didn't have a problem with this. Her mom was human and deserved to find love again.

On the other hand, Elena and Robert were cemented in her mind as true romance, better than anything she could find in a book. She wasn't sure she was ready for her mom to pack their romance away and find someone else, especially someone like Hank, because . . . Well, she wasn't quite sure why. He was just so different from her dad. Plus, her mother and her quenching their thirst within the same family didn't sit right. Not that that's what Naomi was doing—

Anyway, she didn't want to think about it. But maybe this was the real reason she didn't feel particularly warm toward Hank. Obviously, this was a *her* problem.

"You're not leaving already?" Elena asked. "Stay and eat.

I miss you."

"Eh, I'm pretty beat from the weekend and kind of want to go home, put on pajamas, and stream something."

"Did you not get enough sleep?"

"Some." Naomi's skin heated at knowing the reason for her lack of rest.

Elena pressed a palm to her temple. "You do feel kind of warm. I hope you're not getting sick. Are you sure you don't want to stay here and let me take care of you?"

"I'm fine."

After taking some food with her, Naomi drove home. There she found Dex sitting on the sofa while scrolling through his phone. He'd been working a lot lately as a park ranger since it was high tourist season, so she hadn't seen him as often. Selah kept him all to herself these days, spending a lot of time at his place.

He glanced at her when she entered and grinned. "Hey, friend."

"Dex!" She climbed over the arm of the couch to wrap her arms around his neck. "How are you? Where's my sister?"

"Upstairs, taking a quick shower. We're going to the movies."

"Aw, and she wouldn't let you join her in there?"

"No, because, and I quote, *It wouldn't be a quick shower, Dex, and I want to eat before the movie.*"

"That sounds like Selah. Always the practical one."

"Is that food from your mom? It looks really good."

Naomi moved into the small galley kitchen, popping her food in the fridge. "Sorry, it's for those of us unlucky in love.

You can take my sister some place nice to eat."

Upstairs, she ran into Selah in the hallway as she was coming out of the bathroom, her dark, curly hair still damp.

"Hey," Naomi said.

"Hi, welcome back. How was Portland?"

"Yeah, it was, um, great." Naomi was excited to describe how promising things had been at the convention. Except then, she'd have to explain to Selah how everything came to be, including a possible wedding con involving stolen convention badges, a flower wreath, and a makeshift booth. It would sound as if she'd made out like a bandit, which might not be a good thing in her sister's eyes. Selah, who'd always been by the book, wouldn't approve of Boone's unconventional schemes. Nor Naomi, for going along with it.

"Was everything okay with Boone?"

"Mm-hmm. Yup." Naomi made her way to her room, averting her eyes and hoping her flushing skin didn't betray her.

"Naomi," her sister said in a warning tone. Selah might be wrapped up in her own world, but she could be observant at the most inopportune times.

"What?"

"You're acting really weird."

"No, I'm not."

"Look, all I care about is that nothing bad happened—"

"I told you everything was great."

"Ah-ha! You're blushing! Looks like Hailey might be on-to something."

"What!" She hadn't told Hailey anything, but their

youngest sister had the habit of taking nothing, creating a molehill, and turning the imaginary molehill into a mountain. And Naomi, the mole, wasn't even sure where she stood with Boone. "Don't listen to her. You know she digs up trouble when she's bored."

"True, but that doesn't mean you weren't getting into something in Portland."

"I wasn't. It was a business trip—"

"A trip you took with a man who's been into you for over two years."

"No, he hasn't." Had he? It was hard to see past her own perspective.

"Dex?" Selah called, blotting her damp hair with a towel.

"Yeah?"

"Do you think Boone has a thing for Naomi?"

"Was that supposed to be a secret?" Dex hollered from downstairs.

Selah swept a hand forward as though to say *See.*

Naomi released a sigh, leaning against her doorframe. "It's complicated."

"Isn't everything?" her sister replied. "Nothing worth having ever comes easy."

"Now you sound like Dad."

Selah shrugged at this. "Doesn't mean it isn't true."

It did bring something else to mind, and Naomi switched directions. "Hey, have you ever met Boone's dad?"

"He has a dad?"

She gave her sister a flat look. "What? You think he hatched out of an egg or something? Anyway, he was hanging out at the farm when we got back."

"Who was at the farm?"

"Boone's dad."

"Why?"

"I don't know. He said he was lonely and wanted to wait for us with Mom. I didn't even know he had family in town, and this was the first time I'd ever seen him before. Boone hadn't said anything." He didn't look happy about his dad being there and hadn't mentioned to his father anything about finding his sister. Naomi had been careful not to bring it up, either, in case there was a reason for it.

Selah tipped her head in thought. "Huh. Well, maybe he recently moved to town to be near Boone and doesn't know anyone else. Was he weird or creepy?"

"He didn't feel creepy, maybe just overly friendly, like he's trying to charm you."

"So, like Boone?"

"Yeah."

"Huh?" Selah said again.

"If Mom decided to start dating again, would you be okay with that?" Naomi felt nervous about saying it too loudly and turning it into a reality.

Her sister's gaze snapped to her. "Was he hitting on her?"

"No. I don't know. He called her pretty. Like I said, he was really putting it on thick, and, after he left, she admitted she thought he was handsome. I'm not saying anything happened. It just made me think about the theoretical situation."

Selah looked upward as if in thought and then raised her brow in acceptance. "I don't know if it matters if I'm okay with it or not. Mom should be allowed to do whatever she wants, and if someone makes her happy, who am I to deny her that? Hailey is probably not going to take it too well, though, especially if she's still living there. Would you not be okay with it?"

"I don't know. I agree with you that Mom is allowed to be happy and, yeah, it's been almost three years since Dad died. But it doesn't *feel* that long. If Mom starts dating, it would make me feel sad. Like how real was their love if she can move on like that?"

"I get how you're feeling. Some days, it feels like it's been a while, and other times, it feels like it just happened last month. My sense of time is screwed up sometimes. But just because Mom says someone is handsome doesn't mean she's thinking about dating them, let alone Boone's dad. Mom is also just really friendly like that. I think she's trying to find a way to build up her family again, maybe because Dad left such a big hole. It's probably more of a family thing than a romantic thing."

"Yeah, maybe." Selah had a good point. Maybe they all were trying to find some way to fill themselves back up after Robert died. Maybe it was the same thing with Boone and his sister. In their own ways, they were trying to fill themselves, clinging to something that felt like family. Perhaps this was why Boone hung around, even when there wasn't any work to do, and her mother recognized this.

After her sister and Dex left, Naomi slipped into her pajamas, heated her food, and played a comfort movie she'd watched a dozen times already. She checked her phone for messages and found nothing. She thought about messaging

Amber but wasn't in the mood to get into a similar conversation as she'd already had with Selah.

She'd hoped she would have heard something from Boone. If he had a thing for her all this time, why didn't he ever blow up her phone? Why wasn't he messaging her now? He was a hard man to figure out. It was weird how the day had started with them close, literally, only to end in silence.

Naomi tried not to take it personally. He may have had a lot going on with his dad and his sister and . . . he'd acted strange at the farm. Perhaps there was something wrong. She fiddled with her phone before pulling up his number and texting, *I hope everything is okay with you.*

The movie was almost over before she received the response, *Fine.*

She preferred teasing or being called Pinky, or even the addition of a flirty winking emoji to whatever this was. This was less than what he gave her before they'd slept together. This was bluntness. It was nothing.

Giving it another chance, she replied, *Thanks for going with me. I had fun.* She almost regretted it. Would he think she was expecting something from him?

Regardless, her phone remained silent. He never responded, and the longer it went on, the more annoyed she became, both with him and also herself. It was her fault for being disappointed in expecting anything. Clearly, the weekend hadn't meant much to him at all, and she'd do best to treat it the same.

Chapter Twelve

WHEN BOONE HAD left the Moreno farm, he'd gripped the steering wheel so hard he could have snapped it in half. Most of the things that had happened in his life, he'd done his best to brush off. Boone couldn't stand around staring at broken pieces, because what was the point? This time, he wanted to explode in anger, which he couldn't do in front of Elena and Naomi. He had to be careful with strong emotions because it showed weakness, and he didn't want it to be used against him.

He was more exposed than he'd ever been before. Not only because of his desire to dig himself out of where he came from, but also because of the people he valued. He wanted to wrap the whole Moreno family in a bubble of safety. Naomi was the same way. She was protective of the people she loved. He understood her suspicion of him was a byproduct of that protectiveness.

It crushed him to know that welcoming him into their lives might be the thing putting the family at risk. He was connected to someone who didn't care about hurting others and did so with a smile. Boone didn't want to live the type of life where he only chased riches and nothing more. It made him feel like the Tin Man—all hollowed out and missing a heart.

Hank hadn't noticed Boone's dark mood, chatting during the short drive home about something no one cared about but his father. The tension broke when they walked inside the trailer, and his dad said, "I have to tell you, Boone, I think you may have found a gold mine. Do you know what a sweet little setup that Moreno family has? With the Central Oregon housing market booming—First, Bend. Then Redmond. Now Sisters. You know Terrebonne is next. They could be sitting on something really big. Don't know why they keep fooling around with that piddly hot-air balloon business. Here I thought you were sitting on your ass doing nothing, and it turns out you've been doing something all along. Plus, getting that sexy ass as a bonus." Hank whistled through his teeth. "Looks like you finally figured out the lesson on who's supposed to be on top."

Something snapped in Boone. In a whirl of motion, he grabbed the front of his father's shirt, shoving him into the kitchen cabinets. Catching Hank off guard, the Tupperware in his hand fell to the floor. "I told you to stay away. I don't want you near them."

His father smirked as though this was a joke. He didn't seem to take Boone's actions or words as a serious threat. "Okay, you need to settle down. You made me drop my food. What's gotten into you lately? Besides, I got a nice invitation to dinner and—What? I'm just supposed to not go? What sense does that make? When did you get so uptight? Relax."

"You're not going to dinner. You're not going to do anything. I'm telling you to leave it alone, or there's going to be trouble between us. And then I won't care if we both end up in prison."

His father took him in, his expression shifting to something murkier, a dark spark in his eyes as he glanced at Boone's hand gripping the front of his shirt. The mask came off as his lips pulled into a tight smile, as though he had him all figured out. Hank's hands settled on Boone's shoulders with a strong grip. "Son, I know you've been left on your own for a while, and I'm sorry about that. You know I didn't want to leave you. Not me, who'd been taking care of you and raising you when no one else wanted to. Who's always had your back and made sure you had the skills needed to survive in a world that wants nothing more than to chew us up and spit us out.

"And I'm proud of you, real proud. I mean, look at you. You have the potential to surpass me if you stop wasting your time on something that will never get you anything other than a shitty car, a shoebox trailer, and a girlfriend who will want you to settle down, get married, and get a real job like the rest of the suckers. Don't ever forget that I'm the only one who's looked out for you, who will continue to look out for you. You think anyone decent is gonna stick around? With our history? They'll never love you as much as they love each other because you're not family and you never will be. *I'm* your family. I don't know why you can't show a little gratitude. We'll always be on the same side. Nothing you can do will change that."

Boone's anger seeped away, his grip on his dad's shirt loosening. The familiar fear of losing the only person who'd ever been in his corner eased its way into his chest, lodging itself there, trapping him. "Please. Dad. Leave it alone."

"It's okay. Look at me. Will you look at me?"

He managed to raise his gaze, absolute misery sinking into his heart.

"Hey." Hank smiled, patting Boone's cheek with a hard hand. "Now I'm gonna try not to feel hurt that you want to cut out your old man from your plans, especially since I would never do the same thing to you. All I've ever wanted in my life was to make sure you've been okay. But, hey, I get it. Maybe you wanna spread your wings and show you can do jobs on your own, that you're a man. That's great. If you want me to step back, not step on your toes, I'm willing to do that. Just know I'm here for you if you need it. I still gotta lot of contacts. But only if you need it. Otherwise, I'll just step back. Let you work whatever thing you got going on. Okay?"

Boone had trouble processing his father's words, over-whelmed by the guilt and in a daze from the ups and downs of his emotions throughout the whole weekend. "Okay," was all he managed, easing his hold on his father's shirt.

Hank smiled as if all was right with the world again. "Al-right. Good. Well, I'm glad you're back anyway. I've missed you. Did you want some of this food? This good woman is generous. I think generosity is my favorite quality a woman can have." He bent to collect the fallen Tupperware from the ground.

"No." Boone's appetite was nonexistent. He turned and stumbled his way down the steps of the trailer, wanting some fresh air. He sat on the hood of his car, staring off into the landscape in the general direction of the Moreno farm. Cat jumped onto the vehicle, climbing onto his lap and crawling up his chest to butt his head with Boone's chin. He pulled the purring animal closer, providing head scratches as he wondered what he was going to do, ignoring the phone buzzing in his pocket.

He sat for a long while before getting the energy to check his device.

I hope everything is okay with you.

Boone didn't understand why she cared whether things were okay for him or not. She didn't want him—not like he'd hoped. His father had been right. When it came to the Moreno family circle, he'd never get anywhere close to being included inside of it. He'd always be on the outside. There was nothing more depressing than getting a tiny glimpse of what his life could look like and then finding out he'd been conning himself with delusions. He'd only be a secret for her to keep. This was all he was worth, apparently.

It was probably for the best. She shouldn't get mixed up with someone like him, someone who had a father like Hank, who grabbed at every advantage he could and never left an opportunity alone. Boone fantasized about packing his bag, taking off, and starting over. He would have, if he didn't worry about what would happen in his absence, knowing there'd be nothing stopping his father from swooping in. It was a new kind of pressure, a new kind of responsibility. Boone wasn't sure he was strong enough for it.

TWO DAYS LATER, Boone sat in his normal camping chair in the Moreno field, wearing his sunglasses, blinking against dry eyes because his contacts were bothering him. He stared at nothing, chewing on a hangnail, and attempting to keep his gaze from landing on Naomi. His attention returned when it became clear she was talking to him.

"What?" he asked.

"I was just wondering if you messaged your sister."

"No." As excited as he'd been, he began to wonder if it was a bad idea to email Sophie. She was one more person who shouldn't get mixed up with him. Why would she want a brother like him when he couldn't help himself, let alone anyone else?

Naomi sat across from him, her legs crossed as she messed around on her phone. She brushed a strand from her shoulder. Most of her thick, wavy hair was swept into a ponytail. He hated that he remained drawn to her, that he couldn't cut himself off as easily as she could. He rubbed a thumb across his lower lip, remembering how she felt and tasted, how she had sounded when they'd been together. He grew frustrated with every passing minute.

Maybe he owed her. She had helped him find Sophie, after all. If being some kind of pastime toy to her was payment, perhaps the torture of knowing that's all he'd ever be might be worth it.

He heard himself ask, "Rock climbing lesson this weekend?"

Her gaze lifted with annoyance etched on her features. "You can't be serious."

"Come on, Pinky. I know you want to conquer a rock

face, and then you can climb and conquer me afterward." Boone couldn't help himself. He needed this.

Her eyes grew hard and dark, not with lust, but with something similar to anger. "What the hell is wrong with you?" Her brow pressed together as though she was thoroughly confused, which, in turn, confused and annoyed him.

"Just forget it," he huffed grumpily.

"No, seriously, what's wrong with you? You've barely said half a dozen words to me since we got back and—Okay, I'm not like you. I can't just go back. I thought . . . well, maybe you don't want to . . . but I thought we could at least be friends. I don't get you, and I don't know what's going on here."

That made two of them because he didn't understand her as well. Who thought it was important to develop something deeper with a plaything, anyway? Either way, he wasn't cracking himself open anymore. "What difference does it make? You understanding me isn't important, is it? You still get what you want."

"Fine. If that's the way you want it, fine." She didn't look fine. She looked mad.

Whatever. He didn't care anymore. "So, this weekend then?" he asked again.

"What? No. I've been trying to talk to you, and you've completely shut me out for some reason I don't even understand. Why would I want to do anything with you? I really don't know how we went from this weekend to whatever this is. I thought we got to a point where you could let me in, where you could be real with me. Clearly, you're just the same as you've always been, and I don't want to play games anymore. I'm tired of it."

He stood from his chair, the aggravation no longer allowing him to sit still. He needed to walk, to get away, to do something to escape from this conversation, where all she wanted was to do was take more of him and poke at his scabs. He stood away from their chairs, focusing on the landscape with his hands on his hips. "What the fuck do you want from me, Naomi? No, really, what do you want?"

"Boone—"

"Do you know what it's like to have no one?" He couldn't stop the agitation crawling across his skin, making him want to scratch it off so she could see the darkness underneath for herself and finally leave him alone. Because if she pushed him away again, he'd no longer have anything to feel guilty about. He could return to being heartless because it was easier. "No, you don't. You grew up on this farm and had this great family. And even though your dad is gone, you still have your mom and your sisters and your friends. You've probably never had a moment in your life where you were truly alone with absolutely no one to turn to. It wasn't like that for me. The only person who's ever acted like they wanted me around throughout my life was my dad."

If he gave her all the pieces, she'd finally see the truth and stop prodding, and maybe she'd cut him out for good. His shoulders tightened as he stared her down. "And I still ended up with nobody. And you want to know why? It's because you were right about me. All those suspicions you've had about me were right. I'm exactly as terrible as you think I am, and so is my dad. You don't want anyone to know about me being with you? Well, guess what? I wouldn't want anyone to know about me, either. I'm trying to dig myself out, and for what? I live in a rundown trailer on the Crockett farm. It's the first time I've been on my own, and that's the best I've been able to do, and it's still nothing.

The avalanche of truth had broken free, and there was no way to stop it. "My father takes from people. That's how we've always survived. A few days after my eighteenth birthday, he was arrested and thrown in prison. His girlfriend at the time, Sophie's mom, kicked me out. I had no one else. Nowhere to go. No money. No high school diploma yet. I was living on the street, trying to survive. After a few days, I . . ."

He swallowed hard, his jaw working together. Either way, Naomi was going to hate him. He knew it, and he slid a look of disgust in her direction because he couldn't do it to himself. But he'd already revealed this much, and if she wanted *real*, she was going to get it. "I got pretty desperate, went back to my neighborhood to beg Freya, Sophie's mom, to take me in. I promised her everything, that I would be good, change my act around, but it didn't matter. She was done with me because of what my dad took from her.

"So I left and . . . I ran into one of her country club friends, a neighbor, Monica, an older divorcee who'd always had a passing interest in me. I was tired of struggling. I wanted to be comfortable, so I did what any Reyes man would do. I flattered her, gave her anything she wanted, just so she'd take care of me, and she did for several years. She called it payback because my dad had also cheated her out of money. I helped her with her MLM business, using what I could to get other women hooked into it. I did whatever she wanted, and, in return, she gave me what I needed."

Telling Naomi he'd been a kept con man was so difficult, he could no longer look in her direction. There were only the memories of Monica sneering at him, using him, calling him Jonathan, as if he was hers to change into whatever. All this for the chance to stay close to Sophie and the many promises Monica made to help return him to Freya's good graces, to find them after they'd moved away. Turns out *he* was the biggest mark of them all. "So, you see, I've always been someone's dirty secret. Why should I ever be anything different?"

He was done. Finished. Tired of trying—

In a flash, Naomi sprung from her chair, and . . . she hugged him.

Shocked, he didn't know how to react. He'd anticipated her disgust, her hatred. Boone hadn't planned for this. He stood there, a statue, her arms wrapping around him tight, her body pressing to his. He'd witnessed Naomi hug plenty of people. The whole Moreno family were huggers. He'd never been a recipient of one of Naomi's hugs, though. This felt all-encompassing. She engulfed him in her warmth.

"Listen to me," she whispered in his ear. "You're not alone anymore."

Boone had always been a master with words, using them to charm his way into whatever he needed. Naomi didn't use her words like that. But hers were more powerful than anything he'd ever said. Without any effort, her words cracked through his shell, breaking him down. He slumped into her, his muscles softening to form around her, his arms and hands gaining strength to hold her to him in case this was all he got.

"You found your way to us, okay? You don't ever have to feel you have no one anymore," she continued to murmur into his ear, her voice calm and reassuring, making her promises seem possible. He was in a position desperate enough to want to believe them. And maybe that made him foolish, but it was all he wanted.

She pulled away slightly to meet his gaze and tenderly brushed the hair back from his brow. "I'm sorry. I didn't mean . . . I didn't think about how you would interpret what I said in the car. That's my fault because I should have been more clear. I just meant about the sex stuff, Boone. My mom is great, but she's still a little conservative, and I didn't want it to just come out that we'd slept together. That's all I meant. I'm sorry if I hurt you and made you feel like you were some dirty secret. I'm not always great at this either. Is your dad going to be a problem?"

"I don't want him coming around. I don't want him ruining this. I told him to stay away." He hoped it would be enough, despite the pit residing in his gut. If he stuck around and kept an eye on things, maybe this time would be different. Boone was older now. He wasn't a kid. He could keep the farm protected.

"So, rock-climbing lessons?" he asked, his chest daring to inflate with hope.

She smiled warmly. "Yes. Okay. We can go climbing soon." Her eyes sparkled as one of her arms slid from his neck, seeking his hand to intertwine their fingers together.

He tucked their connected hands between their shoulders, feeling that undying spark of possibility he usually only got when one of his plans was succeeding. One couldn't be an ex-con man and not have some level of optimism that went along with the lifestyle. Except this time, it was her giving him that feeling. When Naomi tilted her face to a pleasing angle, all he could focus on was how much he wanted to kiss her.

Boone couldn't resist. Her mouth pulled into a smile as his lips touched hers. She kissed him in return, the June morning growing warmer by the moment as he pushed the kiss further and ran a hand across the length of her spine.

The two-way radio, clipped to Naomi's waistband, crackled to life. "Um. Are you two kissing down there?" Selah's voice was in her standard no-nonsense tone, but there was a hint of humor. The balloon was on the descent and, with them in the open, there was no way their affection wasn't on full display.

Naomi retrieved the radio and, with a grin to Boone, said, "How about you mind your own business, Captain?"

"It's a little hard to mind my own business when I'm pointing out the scenery, and part of that scenery is my chase crew making out."

This was cut off when her mother's van approached, the car horn going off at light intervals, as though being tapped. Hailey, who rarely came out on tour days, popped her head from the passenger window. "Oh. My. God! Has it finally happened? Wait, don't stop. Let me take a video for my social media. Everyone is going to go wild for this."

"Mija! You and Boone!" Elena stepped from the van, rushing to clutch and hug them. "Ah, I've been hoping there was something. Boone, I knew you'd eventually see how pretty and sweet my Naomi is. We need to have a special meal to celebrate."

"Ma! Get out of the shot. I'm trying to take a video," Hailey said.

"Can you guys stop? I still need to land this balloon," Selah said through the radio.

"See," said Naomi. "This is what I was trying to protect you from, but now you're in it whether you like it or not."

Except Boone did like it. He liked it a lot and his lungs filled with full, deep breaths of what felt like a new life.

Chapter Thirteen

"SO, WHAT EXACTLY does this mean?" Amber asked at the end of their Pilates class. "Are you guys together? I mean, officially?"

"I don't know. We haven't actually used the terms of . . . you know." Naomi couldn't bring herself to say it, giving a sheepish sweep of her hands.

Amber pumped her eyebrows, finding the situation hilarious. "Boyfriend and girlfriend?"

"Yeah. That. This is all very new. I think we're just feeling things out."

Her friend smirked. "Yeah, I bet you're feeling things out. I could tell as soon as you walked in that there was a spring in your step. It was either that or a new cleanse."

"No, you didn't." Naomi laughed.

"Let's be honest. As much as you two fought against each other, there was something underneath the surface. He occupied way too much of the conversation. I knew if you got a moment, it was going to come to a head. It had to. Oh, but I'm so excited! It's been a while, and you deserve to have some good lovin' in your life, girl."

"Okay, well, like I said. We're just taking things slow, and I doubt he's even thinking about us being . . . you know."

"God, Naomi. I don't know why saying 'boyfriend and girlfriend' is so difficult for you. You're too funny."

Naomi wasn't sure, either. Amber had been right, and it had been a long time since she'd been in a relationship. Her last boyfriend disappeared after Robert died because she was "*too sad*" all the time. Boone was a guy who'd been through a lot, and if he hadn't been scared off by all her death glares, maybe he had enough resilience to stick around.

She'd always gone into a relationship, expecting a Mr. Darcy, only to be disappointed. Not this time. Naomi had accepted Boone as a handsome, but rough-around-the-edges street cat who needed that sense of home to feel safe. Sure, she didn't like the news about Hank and his history, but Boone couldn't help who his father was. And he had said all those things about himself, things that weren't charming or pretty or remotely flattering, throwing them out like a wildcat would hiss or scratch.

Boone may think he's terrible, but he couldn't do all the things he'd done for them and truly be so. He couldn't care about things like his sister and trying to seek redemption with her. Give Naomi the truth, raw and ugly, and it helped her see past the hissing to find the fear lurking behind it. She recognized the vulnerability and refused to let him define his life with it.

This was a man who made Naomi feel more confident, capable, stronger than she thought possible because that's how he saw her. She felt seen by him, but, more importantly, she felt seen by herself. It was as if she was finally settling into her skin, settling into a spot where she was meant to be. With this new confidence, she could push some of it back on

Boone, embrace him with it, and it felt like . . . she was scared to say love, but it was something warm, deep, and promising.

After class, she and Amber went their separate ways after leaving the Pilates rec room. Naomi found Boone leaning against her truck, holding a tall tumbler. Why did he look hotter now that he wore glasses regularly? "Hey, what are you doing here? And how did you find me?" She didn't mean to sound suspicious, but she was confused, since her own sisters didn't bother to find out when and where she taught class.

"You told me."

"I did?"

"Yup. When you threw that class schedule at me last month. Anyway, I wanted to see you, and I brought you a smoothie. Spicy mango, because I know what you like." He handed her the tumbler, shoving his hands into his pockets while sneaking a peek from beneath his lashes as she took a tentative sip.

"Thank you," she said. The sweet, spicy smoothie coolly slid down her throat and was . . . good. No, it was delicious. "Oh my god, where did you get this? This is amazing." If there was some unknown smoothie place in town with this on the menu, she was about to become a regular customer. She took another taste.

A small smile spread across his face. "I made it."

Her jaw dropped. She was in trouble because she was about to become a regular customer of Boone's. What did that look like, and why was every scenario sexy? "No, you didn't."

"I didn't?"

"No, really? Did you make this?"

"I'm not going to compete with your mom in a cooking competition, but I can use a blender, honey."

She laughed, leaning to embrace him, slipping her free arm around his waist as she drank the delicious spicy mango smoothie he made for her. He gently kissed her temple. "Are you going to go home or . . .?"

"You want to just walk around and hang out?" Naomi was curious about this new side of Boone, one that snuggled and purred with contentment. She wanted to peel back his layers like an onion and know every part of him, find out what other talents he possessed besides rock climbing and smoothie-making.

He offered his hand, and she took it with her free one as they turned and headed to Main Street in Redmond's downtown district, a small-town spot with cute shops and restaurants, each lamppost supporting hanging baskets with brightly colored petunias.

"I sent my sister an email," he told her.

"Oh, good! She's going to be happy to hear from you."

"We'll see," he said, sounding less confident than she was used to.

"What did you tell her?"

"I followed your advice. I said that I know I missed a lot in her life, but I hope we can catch up. And I told her a little bit about my life in Central Oregon. It's not until you need to write an email about yourself that you realize how much you don't have to talk about. So I only talked about climbing, work, and you."

"Me? Why would you want to bore her in the first message?" She bumped his shoulder in a tease, her insides warming at learning she ranked in importance in order to be mentioned in the first email to his sister.

He chuckled in response. "You're pretty tenacious when you really want something. I've always liked that about you. I wish I was more like you." His gaze glided over her in admiration. A warmth crept across her cheeks, and she took another sip.

"You don't feel you're tenacious when you want something?" He may say this, but she had trouble believing it. If what Selah believed was true and he had been pursuing her for two-and-a-half years, that had to be something close to tenacious.

"Eh," he said. "It's different with me. I kind of grew up with a different set of principles. We tended to go for the easiest way of getting what we wanted. Why go for something that took a lot of effort if you can settle for something simpler? I want to break away from that type of thinking, though," he continued. "I'm trying . . . to be different. Be someone better."

While Naomi liked someone who was able to self-reflect, she didn't want him to beat himself up too much. Leaning into his arm, she replied, "Not too different, I hope. I think we all need someone in our corner who's an endless source of confidence."

He barked a laugh at this, turning to face her and brushing back a strand of hair from her cheek. "I'll give you anything you want, Pinky."

"Only if that's what you want too." She flashed him a

grin before sipping from the straw. "Oh, I've been working on fleshing out my idea, the one I workshopped at the wedding convention. And it's really coming together. I'm starting to source out costs and what kind of a package we could offer. I'm getting organized and creating spreadsheets and everything. I even had the courage to talk to Selah about it, and it sounds like she's starting to come around to the idea." Naomi could feel herself getting energized again. "Anyway, there's going to be a convention at the fairgrounds. Sure, it'll be smaller, but it'll be closer to home and I can get a booth. I can be legit this time and not have to flee from an army of cops riding in tanks. Not quite as exciting, but it could be fun."

"Excellent. You should bring the flower wreath."

She wrinkled her nose. "I sent it back. I don't know if I have the constitution for . . ." Naomi leaned closer to whisper, "Wedding conning," before switching back to her regular voice and continuing, "Besides, I felt bad. I sent an email to The Flower Chaise ladies to apologize about everything. They were very nice. In fact, they found the whole thing funny and said it gave them something to gossip about with the other vendors."

"Ah, well, maybe they'll be a good contact for you for the business. So when are we doing this convention?"

"You don't have to help me. I think . . . I think I'm okay doing it on my own. I felt really good in Portland, like I can actually sell someone on this."

"I don't offer because you need help. I know you can do it. I like seeing you making things happen and being a part of it."

"Okay, but as long as we go as ourselves, you know, Boone and Naomi, and not Charlie and Treasure?"

His phony Australian accent appeared. "You didn't like Charlie and Treasure?"

"I'll admit, it was fun pretending to be someone else, but it's also okay being just us too. Who we are in real life, our real names, is just as good as them."

"You do remember that my real name is Jonathan, right? Not Boone."

She'd forgotten. She couldn't see him as a Jonathan, but decided to at least ask, "Would you prefer to be called Jonathan?"

His face scrunched in displeasure. "Nah, I told you, I've had Boone for so long that it feels more like my real name than anything else. Looks like it'll be Boone and Naomi, then. Although, I might still need to sneak in."

"You don't have to. I don't think this one even has tickets."

He stopped, pulling her closer, his hand sliding over her backside. "You gotta let me do a little bit of wedding conning, honey. I need a challenge."

She smiled up at him before pressing a kiss to his lips. They were soft, pliable, and ready to press her further. She didn't hesitate to open her mouth to him, fully committing to the kiss and to him. When they broke apart, she whispered, "Okay, but just a little."

Chapter Fourteen

B OONE'S MORNING STARTED well for a few different reasons. First, he was hopeful things with his father might be turning around. It remained a little tense since their confrontation, but, since then, his father hadn't mentioned the Morenos nor asked about any potential dinner invitation. In fact, the only thing he'd asked this morning was if Boone was going to work or not.

"I'm going climbing. Trying to get an instructor position there."

His father raised his brow in surprise. "Is there decent money in something like that?" Of course, this would be his first question. Hank was about to be disappointed.

"Not really, but I like it. It's quiet and peaceful." He added the last part to discourage his father from joining him. Hank never appreciated peace and quiet.

The man tilted his head in apparent thought. "Well, I'm sure it's a good skill to have, like pickpocketing. You never know when it'll come in handy. Good for you, son. I'm thinking about improving myself too. Might take some kind of class or two."

Boone wanted to be optimistic and believe he wasn't the only Reyes who could change for the better. He grabbed his climbing bag before departing for Smith Rock to meet Naomi. Getting to share his day with her at one of his favorite places made him feel too much—too much happiness, too much contentment. He wasn't sure what he'd done to get such a redemption.

He got there early and hung out in the park, as the summer rays heated the area and the skies eased into a brighter shade of blue. Sitting on the top of a wooden picnic table with his feet on the bench seat, he pulled his phone from his pocket. His heart stuttered.

There was an email from Sophie.

He was half scared, half thrilled. He wanted to know his sister, to have one family relationship that was wholesome and good. Boone was also afraid he'd open the email to discover it'd all been a mistake, and she didn't want anything to do with him. He pushed a quick breath through his mouth to calm his nerves before opening it and doing a quick scan before returning to the beginning to read more thoroughly.

His sister sounded happy to hear from him, asking lots of questions and telling him that she had an old photo of the two of them tucked inside a dresser drawer. She always wondered what happened, but her mom never wanted to talk about it. She didn't mention if her mom knew about this correspondence, but Boone hadn't told his father, either. Maybe it was okay to keep their parents out of it altogether.

Sophie also mentioned her schooling and how she wanted to study climatology at the University of Oregon. She was smart, had her head on straight, and was in a better position than he'd been at that age or now. He felt better knowing he and his father hadn't ruined her life. She was doing okay and hadn't resorted to scamming her classmates yet. He still wanted to help her financially because he knew higher education could be expensive, and he wanted her to succeed.

"Hey!" Naomi called, looking as pretty as an Oregon sunrise with her pink hair and flushed cheeks. She wore tight workout clothes, making him want to forget about climbing up when he'd rather go down on her instead. "Is everything okay? Your brow was crinkled in deep concentration." With her pointer fingers, she pressed her eyebrows together to demonstrate her point.

"I got a nice email from Sophie."

Her concern switched to happiness. "Excellent! I love that you two are reconnecting."

"She asked for a picture." In truth, she'd asked for his social media handles, but Boone hadn't done any social media in a long time. While he thought about opening an account to follow his sister, he had no interest in using it for his own life. Other than Sophie, he didn't want any part of his past reconnecting with him.

"Do you want me to take one with your phone?"

"Can we take one together?"

Her lips scrunched together. "All I did was take a quick shower and throw my hair in a ponytail. I'm not really in picture mode."

"And yet, you're the prettiest person I've seen today. Come on." If Sophie wanted to know about his life, he'd have to include Naomi. She was becoming the most important part of it.

"Okay. Make some room for me." He separated his legs

so she could notch herself between them as she sat on the bench seat in front of him. He leaned forward, sliding his face alongside hers, his arm going around her middle as the hand with the phone stretched before them. Naomi inclined into him with a sweet smile, fitting them together as naturally as could be. Their image smiled back from the phone screen as he took a picture. He liked the way they looked together.

When he brought the camera down, he wrapped that arm around her, too, holding her to him as he kissed along her jawline. "Are you ready to climb today?"

"I'm a little nervous."

"Don't be. I'm going to belay you so good, I'll ruin you for all other belayers."

She snuggled into him. "I hope you do."

They made their way to the river trail at the base of Smith Rock. As they walked, he told her about the different types of climbs and about the Y.D.S., the Yosemite Decimal System, which graded the difficulty on a scale from 5.0 to 5.15.

"So each climb has a name?" she asked.

"Yeah, Smith Rock was sort of the birthplace for sports climbing. Now, there's all kinds of climbing spots, and you can get information about them in guides. The individual routes are named things like To Bolt or Not to Be, Vertical Taco, Purple Head Warrior, Phone Call From Satan . . . weird things like that."

Naomi lifted her gaze, her eyes growing larger at the sight of early morning climbers already high on the walls. "I don't know if I'm ready for this yet."

"We're going to do a nice, easy one for you. A sweet 5.2 single pitch that doesn't take you up too high, and you'll be roped. I just want you to get used to clipping."

"What's the name? It had better not be Text Message From Hell?"

Boone had spent time pouring through his climbing guide for recommended beginner climbs. The one he chose seemed ideal, but he regretted picking one with such an obvious, cringy name, and wasn't sure he wanted to tell her. "Well, um . . ."

When he didn't finish, her features turned worried. "Oh god, that's its real name, isn't it?"

"No. Not even close. It's . . . First Love."

"Oh," she said lightly. "That sounds nice. Hopefully, it will be."

They arrived at First Love as Alan was finishing with another climbing student.

"Boone, how's it going?" the man said, pulling him into a half-shoulder hug with a sturdy pat on his back. "Decided to visit the kiddie pool today?"

"Yeah. I've been showing Naomi the ropes. We had a session at the climbing gym, but I think she'll do well here." He wasn't sure if it would help or hurt him if his student was also someone he was involved with, so he left this information out. Better safe than sorry.

Alan took in the climbing bag and crash pads Boone had brought with them, and his eyes lit up. "No way. You took on a student. Hi, I'm Alan. I'm one of the instructors at Cliff Climbs." He reached a hand to Naomi to offer a handshake. "How are you liking the sport so far? Is Boone teaching you well?"

It wasn't a job interview, but it felt like one, anyway. Just as Naomi was nervous about tackling a real rock wall, suddenly Boone was experiencing anxiety himself. This was worse because it was only their second session, and in the first, she'd fallen off the wall.

Unlike him, Naomi smiled prettily, with no obvious sign of distress. "I've never thought I could do this before, but Boone's been great at giving me confidence, like I can climb anything. I feel safe with him." Boone's chest expanded with her words, hoping they were true.

Alan nodded at her response. "Good. That's great to hear. Well, keep up the good work, both of you." He slapped Boone on the back again before packing his climbing gear, moving through the process slowly. Boone suspected Alan planned to witness some of his teaching style for himself.

The lesson started, and he could feel beads of sweat pop along on his brow. He prepped Naomi, helping her put on the harness and teaching her about the P.A.S., the Personal Anchor System. He triple-checked that her helmet was secured and everything else tightened, clipped, and roped in properly. He was in strict professional and safety mode under Alan's watch. More importantly, he wanted Naomi safe. He'd purchased the crash pads after one too many night-mares of her falling again. Boone was currently kicking himself for not buying more. He should have purchased enough to fill all of Smith Rock in order to protect her.

Alan didn't wait around, leaving with his student soon after Naomi was ready to climb. "Breathe," she said, once the two of them were alone again. He was supposed to be calming her, not the other way around. He leaned against the craggy wall, letting it support his weight as his stress levels returned to normal.

Boone squinted in her direction. "I don't think you have a nervous bone in your body," he observed.

"I think that's because you took all the anxiety for yourself. You've checked my equipment a dozen times by now. Does it normally take this long to get up on the rock? I'm ready."

He chuckled, finding her eagerness endearing. "Okay, let me just get set up with the belayer equipment, and we can get started."

"How do I know where to climb? I'm missing my color-coordinated holds."

"It's the same in that you make sure to look up and read your route, know where you're going to climb before you start. Yes, there are no official holds, but you can see all the chalk residue from previous climbers, and that gives you a hint. The crux, or hardest part of the climb, is right where the yellow vein in the rock runs. You'll have to stretch to reach the next hold. Every time you get to a bolt, pull out one of your carabiners and clip yourself in like I showed you. You're going to do this every time, so if you do lose your hold, you'll only fall as far as your last clip, but I also have you down here. Do you understand?"

She nodded, bravely facing the challenge above her.

"Honey, I need you to look at me and tell me you understand." He felt like an ass saying this, but it was more for his peace of mind than for hers.

She turned her beautiful hazel gaze in his direction, and he knew he wanted a life just like this, one where they'd tackle things together. "I'm going to clip myself in at every bolt." She offered a warm smile. "I can do this, right?"

The desire to kiss her was strong, but he didn't know if Alan was on the hill watching. As the next best thing, he grabbed a handful of chalk from the pouch, giving him an excuse to touch her by prepping her hands. "No doubt you can do it. But just go as far as you can. You know I'm here. I got you."

"I trust you." The words were simple, but nearly knocked the breath from him.

He finally understood the importance of what Alan had said previously about trust, how valuable it was. Having Naomi's trust was heavy, but it secured them to each other, like clipping himself into a bolt, knowing they might fall but not all the way.

She approached the wall, releasing a deep breath while shaking out her hands and stretching her neck from side to side. She started slowly at first, securing her hold before moving on to the next. When she reached the first bolt, she held the wall with one hand, reached to her waist harness, grabbed a carabiner, and locked herself at that point. Her movements were confident, graceful, and full of strength. He had to remember to breathe, to continue to pull, break, go under, and slide the rope to keep tension. He was in total awe. She was a natural. His free solo accomplishments on walls with a grade as high as a 5.14 weren't half as rewarding as sharing in this amazing woman's tackle of a beginner-friendly climb and watching her get to the top.

Naomi released a loud, "Whoo!" while sitting on the ledge like a beacon of triumph. She peered between her dangling legs, shooting him a bright grin. He'd never been so proud, wanting her to soak up her accomplishment . . . and also wanting her to hurry down so he could hug her.

He tried not to rush her as he helped her walk down the wall on her descent. When she did make it to the bottom, he shed his belayer equipment as quickly as he could to haul her into a hug. "I'm so proud of you. You did great."

Her eyes shined, her whole body alight with happiness as she clung to him. "Boone, I think they gave it the right name because I've absolutely fallen in love. Maybe I can tackle Phone Call from Satan next."

He choked on a cough. "While I think you can do any climb, maybe we'll work our way up to that one."

"That's probably smart. My arms are feeling a little bit like cooked spaghetti at the moment. And I'm hungry. Satan's call will have to be put on hold for the time being."

He barked a laughed at imagining her answering a call from Satan and replying, *Please hold*, as if she wasn't already a badass.

They packed their stuff, trekked their way up the hill, and shared a couple of energy bars at a picnic table, relaxing and enjoying the view.

"It's gorgeous, right?"

"Hmm. Yeah," he replied, although he could have said it was infinitely more so when she was included in it.

"I wonder if Dex is working. Do you think we should check? It feels a little weird to come to his workplace and not at least say hi."

Boone liked the friendly park ranger well enough, but he wasn't in the mood for casual conversations. "I'm feeling a little selfish and would rather take you someplace private to celebrate your first climb."

She threw him a coy expression, making a little hum in her throat before leaning forward. "I don't suppose you'd be interested in my home for this private place."

She didn't have to tell him twice. He stood, grabbed her hand and his bag, and they both made a quick escape to the parking lot.

Chapter Fifteen

NAOMI ARRIVED HOME just as a text message came in from Boone saying he had to make a quick stop and then he'd be over. This was fine since it allowed her to take a shower to wash off the chalk and general rock-climbing griminess.

"Hey," she said breathlessly after racing downstairs to answer his knock.

His gaze straight-lined down her body with laser precision. She wore a soft, loose T-shirt and a pair of silky, hot-pink shorts, nothing fancy, but his eyes heated as if it was lingerie. His tongue ran along his bottom lip before his attention flicked to her face. "Selah home?"

"Nope."

"Do you want me, Pinky?" His eyes were already dark and dangerous, exactly the way she liked them.

"That's why I invited you over."

He didn't leave her hanging, pressing into her, his lips finding hers, the door slamming shut behind him. One hand went into her hair, pulling gently at her damp, sloppy ponytail, tilting her head to a more pleasing angle. His other hand spread across her waist. He met her with enough energy to push her against the entry wall with an overwhelming force. A delicious hum of pleasure rumbled in his throat as they kissed.

She kissed, nipped, and caressed him in return, her need for him intensifying. "You wanna go upstairs?" she asked between light pants.

"Mm-hmm." He scooped her into his arms as if she barely weighed anything, and carried her upstairs.

She draped her arms about his shoulders, pressing hot kisses along his neck. "I can walk, you know."

"You scaled a rock face today. I want you to conserve as much energy as possible for what I'm about to do to you."

Her heart beat wildly in anticipation of whatever this entailed.

"Which room is yours?"

At her direction, he pushed the ajar door open before shutting it soundly with a foot. "Well, now, don't you have a very pretty room, honey."

Naomi didn't have a large budget for decoration, but she made do with what she had, this now being one of her favorite rooms to read in. It was bright but cozy, with vintage accents and lots of living plants and books. "You don't have a pretty room?" she teased.

"No. I, currently, don't have any room at all. But I like this one. It feels like you." He deposited her on the bed, pushing off his shoes with his feet before climbing over her and returning to kissing, each pull on her lips intensifying, as though the grade was increasing and he needed to steadily climb to the next height. His hands were everywhere, sliding along her legs to mold them on the outsides of his. When they scaled along her rib cage, under her shirt, and over her breasts, she moaned into his mouth, arching into him.

Naomi was hungry for him, feeling heady and wild as she removed his glasses and yanked off his shirt, tracing the muscles along his torso with her fingers. They were firm and unbelievable. She couldn't believe this man was in her bed. "Oh god, Boone," she sighed, as he made her feel good with nothing but his touch.

Then reality hit her, and she dropped her head onto the pillow. "Ugh. I just realized I don't have condoms. I haven't had . . . something like this in my bedroom for quite a while."

This didn't discourage him as he continued nipping along her throat. "Maybe you should check your front pocket."

"What? Why?" she asked, slipping her hand into her pocket and finding a small, square package inside. "I . . . what? How'd you do that?" A burst of laughter bubbled out of her.

"Rock climbing and giving mustache rides aren't my only skills."

Her fingers went straight for the fastener of his pants, undoing them and shoving them down. She tore the condom packet open and rolled it on him. As frenzied as they'd been before this, he removed the rest of her clothes gently, as if he was savoring the appetizer instead of rushing to get to the main course. He traced a finger along her clavicle, down the center of her chest, brushing his hands across her breasts, squeezing them before bending to run his tongue across each one. "You're so pretty, Naomi."

In her lusty frame of mind, she couldn't understand how

he had this much control. She ached for him while he studied every part, every reaction, every emotion. Naomi wasn't sure she'd ever been seen this much in her life, especially in bed.

He slipped his hand between her legs, stroking her. She bowed into him, clasping his neck and moaning. His touch was everything. "I want this. I want you," Boone murmured. Removing his hand, he pushed himself into her, sinking deep. He nuzzled her cheek, and her lungs stretched the confines of her chest as she felt full of him, both physically and emotionally.

She brushed back some of his hair that had fallen across his brow. Sure, he was handsome, but she felt something more, something deeper and dear. She'd always thought he was busy shaping himself into something that would please other people, but, somewhere, there'd been a switch, and she saw he was attempting to shape himself into how he wanted to be. When he told her during the climb that he had her, it felt true in a lot of other ways too. "You have me," she said. "And I have you."

He met her gaze, eyes searching, before he kissed her again. She held on to those strong shoulders as he began to rock into her harder, sliding in and out with smooth determination. His golden eyes, which at first sparked with heat and fire, became soft and hazy.

The blaze developing in her core escalated from a smoldering brush of embers to a raging forest fire as she adjusted herself to move with him, to get to the cliff sooner and plunge herself off. She arched her neck, giving him access to nip her there, which he took full advantage of. Naomi could feel herself growing more pathetic with her pants and whimpering and clawing. He encouraged this with a "yes" as his strokes grew heavier.

"God, I can't take it," she cried before her body snapped, pulsing around him.

As she caught her breath, Boone pulled her up, positioning her to face the wall. She gripped the headboard as he thrust into her from behind, his movements rougher and almost out of control as he clasped her to him. His voice was gruff and strained as he said, "I like how you take me, Pinky." She pushed back into him, which increased his fervor until he swore and his movement stuttered.

They collapsed onto the mattress, spent. Naomi's inner self was as airy as a balloon. When he rolled to his side, his expression was soft and goofy. It had to match hers because she felt the same. He gently pulled a strand of hair from her damp chest and placed a kiss there. "All I want to do is curl up in this queen-sized bed with you so we can wake up every day and live a life where our only strife is trying to figure out what to eat for dinner and disagreeing about the correct way to load a dishwasher. A simple life is my greatest fantasy."

She smiled as she cupped his cheek, his facial hair prickling her palm. "For once, I don't think that particular dream is so far out of reach. Sounds like a lovely possibility," she replied before pressing a kiss to his lips.

AFTER FALLING INTO the deepest, darkest hole after her dad died, it was hard for Naomi to imagine there were still bright days ahead. The next couple of weeks after conquering First Love, there were so many bright days, it became hard to imagine there could be dark ones on the horizon. Or maybe Naomi didn't want to think of them. She was working, teaching her classes, planning to attend the wedding convention in Redmond, exploring the climbs at Smith Rock, and then spending extra time with Boone. Her life had never been so full, so happy.

Boone didn't always stay over at her place, but she liked when he did. She liked curling into his arms, feeling as though he'd keep her safe, even while dreaming. It was a natural transition for both of them.

One early July morning, her phone on the nightstand buzzed, waking her. She unentangled herself from Boone, crawling across the mattress to grab it.

Can you come to Mom's right away? Hailey had texted.

This wasn't the usual kind of text she'd receive from her sister, and it worried her.

She rubbed one eye while typing, *Something wrong?*

I just need you to come over.

Is Selah coming? Hailey would only involve Selah if it was serious because the eldest sister didn't like getting pulled into ridiculous squabbles. If she felt Hailey was being silly or petty, she'd call her sister out and tell her to stop wasting her time. Naomi was always more willing to listen, which was why Hailey preferred reaching out to her. There was also a possibility Hailey was having some kind of disagreement with Selah, which wouldn't be the first time. Naomi didn't know since Selah never came home the previous night, which wasn't unusual.

No. Can you come?

Okay, I'm on my way. Naomi slid from the bed, grabbed her clothes, and slipped into them. She didn't want to kick Boone out this early, but didn't want to disappear on him either. Kneeling on the mattress, she pressed a kiss below his ear. His eyes stayed closed, but a smile spread across his handsome face.

"I need to go to my mom's house."

He cracked an eye, concern etching on his brow. "Is there something wrong?"

"I'm sure it's fine. Hailey just asked if I could come over."

He propped himself on an elbow before pulling back the covers. "I'll come with you."

"It's okay. I think it's just my sisters squabbling, as normal. You can sleep in and leave when you want."

His arms went around her, pulling her into bed with him. "Come on. I don't want to lose you to your sisters so early. Maybe I can ease you into the day before you have to face all that. You know Hailey can be a bit of a drama queen, anyway." He kissed her throat, his hands sneaking beneath her shirt. "I'll go with you after giving you a proper start."

She sighed blissfully, enjoying the temptation. Her better judgment made her at least say his name like a warning. "Boone."

"Just a little bit, Pinky. You're smelling so good this morning, and I need you."

Naomi laughed. "Nice try, but I told my sister I was on my way. You can need me later." She pressed a quick kiss on his nose, pulling herself from his grasp.

He dropped his head against his pillow with a frustrated groan. "You have no idea how much agony you're leaving me in."

"You need to be teased every once in a while. It's good for you. Just relax, and I'll be back as soon as I can."

Reluctantly, Naomi departed, hoping nothing was catastrophic. She would be mad if this turned out to be something inconsequential. She grew concerned, though, when she parked at the farm and saw her sister waiting for her on the front porch with her arms crossed around her middle.

"What's wrong? Is Mom okay?" Naomi asked.

Hailey lowered her voice as though not wanting her mother, who was likely inside, to hear. "Everyone is fine. I just need you to go inside. I'm sure things are okay, but it's weirding me out, and I need someone else to know."

Naomi shot her sister an odd look. It put her on edge, her heart jumping inside her chest.

"Just trust me, Naomi."

"Okay." She would have appreciated more of a warning of what she should be expecting, but her sister was serious, and she did trust her. Naomi quietly opened the door, making her way inside. There was a conversation occurring in the kitchen, one voice being her mother's, and the other voice was distinctly male, deep and with a soft twang. She didn't like sneaking or spying, especially on her own mother, but she made silent steps forward because her curiosity was piqued. Perhaps her mother was dating again, which could bother Hailey. But if the man was nice, she could get used to it and—

Hank Reyes came into view as she peeked around the corner. He stood close to her mother's side, one hand going to the small of her back, touching in a way that was more familiar than friendly.

"I can tell you're a hardworking woman," Hank said, his smile smooth. "It's not fair for a woman like you to have gone through what you have. When the love of my life, Boone's mother, walked out, I felt like my heart had cracked in two. At that point, you just want to provide for your kids, keep them well, let them have the best life you can give them. Maybe all this other stuff shouldn't be solely on your shoulders all the time. Maybe you deserve to have a break too. Your daughters deserve a break rather than having to worry about all of this farmland and, if you trust me, I can make that happen for you. I can help make things easier, more manageable for all of you."

He swiped a hand across Elena's cheek. "You're a hell of a lady with still a lot to give and take from this life. You have the most beautiful heart. I can see you just want the best for your daughters."

Naomi heard enough, her irritation at an instant ten. "What the hell is going on?"

Elena jumped away, nervous hands adjusting her apron, a blush spreading across her cheeks. "Mija! What are you doing here? Did you want some breakfast?"

"No! I want to know what he's doing here." Hailey crept behind Naomi, but remained hidden beyond the wall. Naomi flipped to full protective mode.

Hank leaned casually against one of the countertops as he turned his smile in her direction, as though this was any other normal circumstance. "Naomi. Morning, darlin'. Good to see you again. Your mother is just so welcoming, I just can't stay away. You girls should know how lucky you are to have her."

Naomi didn't trust anything about the man, remembering how Boone had confessed his father was trouble. She didn't want him anywhere near her sweet, trusting mother. She also didn't like how he said her name, with the syllables elongated, like he could wrap them around her and capture her with his fake goodness. "Yeah? Well, she's lucky to have me, and I'm not as welcoming, so you can get the hell out."

"Mija!" Her mother gasped, looking shocked by Naomi's attitude, but she'd deal with the fallout of her mother's anger later. "I didn't raise you like that. Hank is my guest, and this is my home. You don't talk to people like that."

Hank raised his hands as if he were the most friendly, non-threatening person around. "No, it's okay, Elena. I get it. I like that you have smart daughters who are looking out for you. You should be proud to have raised them as such. And I understand, Naomi, that you don't know me as well as Boone, but like my son, I'm just here to help out. I want the best for y'all. You're like family to us."

"If that was true, you wouldn't be sneaking around in my mother's kitchen."

"Naomi! Hank was just being a friend."

Naomi barely heard her mother's justifications. She didn't care. She wasn't able to stop her father from making bad decisions because of a shady character, but she'd be damned if she'd let it happen again. "Get out," she said, her voice low and hard as she glared at the older Reyes. "Get out, or I'll tell my mom the truth about you."

She hoped he wouldn't call her out. She didn't want to blurt to Elena that Boone's father had been in prison. It made her look judgmental. She didn't want to seem cynical, to believe people couldn't change and they needed to continue paying for their mistakes after finishing their sentence. But she'd use it if she had to, if it meant Hank would leave her mother alone. She crossed her arms, and her jaw was set and determined.

"Honey, I don't know what you think you know, but Boone—"

"Get out!" Hailey shouted behind her.

Hank didn't look bothered or embarrassed, just shrugged his shoulders, cool as a cucumber, as though she were the one making a mistake and overreacting.

"I'm so sorry, Hank. I don't understand," her mother said in a hushed tone. Why did she feel the need to apologize to him? And how often had he been coming around? Naomi had been so wrapped up in her own stuff lately. Had she been missing all the signs there'd been something wrong at the Moreno farmhouse? She felt terrible.

Hank took her mother's hand. "It's okay. Your girls are clearly upset, and I don't want to cause any trouble. I'm sure they're afraid of seeing anyone moving in on their dad's territory. I get it. I want to thank you for your hospitality and for making a lonely guy feel so welcome. It's been a long time. I don't think there's anyone quite as lovely and nice as you."

He said this to Elena so gently, Naomi almost regretted taking as hard of a stance as she had, doubting herself. What if she heard wrong? Or perhaps it wasn't as bad as she thought. What if her mind tricked her into jumping to the worst conclusion, and she was again making someone into a villain who didn't deserve it? What if her mom and Hank had indeed struck up a friendship, and Naomi was coming in like a spoiled child and throwing a tantrum because he wasn't her dad?

She was close to changing her mind, but when Hank made his way from the kitchen, he stopped near her. He didn't make eye contact, staring straight ahead, those light, gray-green eyes no longer warm, but cooler, emotionless. "Looks like my son is losing his touch and not able to keep you as *distracted* as we had hoped. Shame."

Without any further reaction to the grenade he dropped on her heart, Hank slid on a pair of sunglasses and strode out the door, shutting it soundly behind him.

Chapter Sixteen

AFTER NAOMI LEFT, Boone dozed off again, pulling her pillow to him so the delightful scent of berries could continue infiltrating his sleep, even in her absence.

When he woke again, he stretched and yawned, feeling the spoils of having a real bed in a real home. Reaching to the nightstand, he grabbed his glasses, sliding them on before checking his phone. It was later than he'd expected. He was surprised Naomi hadn't returned yet. He considered sending her a text to ask what she wanted if he went out and got some coffee and pastries for breakfast. Except, knowing her mother, she might already be at the table, being fed.

Before he could send any message, his phone received a call from Naomi.

"Hey, honey, I was just thinking about you and—"

"How long has he been coming around?" she cut in, the question accusatory.

"What? Who?" There used to be days when he'd been in all kinds of trouble and handled phone calls like this without a care in the world. Now his gut froze.

"Your dad. You said he wouldn't be coming around, but that's obviously not true, is it? Now all I want to know is how long it's been happening behind my back."

Oh shit. If Hank was involved, Boone was definitely in trouble. "What's wrong? What happened?" In the background, he could hear Hailey talking loudly and Elena sounding tearful. He scrambled from the bed, grabbing his clothes and shoving them on, not checking to see if they were right side out or not.

"I don't know, Boone." He didn't like the way his name had a hard edge to it. "Maybe you did too good of a job keeping me *distracted* because no one was more surprised than me to find Hank in my mom's kitchen this morning, making himself at home, and putting his hands all over her as he talked about his big plans for our farm."

Boone held his phone to his ear with a shoulder as he put his shoes on, the dread already filling him up. "I'll handle this. I'm just getting my clothes on, and then I'll be over."

"Don't bother. I'm just calling to tell you to get out of my apartment and leave us alone." The call disconnected.

She was upset, and for a good reason. If he had gone with her and found Hank in the kitchen, as she had, he would have been mad as well. In fact, as the minutes ticked by, the angrier he became. He felt horrible because, even though he'd warned Hank to stay away, he still felt responsible for this.

Boone had given himself one job and he had failed.

He'd spent too much time with his focus elsewhere, his love for Naomi so bright, everything else was eclipsed by it. He only went home these days to take care of his pet. He'd already been dreaming about a future where he could pack up his few belongings and Cat, and make a home with Naomi.

217

There was a side of him worried he was falling into his old pattern of using Naomi as a life raft to keep himself afloat. But this had to be different because he loved her, wanted to build a real future, and support her as much as she supported him. They'd keep each other afloat. With this new horrible wrinkle, she might not see that.

Despite the finality of her words, Boone needed to see her, talk to her, and make sure Elena was okay, if only because he had to know their lives weren't going to be ruined by one of the Reyes men. All this might still be fixable. If he ever needed to talk his way into something, this was the time for it.

He grabbed his keys and headed to Terrebonne, arriving at the same time as Selah. She gave him a sideways glance, looking about as confused as he was. Elena was on the porch, waiting for Selah because she cried out, "Mi roca," and opened her arms.

The eldest daughter jogged to her, pulling her mother into a hug. "It's okay. I'm here. Tell me what's going on."

"You need to talk to Naomi. She's very upset. I didn't know I was going to make her so upset." Elena sniffled through tears before noticing him. "Oh, Boone. I'm sorry for causing any troub—"

In an instant, Naomi pushed through the screened door, striding out like a woman on a warpath, with Hailey trailing behind her. "When I told you to get out, I didn't mean to come here. You need to leave."

"Naomi! Boone didn't do anything. Don't be mean to him," Elena cried.

He could feel his chest squeezing tight. "Look, I understand you're upset, but I'm just trying to figure out what's going on."

"Oh? You're just trying to figure out what's going on, like you haven't been a part of everything the *whole* time." Her words were spit out in red-hot anger.

"I haven't!" Boone's sense of calm, his careful plan to talk sensibly and she'd see the truth, evaporated as he panicked at the possibility of losing everything.

Her hands went to her hips, not giving an inch. "That's not what your dad said."

"He . . ." Boone ripped his hands through his hair in frustration before starting again. "I don't care what he said. That's not what happened. You have to believe me, honey. I don't like this any more than you do. You think I'd work for two-and-a-half years wrangling hot-air balloons for some deeper, darker plan? I'm not that patient!"

Naomi rolled her eyes. "That's so reassuring."

"It's the truth. I did it because I needed a job that wasn't going to look too closely at things like my past or my credit and see me as a liability. I rolled the dice and landed here. But this is the best thing that ever happened to me. Your family, your mom, *you* are the best things to ever happen to me. Why would I throw that away?"

"So, are you saying you haven't been trying to distract me, as your father said? Because you were trying awfully hard to keep me in bed this morning. I wonder why that was. Maybe getting me into bed was the plan all along."

"That's not true." It was as if Boone was climbing a sandy cliff, and the more he clawed, the more his hold disintegrated.

"Then why did you do it?"

"Because I love you!" His confession could have been followed by a pin drop if it weren't for the gasps from Elena and Hailey. "I love you, Naomi. I hardly have anything of value in my life, but I have you, and for the first time, none of that other stuff matters to me. I'm willing to give up everything I own to continue having you."

Some emotion must have cracked through the anger because a tear spilled down her cheek, but she dashed it away with a hand. The rest of her family stood there in rapt interest, unable to look away from the chaos of their relationship. He wanted nothing more than to wrap his arms around her and take away every bad emotion she was experiencing. He took a step toward her, but she stopped crying, straightening her spine.

"Hank can also use beautiful words," she said, his heart dropping. "And then, in the next moment, he can say something hateful. My dad got taken in by someone like that, but that's not going to be me. You're the only one who brought this man into our lives. Leave." She strode back into the house, slamming the door behind her.

Boone had opened up, revealed himself to her, and in doing so, he'd given her all the ammo to use against him. He was left there, with Elena staring at him with sad eyes, her arms clinging to her oldest daughter. Only one other time had he ever felt so small, so alone, so completely cut off from the life he'd established. He didn't know how he'd be able to handle it this time, hoping the other members of the Moreno family wouldn't close ranks and leave him on the outside.

Selah spoke first. "Okay, I think we're all a little upset

and just need time to calm down. I think you should leave, Boone." She said this matter-of-fact, not in the hateful way Sophie's mother had when she kicked him to the curb. It didn't matter. The result was the same. He was out.

Naomi had cut the rope. He was in freefall, and this time, it was a screamer.

Boone didn't have anything to do but slink away to his car, looking guilty even when trying to be his best. When he arrived at his trailer on the Crockett farm, he found Hank reclining on the couch. He ate an apple while flipping through one of Boone's paperbacks, appearing as if he hadn't just firebombed the rainforest flourishing in Boone's life. He offered a carefree smile. "Hey, son. What do you think about going out tonight? My treat. I think we both could have a little fun, meet some new prospects."

"Get out." Boone didn't yell, didn't throw things, didn't punch anything, but his hands fisted at his sides.

Hank chuckled, as if Boone's demand was a punchline and not anything to be taken seriously. He didn't even stop eating the apple in his hand.

Boone didn't wait for it to sink in. He strode to the single bedroom, grabbed a duffel bag, and began shoveling his dad's possessions into it. It wouldn't take long because Hank didn't have a lot, but the number of items had grown since he'd first moved in, and most of them were of better quality than Boone's stuff.

"What the *fuck* do you think you're doing?" his father said, getting up. "Hey, some of those are nice pieces. I don't want them balled up in a bag."

Boone didn't answer, determined to finish the task as soon as he could.

"Kid, if you want to use the bedroom for a little sleepover with a friend, you just have to ask. I don't mind sleeping on the couch for a day or two."

Finished, Boone zipped the bag and shoved it into his father's chest. "Get out."

Hank's mouth fell open, the words finally hitting the way Boone intended them to be taken. But then his brow raised in a sympathetic look. "Look, I've been hearing that a lot lately, and it's all been a silly misunderstanding. I didn't expect to hear it from my own son. We're a team, remember? It's just you and me, boy, against the whole rotten world that won't give us what should be ours."

Boone had fallen for this attitude before because everything around him showed him the world wasn't nice. No one would ever give him anything out of the goodness of their heart. Except this wasn't true. He knew that now. The Moreno family had been nothing but kind to him. They didn't deserve someone like Hank taking advantage of that. His father had always seemed big, charismatic, and optimistically undefeated, but it was a pretty shell to hide the cockroach underneath.

Boone pushed him from the bedroom doorway and down the hall to vacate him from his home.

"Come on, Boone. I love you, kid. I've loved you longer and more than anyone else. And this is how you repay that?" His father's tone had turned desperate. "I, who took you under my wing when no one else wanted to, when you could have been someone who moved from foster home to foster home. I admit, I'm not perfect, but I've always done the best I could."

As strong as Boone tried to be and as angry as he was, his heart—whatever remained of it after Naomi had stripped it down—continued to be shredded by his father. At this point, it functioned as nothing more than a scratching post for everyone else to use. With much more care than his father deserved, Boone opened the front door, grasped his dad by the shirt, and shoved him outside with Hank clutching the duffel bag to his chest.

"Well, fuck. What am I supposed to do now? Where am I supposed to go? You're just going to throw your old man out on the street? And for what? For a bunch of hysterical women?"

Boone looked him straight in the eye. "Now you'll know what I went through when Freya kicked me out after you got arrested. I'm sure you'll figure it out just like I had to do." Then he shut the door in his father's face.

Chapter Seventeen

ELENA CONTINUED WEEPING on the sofa, using Selah as a support beam. Hailey had told her sisters the whole story about how Hank had been a frequent guest over the last few weeks at odd hours, always wanting to talk to and befriend their mother.

"He's just lonely, like me. He's a nice man. Really," Elena cried. Naomi did not enjoy being the bad guy in this situation. Her mother didn't see anything wrong. It was the first time in her life she felt like the parent and her mother was the child.

Selah rubbed Elena's shoulder. "It's okay. We're not blaming you at all."

Naomi swallowed hard. It wasn't that her mother wasn't smart. Rather, her mother was too gullible and trusting. Naomi didn't want Elena to change because she was lovely as is. The only solution was for her to watch out for her mother more.

"But do you want to date him? Are you over Dad?" Hailey said, her face contorted in pain, the only one gutsy enough to blurt out what had been on all their minds.

Her mother's tears stopped, her expression one of shock. "Dating? Me? No. Your father, my Robert, was the love of my life." She looked at each of her daughters. "You think I wanted to marry Hank?"

Naomi wasn't able to maintain eye contact, choosing to study her hands.

"Mijas. Hank was just very nice and charming. He's handsome, yes, and seems to be very knowledgeable about business—"

"Mom," Naomi inserted.

"You don't know him, Naomi, and you were very rude when he's been around to keep me company. I just get lonely all the time with you girls doing your own thing. I don't have your father anymore, and I just like having someone around."

"Okay," Selah said gently. "We understand you're lonely. Maybe Naomi can help you sign up for some classes in town, and you can make some new friends."

"I don't want to do Pilates. That's too much for me."

"There are lots of other classes besides Pilates, Ma," Hailey replied. "Maybe we can do a class together or something. We'll both meet some new people."

"Yes, that's a great idea. You don't need Hank. I know he seems nice to you, but he's not necessarily someone you can believe. You just have to trust me," Naomi said.

"But Boone." Her mother's eyes became shiny with tears again. "He's going to come back, right? Boone's like family."

Hailey and Selah both glanced in Naomi's direction. She understood her mom was attached to Boone. She'd always treated him like he belonged in the Moreno household the whole time. Telling her mother he was out and not welcome at the farm anymore would devastate her. As angry as she was with Boone and Hank, she didn't want to hurt her mother. She'd also been so concerned with her mother, she hadn't had time to process what it meant for her to lose Boone.

When she didn't answer, Selah replied, "We'll see." She didn't want to disappoint Elena either. "We do have to talk about bigger issues. Because Naomi had to"—she cleared her throat before continuing—"fall in love with one half of our chase crew—"

"I didn't fall in love!" Naomi didn't want to believe she could be as gullible and persuadable as her parents. This was worse because Boone hadn't even offered her promises of wealth and success. He'd only made her believe there were real emotions between them, something meaningful and full of hope. But it was easy to believe that a man who was willing to do things like a wedding con was capable of tricking her as well.

"Well, for the sake of the business," Selah continued, "what exactly are we supposed to do now? Your fight now affects all of us."

"Excuse me? I'm the only one here who didn't want to hire him in the first place."

"Lay off her, Selah," Hailey replied grumpily. "You can't help who you fall for. We've all made—uh, could have made bad decisions when it comes to love. What if someone had said that about you and Dex?"

"I don't work with him, and when Dex and I broke up, it didn't mean we had to shut down the whole business. This is the reality of our predicament, and we need to make decisions. We're going to have to put tours on hold until we hire someone else."

"Really?" Hailey crossed her arms. "That's all Boone meant to you."

"No. I like—Okay, fine." She raised her hands when Naomi glared at her. "I *liked* Boone, but it doesn't matter because the situation is still the same, and bills don't stop because of a love crisis."

"I don't love him!" Naomi yelled again.

Selah leveled a look at her. "Then what exactly were you doing with him?"

She didn't have an answer, but then all the things she would miss started to hit her. It was ludicrous. It didn't make any sense. She wanted to hold on to her rage because it made her feel in control. Naomi didn't like this weak slide into depression at realizing she'd never see him again, never talk to him, never feel his arms around her, never hear the pride in his voice when she tackled a new climb, and never feel the soft brush of his hand through her hair as they lay in bed. None of these things should be more important than her mother. She should be able to live without them. But knowing she'd never experience them again made her shoulders cave into themselves.

The dam on her emotions broke, and she sobbed.

Chapter Eighteen

H E FELT LIKE a jewel thief casing out a store to rob.
Boone observed the tourists in the Smith Rock visitor center yurt while trying to pretend to be normal by casually flicking through a local bird-watching book. He failed in his objective after realizing a few minutes later he'd been flicking through it upside down.

It had been almost a week since he last saw Naomi and he'd kicked his father from his trailer. He didn't know what he expected to happen. He'd been too optimistic to believe the latter would somehow fix the former. That had not happened, nor had she responded to any of his texts. He was becoming miserable, realizing he held more hope in people than they ever had in him. They'd always given up on him so easily.

His only company these days was Cat. He wondered if the feline could sense his misery, never venturing far from his side, preferring to snuggle into his chest and purr loudly against his throat.

This was the first morning he felt the need to climb. He chose one of the more difficult ones, one with a grade of 5.14. He'd never attempted it free solo, but the intensity of it would push everything else from his mind.

Before he got to the wall, he'd run into Alan. It didn't help Boone's mood when he asked, "No Naomi?"

"No. Thought about hitting Assassin. I really need a challenge today."

"Listen, Boone, I, uh . . . the thing is, about that job—I think you'd make a great instructor, but the boss already had a favorite, and they hired someone else. But I want you to know that I really fought for you, and they said maybe next summer they might be looking for someone. I know you've been really trying, and if you ever go for a similar job with another outfit, feel free to use me as a reference."

The news should have been devastating, but he'd been so overwhelmed by emotions in the last week, it was one more thing to hit him when he was already numb. "Oh. Okay. I appreciate you trying."

Alan frowned. "Everything okay with you? You want a climbing buddy today? I just finished with a client, so I'm free, and we can hit Assassin together."

Boone did his best to throw him his regular grin, patting the guy on the shoulder. "Yeah, I'm good. Everything's great. Just want my own company right now."

It didn't appear Alan believed him, but he nodded. "Okay. Well, you be careful. You don't need to go back to the free solo thing. Let me give you my number. If Naomi isn't available, and you ever want a belayer or something, text me."

He assured Alan he was okay, but took the guy's number anyway. Except, afterward, he stood at the base of the rock and didn't want to climb anymore. He considered leaving and going home to Cat.

When a park ranger passed him, his mind went to Dex, and he had the wild idea of trying to find him to talk. While Dex was inside the Moreno circle as Selah's fiancé, he was also enough outside of it that he might be willing to listen to Boone. It was worth a shot. He asked a female park ranger wearing a campaign hat about Dex, and she communicated with someone through a walkie-talkie. This was how Boone found himself flipping through an upside-down bird book in the visitor center.

After waiting fifteen minutes, the man in question came through the door, removing his baseball cap to swipe his forearm across his forehead, blinking his eyes as though adjusting to the dimmer light. As soon as his gaze fell upon Boone, his friendly expression dropped away. "Oh god," he said, which wasn't the reaction Boone had hoped for.

At least Dex was decent enough to walk toward him. "I'm not getting in the middle of anything because I'm already on their side, no matter what."

"Good," Boone replied. "Because I'm on their side as well."

The park ranger's brow rose.

"Five minutes. That's all I'm asking for."

Dex seemed to consider this before breathing out a groan. He tipped his head in the direction of the door, shoving his hands in his pockets as Boone followed him out. The ranger took him to one of the split rail fences along the dirt path that overlooked the park, leaning his backside against it and folding his arms. "Five minutes."

A second ago, five minutes had seemed like enough time to explain his whole life story, but now it was nothing. He was overwhelmed by where to start and which set of words would give him the best chance. Boone asked one of the more pressing questions on his mind rather than jumping in to defend himself. "Are they okay?"

"They're fine. You know how protective they can be of each other. I think there's a lot of high emotions happening right now because of that protectiveness."

Boone nodded. He got it. He knew if there was a threat, they'd cling to each other as though their collective force could ward it off. Perhaps they were right. They were strong, a lot stronger than he ever thought possible from his first impression. The Moreno women were something to be admired as a whole.

"My dad . . ." He cleared his throat before starting again. "He's not someone I would want around them. I blame myself because I thought—I was arrogant enough to think I had control of the situation, that I could keep these two parts of my life separate. I know my dad is problematic and, yet, he's still my dad and . . ." Boone paused, running a frustrated hand across the back of his neck. "There's nothing worse than being completely fucked, even when trying your best, knowing you're partially responsible for the pain they're going through and feeling helpless at being able to fix it."

Dex stayed quiet during this, not reacting much at all. The park ranger would do whatever was best for the ladies. If he came away from this conversation believing he was a threat, Boone would want him to protect them, even if it left him with nothing.

"My mistake was I should have kept a better eye on him. I shouldn't have let myself get so wrapped up in Naomi and everything else in my life. I was more *hoping* things would be okay instead of ensuring they were. Whatever my father told them, told Naomi, about me, it's not true. It's just his way of burning things down whenever things aren't going his way. I gave him a place to crash because he's my father. Other than that, we weren't interacting much. Whatever plans he'd made, I wasn't a part of it."

"You didn't know he was going over to see Elena?"

"I swear, I had no idea. When we got back from Portland, that was the only time I knew he went over there. And I told him then I didn't want him anywhere near that farm. But when Naomi called, when I went over there . . ." It was hard to think about it. He continued feeling raw at being cut off from the Moreno family. "Anyway, afterward, I went home, packed his bags, and kicked him out."

Dex studied him, his stance softening. "It's gotta be tough kicking out a parent, even the bad ones."

"Surprisingly, it was goddamn easy. I'd cut every part of that man out of my heart with a fucking spoon for the things he's done—not necessarily because of what he's done to me, but to other people. I can't live with it anymore. I'm done."

Dex's lips pulled into a frown. "You doing okay?"

Boone never had this many people ask him before. First Alan and now Dex. He must have looked terrible. "Hanging in there. I just want to make sure they're okay."

Giving him a half smile, the ranger replied, "They're fine. Selah and I have been going over to check in and visit in the evenings. I think Naomi is there with Hailey all during the day now."

He nodded. It would have been nice to see and talk to

them himself, but Dex's words were reassuring. Boone squinted toward the landscape, taking another chance. "I don't suppose they're hiring park rangers right now."

"No, I don't think they are. I thought you were trying to get a rock-climbing gig."

"Yeah, I, uh, didn't get it."

"Oh." Dex scratched the back of his head, adjusting his park service ball cap. "My coworker's brother runs a local landscaping business. They always seem to be looking for people. I can check with him if you want."

"Yeah, thanks. I'd appreciate that." Boone would never be presumptuous enough to refer to Dex as a friend. The man was one of those people one could say, *he's a good guy*, and not worry about being proven wrong. He suited Selah well and was a natural fit into the Moreno family, better than Boone had ever been. If he needed a friend, he'd be a good one to have, but Boone would probably mess that up too.

"I better head back to work," Dex said, standing upright.

"Yeah. Thanks for those five minutes."

The ranger started to walk away, but had only taken a few steps before turning to say, "I'll talk to Selah."

It wasn't everything, but it was something. The eldest Moreno daughter had always been levelheaded, and if it was coming from Dex, she would at least listen. If Boone was lucky, word would get to the rest of the family, especially Naomi.

He departed the park after writing a reply to his sister. He'd received a message from Sophie the day everything blew up, but things had been too chaotic for him to focus.

He hadn't been in a good frame of mind to respond. What would he even write about? His life had fallen apart, and he didn't want to burden his sister with his problems. She was a kid. She didn't need any more of the Reyes's poison.

Today, he apologized for not responding sooner because things had been busy. This seemed to be a good compromise. While he didn't want to unload on his sister, he wanted to be the way Naomi liked him—authentic and not someone who hid behind fake bravado. He owed his sister and himself a relationship that had weight to it, something real. He told her he was enjoying getting to know her again and asked her questions about what kind of books she liked, and if she ever watched those historical romance shows. When everything else in his life sucked, he wanted to focus on the things that made his sister happy, to know what those things were. Developing this relationship felt wholesome, and he needed that right now. He needed his sister's eagerness and optimism to survive, even when things got dark.

Afterward, he stopped by the local grocery store to buy some food both for himself and his cat. Things were looking bare in his fridge and cabinets. He took his time, avoiding returning to his sad, empty trailer for as long as possible. When he got home, he was surprised to find Cat outside the door waiting for him, doing his cute, chirpy greeting when Boone got out of his car. He didn't remember letting the cat out when he'd left this morning, but these days, his mind wasn't running on all cylinders.

Upon entering, there was Hank in the kitchen, making himself a sandwich with two heel pieces, all that remained from a loaf of bread.

"I was wondering when you were finally going to get back," his dad said, as though he'd never left at all.

Boone tensed. "What the hell are you doing here? I told you to get out."

"Come on, son. Are you still angry about that little misunderstanding? I thought you'd have cooled off by now. You never were one to hold a grudge."

Hank hadn't taken him seriously. He must have thought if he stayed away a week, Boone would forget everything and let him into his life again. It was logical, since it had happened this way before. That's what *always* happened when it came to Hank.

Not this time.

This time, the gloves were coming off.

Chapter Nineteen

"WHAT'S GOING ON here?" Selah said as she entered the Redmond townhome with some late-morning coffee, dropping her keys on the kitchen counter and removing her aviators.

Her sister treated their shared townhome as more of a pit stop these days than her place of residence. It must have been a shock to see Naomi packing things in a box and adding it to a stack. Now was as good as any other time to talk to her sister about her new plans.

"So I'm thinking about not renewing the lease when it expires in two months. If you want to transfer it to your name and take it, we can check with the management company, but I figured you might not be interested since you pretty much live at Dex's, anyway."

"You're moving? Why? Where are you going?" Her sister's brows knitted together.

Naomi taped the box, acting nonchalant. "I'm, um, moving back in with Mom."

Selah tilted her head, her frown deepening. She'd always been independent. It wasn't surprising she didn't understand. "Does Mom know about this?"

"I was going to talk to her about it today. I don't think

she'll say no." Their mother was the most welcoming person in the world, after all.

"I don't think she'd say no either, especially if she thinks you need help. But I don't think she's going to like it if the real reason is because you think *she* needs help. Mom loves us, definitely loves us nearby, but I don't think she wants us to give up our lives and treat her like she needs to be protected or something."

"That's not what's happening," she replied defensively, having just gone through a similar conversation with Amber after their most recent Pilates class.

Selah shook her head, not appearing convinced. "Naomi, stop. What are you doing?"

"I just . . . would feel better if I was there to keep an eye on things."

"You don't trust Hailey?"

"I do, but Hailey is still young—"

"Look, I know I haven't given her a lot of credit in the past, but Hailey's doing okay. Yeah, she can be a little flighty and immature, but she's smart and perceptive. She suspected something was wrong, and she reached out. Hailey did exactly what she was supposed to do, which should be more reassuring, not less." Her sister had a point.

"What if Hailey finds someone and wants to leave? She was dating someone before."

"She was? Who?"

"I don't know. I just know she was seeing someone before Dad died, and she was being really secretive about it. She could be dating someone right now, for all we know, because we're not there."

"And? We can come up with 'what-if's' all day long. I don't think we need to worry about it until we're actually faced with that situation. Mom is going to be fine. And if something comes up, we'll figure it out."

Selah made it seem simple, but she'd always been the strongest one. Perhaps it came easier to her. There was a reason her mother always called the eldest daughter her rock. She'd been all of their rocks at different points. Naomi wasn't like that, though. This could be why her dad didn't listen to her.

She took a breath. "I need to protect Mom because I wasn't able to with Dad."

"What do you mean? You can't stop a brain aneurysm from happening."

"No, I know. There's something I need to tell you. He used to watch this YouTube channel—"

"Sure Shot Money? Naomi, I know."

"You do?"

"About how much he gave for private online seminars and the refinancing at high rates? Yeah, I know. I dug through all of his finances after he died. I had to find out where all the money had gone to."

"Why didn't you say anything?"

"Probably for the same reason you didn't. I didn't want to ruin Mom's, or my sisters', perfect image they have of him. I was trying to protect you."

Naomi's shoulders dropped while the burden of this secret lifted. Here, she'd been carrying this guilt when she could have talked to Selah the whole time. Tears sprung to her eyes. "I tried. I tried to talk to him because I was there when it was happening. I knew something wasn't right."

"Come here." Selah took a spot on the couch, opening her arms as an invitation. Her older sister was petite, smaller than herself, but Naomi could curl in her sister's arms, her persona making her seem bigger. "You didn't do anything wrong. Dad made his own decisions. There was probably nothing you could have said that would have changed his mind because he wanted to believe in things so badly. Sometimes it worked and sometimes it didn't. But that's not your responsibility."

Naomi couldn't help crying, knowing her sister's logic was sound, but having a hard time believing it, anyway.

Selah continued, "Mom is an adult and her own person. We can help her if she wants it, but just as she wants you to live your own life, you have to afford her the same thing. Obviously, we can talk about it, but at the end of the day, it's her choice on what she does. You can't always protect her. I know it's hard to accept because I want to do the same thing. I don't know when things switched, and I started to feel more like the parent, but I get it. Trying to control every little aspect is impossible and exhausting. Sometimes, you just do the best you can, and then you have to let it go. It's just like flying a hot-air balloon. You can make plans, but at the end of the day, you can't control the wind. You just have to let it take you where it wants to go, and sometimes you land in a totally different spot than you expected. This isn't necessarily a bad thing."

Naomi did a watery laugh. Of course, her sister would relate everything to flying.

"Since we're already having a tough chat, maybe we

should talk about Boone."

"What? Why?" Naomi did not see why it was necessary to talk about things that might make her cry harder.

"Well, it's either with me or Mom, because she won't stop asking about when he's going to come back. And since you're supposedly planning on moving in with her, you're probably going to hear a lot more about it. I think we should just talk now."

Naomi pulled away from her sister, done being comforted, and crossed her arms tight around her middle, the anxiety building. "He's not coming back. Ever."

"Naomi—"

"You, of all people, should understand. I already feel bad enough falling for a con artist. I should have known better. I'm no better than Dad."

Her sister pressed her lips together. "Okay, let's just step back and think about this for a minute—"

"I'm not wasting my time giving him any more thought."

"This isn't for him necessarily. This is for you. Okay?" She raised her hands in a calm-down motion. "So you're saying that Boone is a liar, right?"

"Yes."

"Would you say that Hank is a liar?"

"Yes," Naomi replied, annoyed at having to state the obvious.

"But if they're saying two different things, Hank implying Boone is involved in whatever his plan is, while Boone saying he is not involved, it stands to reason, then, that one of them must be telling the truth and is, in fact, not lying. Right?"

Selah had her there. "It doesn't matter. Boone is still a liar."

"Okay," her sister said. "What has he lied about?"

Naomi opened her mouth to respond, but no sound escaped. Her mind scrambled to produce a bunch of evidence to be used at Boone's trial.

Her sister leaned against the couch back, resting her head on a hand in the casual pose of a pretend lawyer who wasn't the least bit worried about losing this case. "The guy has been helping us at High Desert Tours all this time. You must have a long list of lies you've caught him in that I've just never heard about."

"Just because he's never been caught in a lie doesn't mean he hasn't lied. He's from a family of conmen. He's probably really good at it." She didn't like stooping to this level of petty, but it was all she had.

Selah barked a laugh. "Are you listening to yourself? You know that isn't fair. I did a thorough background check on him, above and beyond what is normal, after the interview. You were so against him, and I thought maybe you were right, and you were seeing something I wasn't. Besides his weird lack of work history and horrible credit, there wasn't anything."

Her sister had listened to her, after all? This surprised her more than the fact Boone had a cleaner past than she'd given him credit for. Naomi was desperate for anything at this point. "Alright, fine. You want to know when he lied? When he said he loved me."

"He kicked his dad out."

Her brain stopped in its tracks. "What?"

"Boone kicked Hank out that day."

It took Naomi time to process this. "How do you know?" She'd feel betrayed if her family had been talking to Boone behind her back this whole time.

"Dex saw him this morning."

"Oh." She resisted the temptation to ask how he was, trying not to worry about him, but failing anyway. All the anger she had was missing. She'd been so worried about what could have happened to her mom, she hadn't stopped to consider if she believed Boone had done the things his father—and worse, she, herself—had accused him of. Selah was right. They both couldn't be lying when they said opposite things. One of them had to be telling the truth, and she yearned for that person to be Boone.

Naomi had one stubborn point remaining. "Look, even if Boone wasn't involved, he should have worked harder at keeping his father away. He should have stopped him. It's because of him that man had the chance to prey on our mother."

Her sister nodded, but appeared as if she'd already won the argument. "Right. He should have been able to control his father from doing something bad . . . just like you were able to control our dad from doing something he shouldn't have."

Naomi glared at her sister, wanting to be mad at someone but not knowing where to direct it. She didn't know why, but none of this felt fair. Selah had lit a match on a list of Naomi's grievances, and all she could do was watch it turn to ash.

Her sister left soon after, but Naomi was restless and

couldn't return to packing. She got in her car and drove straight to Terrebonne. She could go to the Moreno farmhouse, her mother would offer her lunch, comfort her, and make her feel as though she was still a good person. She was beginning to have her doubts.

Instead, she continued to the Crockett farm. She was unsure where Boone lived on the property as she'd never visited before. Naomi had to see him for herself, curious if she could detect his true guilt or innocence from sight alone.

"You lost?" An older man, his aging white skin drawn tight over his bones, stepped from a dilapidated farmhouse, surrounded by old junk and garbage. He wore dirty denim overalls with no shirt, and tufts of graying chest hair were on full display.

"Hi, I'm one of the Moreno daughters from the farm next door." She pointed in the general direction and nervously slid some hair behind her ear. "I'm . . . I was told Boone lives here, and I'm looking for him."

"Boone?" The old man gave her a good once-over before answering. "Yup, he lives here. He's in the trailer on the other side of that barn over there."

It wasn't too far, but she'd have to venture through a maze of rusty, broken farm equipment, like a character in a horror movie. "I think I'll just walk over. Is it okay if I leave my car here?" she asked nervously.

He nodded and left her on her own. She was never more relieved when she spied Boone's car beside the tan, outdated, single-wide trailer with dead wild grass growing around it. As beautiful as the High Desert could be, this view was depressing as hell.

Naomi stopped in her tracks at the sound of a heated argument spilling from a cracked window on the side of the trailer. She recognized Boone's voice, and the other sounded like Hank's, but it lacked its soft, twangy drawl.

There was a moment of vindication. She was tempted to throw the door open and shout *I was right! You are a liar for making everyone believe you kicked that man out. You are working together!* It only lasted a second before disappointment filled its space. Naomi wanted to be wrong, wanted to believe she'd known the true Boone, wanted to be able to love him.

If this was all there was to learn, she would have left. Except... Boone's tone wasn't happy. In fact, he sounded angrier than she'd ever heard from him before. Naomi sneaked closer, pressing herself beside the window on the trailer wall. An orange cat crawled out from under the home, weaving through her legs until she scooped it up and held the feline to her chest while she eavesdropped.

"Can I at least finish my sandwich before you get all worked up? Do you want me to starve?"

"Does it look like I care? I wasn't kidding before. You don't live here anymore. Take the sandwich, get out, and don't come back."

"I really don't know what's gotten into you lately. After all we've been through, after all I've done for you. And this is how you repay your old man? I keep telling you, it was all a misunderstanding. I can understand the women getting a little hysterical, but not you. You know how these things are."

Boone released a bitter laugh. "All you've done for me?

244

You've ruined my life."

"Oh, don't be so dramatic. It's because of me you got to enjoy some of the richer things in life. You think we would have gotten half of those experiences if I did blue-collar grunt work? What about all the trips and clothes and food we got?"

"While we're reminiscing, let's not forget about all the times I got to visit you in prison or when I was homeless and had to steal to eat."

"I taught you survivability. And you were on the street for less than a week before you figured it out and got Monica to take you on. Don't act like that was some great hardship. When I came to get you, you didn't look like you were suffering too badly."

Naomi released a shaky breath, snapping a hand across her mouth, fearing someone might notice her snooping.

"You don't know what I went through or what I've been doing to get out—"

"And, as I keep telling you, now that I'm here, I only want to help you."

"I don't want your kind of help. I want you to leave. Whatever plans you've had or currently have, I don't want any part of it."

There was a long pause before Hank spoke again. "Is this really because of me, or are you just hung up on that pink-haired Moreno girl? Look, I admit, it's easy to get taken in by a pretty girl with great tits, but—"

There was some kind of scuffle, as if something slammed into a cabinet. "If you don't fucking shut up about her, I'm going to—"

"Rule number one! What's the number one rule I've always told you, Boone? You keep your emotions out of it. Because as soon as you let yourself feel things, *you* get taken in. You're the one who is being played. You think she's ever going to stick around with someone like you, living the way you do, with no money, shitty car, no job possibilities. I don't care what they say, all women want the same thing, and you don't have it. Stop using your dick and use your brain. Invest in you, and the money tree will grow. Hasn't it always worked that way? They're not worth it. They're *never* worth it."

It was quiet again. Naomi prayed Boone wouldn't listen to his father. She pressed her face into Cat's fur, hoping Boone would realize his dad was wrong about everything.

"Look, I know this wasn't your fault. I didn't know those girls sunk their claws so deeply into you. But you cut me out, Boone. Me, your own dad. After all I've done, raising you when no one else wanted you. You just cut me out of your plans."

"There was no plan! I keep telling you, I was just trying to live my life."

"Well, I know that isn't true. There's always a plan. And I was starting to feel a little desperate for something. But that's alright, that's fine. I forgive you. But if we're going to be partners, real partners, not just a father and son, but equals, we need to be better at communicating."

"I don't want to communicate. Don't you get it? You've ruined my life. You've taken *everything* from me." Boone didn't sound angry anymore, only defeated, his voice cracking the shell around her heart as though it was made of thin glass.

"Boone—"

"Get out." His voice returned with a hard edge, as though it had become a razor capable of cutting anything from his life.

Hank's tone switched to one more menacing. "Don't think I'm going to forget about this. You don't want to partner with me? You want to do your own schemes? That's just fine. But know that I always come out on top because, unlike you, I'm willing to do anything. Maybe all you're good for is being some kind of boy toy to rich, lonely bitches." The older man clucked his tongue. "It's a shame, a real shame. You had so much potential at the beginning and now look at you. Don't come crawling to me when you get tired of being nothing. I don't know you anymore. You're not my son. You probably never were mine. I only took you in because women like single dads."

"Fine. You don't claim me, and I don't claim you. Leave."

Footsteps made their way to the door. Naomi, terrified of getting caught, hurried around the corner of the trailer. The door opened, and heavy stomps came down the steps, crunching dirt and dried plants beneath them. Hank stalked away from the trailer, body stiff, hands fisted. If he turned, he'd see her. Except, he didn't. The man never once looked back, as though Boone had left Hank's universe and had already been forgotten.

Naomi leaned against the trailer's wall, realizing how wrong she'd been. She considered knocking on his door and talking to him, but she must have hurt him as much as his so-called father had. Guilt as big as the boulders at Smith

Rock weighed heavy on her shoulders. She had told Boone he wasn't alone, that he had more than a shitty father in his corner. She'd insisted he had Elena and her sisters and her. But at her first moment of panic, she'd cut him off and left him alone.

No wonder he was a free solo guy, no wonder he was alone. If she'd been his belayer, she would have dropped him, left him to dangle on the side of a cliff because she'd been scared of making the same mistake as her father. She'd learned the wrong lessons from rock climbing. While she may be stronger than she assumed, she'd only been able to discover her strength because he'd been at the bottom of the wall. He'd had her, but she hadn't done the same for him.

Selah's parting words from that morning haunted her. *"Maybe you're scared to realize that if Boone hadn't lied about the other stuff, then maybe he hadn't lied about loving you either."*

She couldn't go to him and say, *Never mind. Everything is fine now that I know the truth.* It wasn't good enough. She had to give him something more. Something that said if things got scary again, she'd belay for him. She'd keep him from falling.

Chapter Twenty

A NOTHER WEEK AND a half passed after Boone kicked out his dad a second time. This time, Hank kept his word and didn't return.

He wasn't completely alone, as it turned out. His sister responded to his messages fairly regularly. It was becoming a bright spot in his life. If he had exchanged his relationship with his father for one with his sister, it was an upgrade. Their relationship wasn't one of manipulation or how one could use the other. It was nice and genuine, and he loved learning more about her life.

Dex had also reached out to him, giving him contact information for the landscaping job. Sure, it wasn't what Boone wanted to do forever, but it was fine and brought money in. He had no reason to complain, especially when he hadn't expected Dex to follow through and help him. He was eager to know if there'd been any discussion with Selah, but assumed the silence was answer enough. Dex was nice enough to text him and make sure things were going okay with the job. This was at least some kind of connection to the Moreno family, however small it may be.

Alan checked in on him, asking if he ever wanted to go climbing together. Boone hadn't been in the mood lately, but he considered taking him up on his offer at some point. All these things weren't a whole lot, but it did make him feel not entirely friendless.

One night, while he was lying on the couch and watching TV, his phone rang. He checked the ID on the screen.

It was Selah.

His heart beat heavily in his chest, and it took him several seconds to answer it. "Hello?"

"Hey, Boone. It's Selah." Her voice was her typical no-nonsense candor, and he couldn't distinguish if she was happy or angry. It was strangely normal, as if the last few weeks hadn't happened, and she called for a casual chat.

"Hey. How are you?" He tried not to jump in to ask about Naomi.

"Doing okay. How are you?"

"Fine. How's your mom? And Naomi . . . and Hailey?" Okay, so he didn't last long with playing it cool.

She laughed lightly. "They're fine too." There was a brief, awkward pause before she continued, never being much of a small talker. "So, I was wondering if you wouldn't mind coming out to the farm tomorrow."

Was he getting his job back? He wanted to return, if only to see Naomi. He'd even take it back if all she gave him were curt responses and rolling eyes, like in the old days. He could work with that and, hopefully, dig his way out of it as he had once before. "Do you need help with a tour tomorrow? I would say yes, but I'm, uh, working at least until noon."

"With the landscaping company? Oh, yes, Dex told me about that. No, that's fine. You can come after work if you want."

He was befuddled but couldn't quite bring himself to ask, *Why?*

She appeared to have read his mind when she jumped in with, "I understand if you'd rather stay with the landscaping company, but I do want to talk to you about possibly coming back, if that's something you're interested in. I'd just rather do it in person, and my mom keeps asking if she can see you. If tomorrow doesn't work . . ." She let the sentence drop as though letting him decide how it should finish.

"No, I can come tomorrow after work. I . . ." He wasn't sure what to do with this information, not believing everything he wanted might become a reality. One part, though, remained a mystery. "Does Naomi know? She's okay with me stopping by?"

"Oh, yeah, she knows," Selah responded, which didn't fully answer his questions. They ran things like a democracy. It was possible she wasn't okay, but was outvoted.

Selah finished with, "Okay, great. We'll see you tomorrow then. Bye," disconnecting the line and leaving Boone wondering what he could expect next.

"BOONE!"

Hailey sat sideways in a chair on the Moreno front porch, her legs dangling over one side. She removed her attention from her phone, which was always glued to her hands. Her face brightened with a smile as she jumped from the chair.

Boone hadn't known what kind of greeting he should

have expected from the family when he parked at the farm, but this already exceeded everything.

"Ma! Get out here. Boone's here!" Hailey shouted through the screen door before bounding toward him. She pressed the sides of their faces together, knocking his glasses askew as she held out her phone. It was in recording mode. "Guess who's back, everyone? Boone, did you miss me?" She continued smiling at the phone screen, reflecting both their images.

His own expression was somewhat surprised and bewildered. Then he fixed his glasses and switched to his most winning smile. "Of course I missed you, darling. I missed all the Moreno women. Some more than others. Have you been keeping yourself out of trouble?"

She giggled, making a faux shocked expression at the camera. "Some of us like trouble," Hailey said with a smile. "It provides some of the best content."

"Boone!" Elena pushed through the door, with Selah following calmly behind her. Their mother was already weepy, as though Boone had been lost at sea for months and had finally found his way back. "Boone!" she cried again as she rushed to him.

Hailey released her grip before the older woman threw herself at him, wrapping him in the tightest hug. "You don't know how much we've missed you. I'm so sorry for causing so much trouble for everyone. I've been wanting you to come back."

Not expecting this, he was taken aback by her apology. "You didn't do anything wrong. This is my fault. Okay? I should have . . . I should have done more—"

"Stop." Elena pulled away, taking his face between her palms as she forced his attention on her. "I know you wouldn't do something to hurt us. You're good. I know you are good. And I want you to know this too. You're welcome into my home anytime, okay? You're a part of our family. You understand?"

A tickle in the back of his eyes developed, the emotion growing stronger. Boone tried to hold it back because Hailey was recording this moment with her phone. His only response to Elena was a nod, and he hoped it was enough.

"Good." Her face lit with a warm smile as she hugged him again. "Are you hungry? I have no idea what you've been feeding yourself, but it looks like nothing. How are you skinnier? Doesn't he look skinny, Selah?"

The eldest daughter laughed before saying, "God, Mom, leave him alone." She pulled him into a light hug, which wasn't easy with Elena hanging onto his arm. "Welcome back."

"Thanks." Boone, overwhelmed by it all, could barely find any words to use.

"You are coming back, right, Boone?" Elena asked.

"I, uh, would like to but . . ." He cleared his throat. "Only if it's okay with everyone." Despite receiving a happy welcome from them, the most important person in the group remained missing. How much would he have given to see Naomi walk out the door with the rest of her family, to know he'd received her . . . well, maybe not love because that was a lot to ask for, but at least her blessing to return. Her absence had to be a bad sign.

"Oh, wait." Hailey tapped her chin. "Where is Naomi? Has anyone seen her?"

"I think I saw her over on the other side of the barn. We should go over there," Elena answered in an unnatural tone, her daughter being the better actress. He gave them an odd look, but Elena looped her arm through his, pulling him in the direction of the barn. "Come on. Let's go find Naomi," she said, way too loud to be normal. As they walked, Elena dominated the conversation with all the things he'd missed the last few weeks. Most of it being a visit from her sister, and she and Hailey taking a knitting class together in town.

As soon as they turned the corner, Naomi was there, waiting like a highly anticipated vision. Her pink hair was partially pulled back into a loose style, with soft curls gently playing on a breeze. She wore a long, summer floral dress, the neckline pushed off her beautiful shoulders, showing her golden-tanned skin. Her gaze flicked to him when he came into view, those soft lips parting on a breath.

"There she is!" Elena said. "Isn't she pretty? You should go talk to her, Boone. I, uh, have something in the oven I need to check." She encouraged him by pushing him forward without her. "Come along, mijas. You can help me in the house."

Then he and Naomi were alone. He had so much he should have said, and could have apologized for, but he didn't know where to start. Perhaps he should simply fall to his knees, wrap his arms around her waist, and beg.

Before he could decide, she spoke first, approaching closer. "You know what this means, right? The negotiations for your return have been left in my hands." Her lips tipped into a sly smile, which was his first hint she no longer hated his guts.

His body eased from feeling as if he were about to face a firing squad to finding relief that he'd possibly survive this and end in a better place. He stuffed his hands in his pockets, leaning a shoulder against the side of the barn. "It probably should have been that way all along, don't you think? You seem to be perceptive as hell."

"Sure, I'm perceptive, but not infallible. I've been wrong about people once or twice in my life."

He gave her a warm smile. "In my expert conman experience, telling people you're not infallible isn't a good strategy when you're about to negotiate, honey."

One of her shoulders lifted in a subtle shrug. "I think it's more important that both parties come to the table or, in this case, the barn in good faith. Obviously, neither one of us is perfect, but maybe that doesn't matter. We can compromise enough until we both end up happy and get what we want."

His brain latched onto the phrase *both end up happy*. She approached closer, and he itched to touch her, to plunge his fingers into her hair to the very roots. He ached for her. "I'm afraid you have me at a disadvantage because I'm liable to say yes to almost every one of your demands."

"Good, then this won't take very long. Here's my first request." She was directly before him now, so close he was invaded by the delicate smell of berries. Her gaze rose, looking less coy and more sincere, her delicate brow lifting. "Forgive me?"

His forehead furrowed. He'd come here today ready to plead with each member of the family for mercy and forgiveness for Hank's transgressions. Them turning it around and apologizing *to him* wasn't part of his plan. He hadn't prepared for this. "I don't blame you for being upset, Naomi."

She took his hand in hers. "That's sweet but . . . I should have given you a chance. I shouldn't have cut you out like that. I lumped you two together, just like Sophie's mom did, and that wasn't fair. I'm so sorry, Boone." Big tears splashed across her cheeks like broken bits of glass. "What I did to you wasn't okay." She roughly wiped away a tear from her face. "And I want you to know that it wasn't my family. It was me. I was the stubborn, scared one here. They supported you. I understand if you don't want to come back. Just don't blame them when it was me."

Boone couldn't listen to this anymore. Everyone was fighting to take the blame instead of putting it directly on Hank's shoulders, where it belonged. He realized they all deserved some mercy. He took her by her shoulders and pulled her into his arms, her own going around his lower back as they held each other. "I do want to come back. I've always wanted to come back. I've missed this hot-air balloon business and this farm and your family and sitting with you in those damn camping chairs as we wait in a field for Selah to land. I miss the climbing and meeting you after your class and talking about your wedding stuff. I just miss *you*."

Her laugh was blubbery with tears. "I want to kiss you, but I'm not done. I've been tasked with more negotiation, and I don't think it would be fair until you hear everything."

"There's more?" What else could there possibly be? Everything until this point had been exactly what he wanted.

She pulled back to look at him. "I heard about the

climbing job. I'm really sorry. That must have been disappointing, as I knew how much you wanted it."

Boone tried to brush it off. "I'm sure something else will come along."

"Especially since I know how much you hate Tom."

"What about Tom?"

She cringed. "Oh god. Sorry. You didn't know? The guy at the climbing gym got the job. I ran into Alan, and he told me."

He supposed this news should be annoying. Maybe the universe thought it was a fair exchange if Boone got the girl and Tom got the job. Truth be told, he got the better end of the deal.

She covered her cheek with a hand. "Just . . . I'm sorry. But I want to show you something. Come with me."

With this, she took his hand, pulling him alongside the barn before taking him to the backside. "We all want you to be happy. You deserve to finally find your place, and I hope that it'll be here."

When she stopped, sweeping her hand to the barn wall, his confusion shifted to amusement and then back again. The whole backside of the tall barn was covered in colorful climbing holds bolted into various patterns. "Wait . . . what's happening?"

"So we've been talking and, for once in our life, we're all in agreement. We want to support your dreams, at least as much as we can. If being a climbing instructor is your dream, then we want to help you. If you want to try being a private instructor, we'll fold it under High Desert Tours. Maybe we'll change our name to something more encompassing, so it can include the hot-air balloons, private climbing lessons, and my event side. We have a farm. We have room for all of this. Hailey even said she'll help set up your website and social media if you want. Selah has agreed that we can give up some of this old farm equipment we've been holding on to and sell it so we can invest in you and get things you need, like safety mats or whatever. Alan and Dex both helped bolt all these holds on the barn. Alan also said if they run out of room in their classes, he'll slip people your business card to help you get started. You see? We're all rooting for you."

Boone could feel himself getting emotional again, rubbing the corner of his eye. No one in his life had done so much for him, been so kind, just for the hell of it, because they wanted him to be happy. He wasn't sure how he'd ever make it up to this family, or what he'd ever done to deserve it. It was too risky to speak.

She seemed to understand, her hand rubbing his arm, but she continued the emotional hits. "Oh, and if you don't want to live at the Crockett farm anymore, Mom said she's okay if you want to move into the farmhouse with her and Hailey for now. You can take my old room if you want. You can even bring Cat with you."

"Um." He did this weird cough-sob, clearing his throat to cover it, never feeling more like a vulnerable, weak baby than he did at this moment. This was more love than his heart knew what to do with.

Naomi wrapped him in her arms again, and he pressed his face into her neck. "I know," she said. "It's a lot, so you can think about it if you want. There's no pressure or anything. It's whatever you want."

He couldn't help but laugh at this. "Are you kidding? This is the nicest thing anyone has ever done for me."

"So, you love it?" As if there was any doubt and he didn't love everything. His chest might burst because it was so full of love, especially for her. Naomi always went a little extra with things, and he couldn't believe she went through all this effort for him. She was a storm of getting things done, which is how he knew her event business would be a success. When it came to her future, he only wanted to be along for the ride.

"Yeah, I do," he answered. "Question, though. This invitation to take your old room in your mom's house... Does it come with you? Because you know I want nothing more than to wake up early in the morning, to find you there, the warm glow of the sun spreading its way across your soft cheek, highlighting your hair like strands of rose gold. Those sunrise colors make you look like a watercolor that I wish I was talented enough to paint." He grinned as her gaze darted away and she blushed. "Your mouth hanging open in an adorable snore—"

She punched his arm playfully, a laugh bursting from her. "Excuse me! Now your fantastical scenarios are too rude. And, no, I won't be living in my old bedroom. I'm still going to be at the townhome, which is also an option for you, but the trade-off will be more me and less of my mom's cooking. I don't know if it's a fair deal."

He plucked a strand of windblown hair that had plastered itself to her forehead as his attention swept over her. "You'd let me come stay at your place?"

Her hazel eyes warmed. "Mm-hmm. Because I love you."

This was all he needed. His life was complete. "And because I love you, I'm willing to give up your mom's cooking. I'd rather have your adorable snoring."

"If you don't knock it off—" He didn't let her finish before he was clasping the side of her face and bringing her in for a long-overdue, grateful kiss. Her hands gripped the fabric at his waist, his hold sliding to the nape of her neck. Her lips opened as she released a moan, letting the kiss deepen into delightful sparkles of chemistry.

"I love you, Naomi," he whispered as he parted from her to adjust his angle to a better one. They stayed, making out and making up for lost time. He pressed her into his new outdoor climbing wall, gripping the holds on either side of her, feeling this was the best of both worlds and wondering if it would be possible to make love to her there.

When they finally parted, they walked hand in hand toward the farmhouse, toward his new, adopted family. Hailey cheered a loud, "Woo! Finally!" from the porch when they emerged, pulling out her phone again to what he could only assume was to document the moment further. He didn't care. They smiled at each other, and he brought her hand to his lips, kissing her knuckles before raising it victoriously.

This moment was his biggest success to date, like he'd pulled off the biggest heist in history and walked away with the most glittering jewel he could find—Naomi Moreno's heart.

It was a treasure he'd value forever.

Epilogue

The following May

"DAMMIT," NAOMI HUFFED as a hairpin slipped and clattered into the bathroom sink. She didn't understand how the YouTube hair influencers she'd watched made this appear effortless. Scammed again. It was downright laughable, as her hair didn't look even close to the style demonstrated.

She released a frustrated breath, scrapping her whole hair plan and sticking with something she could manage. Probably for the best, anyway. She was removing the rest of the hair clips when Boone's reflection appeared behind her in the mirror.

He leaned in the doorframe, doing an obvious perusal as he checked her out from behind. Not surprising, as she was wearing a drapey, white summer dress that clung to her figure. He was much more put together than she, in regards to getting ready, but to be fair, he'd started with good bones. Bastard. His hair was neatly swept back, and he wore a pair of dark jeans and a nice shirt, opened at the collar. She couldn't help checking him out for herself as she pulled another pin from her hair.

"You sure wearing that today is a good idea?" he said

while adjusting his glasses. Since he wore them exclusively now, Boone had reached his "hot professor, too busy to shave" stage of life. He had a bit of a scruff on his jawline, and then she noticed the mustache.

Naomi ignored his question because, even if it was kind of a workday, she wanted to look cute, giving his reflection a flirty grin. "Well, well, well. If it isn't Charlie darkening my doorway after all this time. Guess what? You're too late. Someone else has come along and claimed my heart."

Creases indented his face as his lips curved upward. "Hey now, Treasure. Don't be this way," he replied in his fake Australian accent as he approached, sliding his arms around her waist. She tipped her head to the side, giving him access to dip his head there and press a kiss to her skin. "You think he can give you everything that I've given you?"

"I don't know. He's pretty great, even if he doesn't know how to properly load a dishwasher."

"He's clearly a silly wombat. If he can't load a dishwasher properly, how do you expect him to bloom your onion down under?"

She laughed. "I have no complaints. I love him, anyway."

"Aw, Treasure. Well, I don't think I could have parted with you to a better scoundrel. Although, I might still come around from time to time. You never know when you'll need a ride." He winked at her reflection as she leaned against his chest and he rested his chin on her head. They stayed like that for a moment, savoring it.

"You don't think anyone suspects anything, do you?"

His eyes twinkled, the accent replaced by his normal voice. "Not if Dex can keep his mouth shut."

Soon after Boone and Cat had moved in with her, Naomi received an email from the couple they'd spoken to at the Portland wedding convention. They asked to tour the farm on a pit stop as they traveled to Crater Lake. They arrived on a tour day, so Selah offered to take them up and the couple fell in love with the idea. They went ahead and made their reservation. High Desert Events had their first wedding coming this summer. Naomi also booked another wedding for early fall and a couple of more reservations for the following year. It was a quiet start, but she was excited.

Dex volunteered to go through the process to get ordained so it could be an included service. It was cute how excited he was about it, eager to marry someone, once it was official. Selah still hadn't set a date for their own wedding, which was okay because neither one seemed to be in a big hurry since Selah had finally moved full-time into Dex's house, anyway.

Either way, Selah insisted on a test run of everything when the tour schedule opened up in order to work out any kinks. Everyone agreed it was a good idea. They'd go up with Selah piloting and Dex officiating. Hailey would be there as a "photographer," Elena as the witness, and then Naomi and Boone were the stand-ins for the bride and groom.

After the date had been set, later that night, Naomi and Boone had discussed it in bed. "You know what would be funny?" he had said. "What if Dex married us for real?"

"Oh my god. Ha! What a good joke that would be. We just happen to have the marriage license and then go, *Surprise! We're really married!*" Naomi wanted to laugh at how shocked her family's faces would be, even while knowing they'd be happy once the emotion wore off. Come to think of it, she'd also be happy with this outcome.

"We should really do it."

"Yeah, *we should* really do it. After all this time of my mom bugging us to get married, we'll just beat her to it."

"We can get a marriage license, a couple of rings, and then I'd marry you so good right under your family's nose. It's like an elopement they didn't know they were invited to."

She laughed and kissed his lips before snuggling into him. Usually, these types of jokes died, but this one didn't. This one they kept talking about it amongst themselves, and maybe it was because both of them really did want to get married. They went to the Deschutes County Clerk's office to get the marriage license, they secretly picked some simple rings because there wasn't a lot of money between them, and they decided they were going to do it. The only person they told was Dex because they weren't sure if it would be legal if he thought the vows were fake. Better not to take the risk. Dex was a good sport about it and promised he wouldn't breathe a word to Selah.

So now it was the day of their supposed surprise wedding. Butterflies fluttered in her stomach all morning—not because she was nervous, but more because she was excited to officially claim Boone as her husband and start a new chapter in their lives. His climbing business was steadily rising. Naomi could say the same about High Desert Events. Everything was good for the chase crew. Why not make it better? Boone and Naomi drove out to the field where everyone was already there for balloon setup.

"Oh, Naomi," her mother said. "You're looking very pretty. But aren't you going to be cold? Do you want me to run back to the house to get you one of my sweaters?"

"Why in the world would you wear a dress today?" Selah asked.

As much as she wanted to burst with glee, she tried to maintain a neutral expression. "I brought a little cardigan to wear. I should be fine. Besides, if this was a real event, it's likely the bride would be wearing a dress. I thought you wanted to do a real run-through."

Selah gave her an odd look. "Well, I hope you don't plan on wearing a white dress as the wedding coordinator. We don't need any unnecessary drama."

"You do look very pretty. Boone, doesn't my Naomi look pretty today? She would make such a pretty bride," her mother said.

"Huh," he replied. "Maybe someday someone will marry her then."

Elena's lips flattened. "No. *You're* supposed to marry her. Why do you enjoy teasing me like this?"

Boone only grinned and waggled his eyebrows.

Once everything was ready, everyone climbed into the gondola. Selah turned on the burner, and they lifted into the air as far as the tethering would take them.

"Okay, so I think since Selah needs to stay in the center with the burner, we can put the officiant, Dex, in this case, at one end with the bride and groom. If we have a photographer and guest, they should probably be on the other end. Let's just stand in the spots for now," Naomi said, directing this like a mini production. "Hailey, if you were the photographer, does it look okay?" Their basket was meant to fit about six people, and it was a cozy fit, with not a lot of room.

"Selah, move your elbow. You're right in the shot," Hailey said, looking with her phone. "No one wants wedding pictures with you partially in them, looking like an intruder."

"The ceremony hasn't even started yet. I'll move my elbow when it starts. And we'll have to make the stipulation that the wedding couple can only go up if the bride doesn't have a really long train or a huge puffy dress. How would she even get in the gondola? Did you even consider this, Naomi?"

"I know. There's barely room to turn around. I've already discussed this with the bride. Let's just go through the ceremony so we can see how long we can go without the burner interrupting. We don't want them declaring their love, and then Selah turns on the burner with—" Naomi made an impression of the sound the flame made when it turned on.

"I'll use the quieter burner during the ceremony."

"But is it still going to be an interruption?"

"I don't know. How long is a ceremony?"

Dex pulled out a piece of paper from his pocket. "Everyone calm down. Let's take a deep breath and just run through it. Okay, bride and groom, let's do this." Boone and Naomi stood before him, taking each other's hands. When she lifted her gaze to meet his, his eyes were filled with adoration. She blushed and couldn't help smiling.

"Aw, mija. This is so sweet. Like a real wedding. Hailey,

take a picture so I can send it to your auntie. She'll want to see how pretty Naomi looks with her hair today, like a real bride."

"Ma, stop talking. You can't do that during a real wedding."

"*Dearly beloved,*" Dex said, interrupting with good-natured sternness. "We're gathered here today to join Boone and Naomi in holy matrimony. Marriage is not only about finding your soulmate, your love, the person you want to spend the rest of your life with, but also the start of building a new home within each other. It's not just you gaining a new family, but it is a family gaining you as well."

Boone swallowed hard. She understood how he felt, choking on her emotions too.

"Ah, Dexter. That is so beautiful."

"Ma, stop," Hailey said. "You're going to be banned from these things."

"I'm trying to be encouraging. I want Dexter to know he's doing a good job."

Dex continued. "Naomi and Boone, your love and respect for each other is clear. Like a hot-air balloon, you can rise to any challenge together. There is no rock face you cannot climb with each other. You've taken your love to new heights, and we know you'll continue to grow, support, and love one another. Because why go through life solo when you can go together? Are you ready to commit to marriage? Do you have the rings?" Boone reached into his pocket, pulled out the small black jewelry box that held both their rings, and opened it.

All the women gasped. "Wait . . . you actually brought rings?" Selah asked.

"Oh my god," Elena waved a hand in front of her face as if to keep the tears at bay.

Boone repeated the wedding vows after Dex. "I, Boone, but really Jonathan Henry Reyes, take you, Naomi Josephina Moreno, to be my wife, to have and to hold, from this day forward, for richer... but probably for poorer... in sickness and in health, to love and to cherish, until death do us part." His hands trembled as he slipped the ring on her finger.

"Okay, what exactly is going on?" Hailey said in hushed excitement, her mode back into phone photographer. She could have been streaming, for all Naomi knew. She didn't care. All Naomi saw was Boone, her eyes growing teary. She took the band meant for him, took a deep breath, and repeated the vow back to him, saying every part of it with conviction, knowing her heart didn't want to do this life with anyone else.

"I now pronounce you husband and wife," Dex said, lifting his hands as though his job was done, his smile big. "You may kiss the bride."

Boone took her face between his hands, pulling her close, pressing smiling lips to her mouth. "I love you, Pinky."

It was a little messy and teary and giggly. The wind kept sweeping her hair into their faces, but it was perfection too. "I love you," she told him.

"Ahh! What? Did you really marry them, Dexter?" Elena asked.

"That did feel real," Selah said. "What is happening right now?"

Dex merely swept a hand toward Boone and Naomi.

"Surprise!" she said. "We're actually married."

"WHAT?!" screamed the other three women.

Elena yanked them into a hug, the basket swinging from the force. "Oh my god! Oh my god! You and Boone are married?"

"How is this possible?" Hailey said, as she recorded them. "This is the wildest thing ever!"

Selah also pulled her into a hug. "God, Naomi. I . . . I'm still trying to process this. My sister just got married! And Dex—Did you know about this the whole time?"

"You're not mad, are you? I still need to sign the marriage license but they said they really wanted this."

"No. That's hilarious. Oh my god."

"Why did you not tell any of us? I could have made a big breakfast for everyone. We could have had a party with the rest of the family," Elena said. "But you two are really married, right?"

"Yes, we're married. We just wanted to do something small. And we wanted to surprise everyone!" Naomi laughed at how much they were carrying on. What started as a joke, turned into the most beautiful moment she could give her family and to her and Boone.

They continued to be a lively bunch as the balloon descended to the ground so they could all dismount. "Oh my god, Selah," said Hailey. "Can you believe your younger sister got married before you did? When are you and Dex finally going to tie the knot?"

"I don't know. Maybe soonish. If Naomi can do a small surprise ceremony, maybe we can do one, too, but at the park."

"Oh, we can go there right now, and you guys can get married," Elena suggested.

"I don't think Dex can officiate his own wedding," Selah said. "That would be weird. No, I think we're good, letting this be Naomi and Boone's day. They deserve it. We'll plan something, though."

Dex wrapped Selah in his arms, pressing a kiss to her temple. "I can't wait to marry you, Captain."

They landed the balloon, secured it, and began breaking everything down. After it was packed away, they got into their vehicles and made their way to the farm, where they could continue the celebration. As Naomi drove her and Boone in her truck, she noticed him focused on his left hand, where the new band shined on his finger.

"Everything okay?"

"Yeah, of course." He glanced at her. "I just realized that, as far as I know, Hank has never been married. I'm already doing something differently than him."

They hadn't seen or heard from Hank since he left Boone's trailer that final time. They had no idea what he was up to. Naomi wondered if Boone ever missed him. As bad as he was, the man was the only parent he'd ever known. It had to be rough.

"Are you having any regrets?" she asked after they parked. They got out and stood next to the vehicle, wanting to have a moment alone before joining the rest. He loved her—she felt it as much as the sun—but her heart couldn't help but wonder.

His expression warmed. "Are you kidding? I get to tell Tom that you're my wife now." His expression sobered, turning earnest. "Marrying you is unbelievable. You are the best thing to ever happen to me. I want to be the husband that you deserve."

"You already are. You're an infinitely better man than Hank. I hope you know that. You actually have the capacity to grow and to love. Your sister is going to be excited to meet you next year."

Sophie was finishing her last year of high school. Her mother hadn't given her permission to travel all the way to Central Oregon yet, but they FaceTimed quite a bit these days, their relationship continuing to grow. Sophie wanted to spend part of her summer before college in the High Desert, to hang out with Boone, learn to rock climb, and maybe take a few hot-air balloon rides. She treated Boone like he was the cooler, older brother, and Naomi was glad he had this. The family couldn't wait to meet the girl herself and make her feel at home.

"Did you tell her we were getting married?"

"Not yet. Hailey texted us a wedding picture, though, so maybe I'll send it to her. That was pretty great, right?"

"Yes! It was perfect."

He grinned, offering a wink. "I'm glad I was able to convince you to elope with me. I can't believe how persuasive I am. In fact, I'm going to be persuading you to do all kinds of things tonight."

It dawned on Naomi that, just like Lydia Bennet from *Pride and Prejudice*, she'd also secretly eloped with a scoundrel. It made her want to laugh all over again because the joke was clearly on her. "Was this your final wedding con, Mr. Reyes?"

He leaned closer, his eyes sparking with mischief. "You got it backwards, wife. It was you who had me hooked from the very beginning." He pulled her in for another kiss.

Turned out Naomi Moreno was a George Wickham girl, after all.

The End

Want to read a bonus chapter when Boone moves into Naomi's place?

Sign up for Janine's newsletter at www.janineamesta.com

Acknowledgements

You would think writing acknowledgements and thank yous would get easier the more I do this, but, alas, it's still difficult. Not because I don't know who I should be thanking. It's more of a case where I don't know where to start in expressing my gratitude. I'm going to give it my best shot.

First and foremost, there is one individual who stuck with me every single day of drafting and revising this book. And that is my cat, Hitchcock. Every single day that I'd gather my laptop and go into my office area, my cat would follow me, curling up next to me to nap. He did this even when I did not have treats stashed in my pocket. In fact, he's sitting next to me right now. I'd like to take this as evidence that he truly loves me. Hitchcock also provided me with inspiration for this book. Just as with Boone's pet, Cat, mine is also a former street cat who weaseled his way into my home. I hope he lives forever.

Now let's talk about some of the humans that helped with the creation of this book. As always, I want to thank my editor, Sinclair; my copy editor, Kay; and my proofreader, Marlene. Thank you for your notes to make sure my book is the best that I can produce.

I also want to thank the rest of the Tule team that always

comes through for me and patiently answers all my questions. I'm a girl that asks a lot of them. Thank you to Mia, Kelly, Meghan, Cyndi, and Lee. Also, a warm virtual hug and special thanks to Sugam for drawing the most beautiful covers for me. Your drawing hand must be magic. 😊

The writing friends who let me join them for writing sprints and listened to me cry over story plot points as I tried to figure things out—you were such a lifesaver! Thank you so much Denise Williams and Sarah Smith.

To my Pen Pals friends for giving me a group to laugh, vent, and just discuss writing and life in general, you're the best, and I don't know what I'd do without you—Katy, Colleen, Abigail, and Natalia.

Being a writer isn't all sitting in a room with a laptop and a cat. These days it can be a lot with social media and marketing aspects, making it overwhelming. A very special thanks to Lisa Christianson, who's been helping me behind the scenes, taking some of these things off my plate. You have no idea how much I appreciate all your help.

You're never lonely when you have romance book groups to chat with. I love my Romance Fight Club with B, Allie, J, and Denise. You're all amazing, and I admire you so much—but also, I'm not above taking you all down in order to win Victor and have him live at my house again.

Also, all my fellow Tule authors always give the best camaraderie. A shout-out to Heather, Rebecca, Stacey, Denise, Kelly, Lisa, Mia, and Fortune. You ladies are always a good source of information and are a blast to chat with.

I can never write anything without the love and support of the one person who believed in my writing before anyone else did. And that is my husband. He offers words of encouragement, listens to all my complaints and writing community gossip, and is willing to pick me up when I happen to be spiraling...sometimes all in the same day. Thank you for always being there. Mwah! Love you!

And, lastly, of course, the readers! Whether you are excited to read all my books or have decided to give me a chance by picking up your first one, thank you for giving me your time to read the characters and world I have created. I know there are a lot of romance books out there (maybe about a gazillion), so it means so much to me that I have made your reading list. The nice messages and reviews I have received from people give me life and the encouragement to keep typing. When days are tough, sometimes this is all I need.

If you enjoyed *The Wedding Con*,
you'll love the other books in...

Love is in the Air series

Book 1: *Love at First Flight*

Book 2: *The Wedding Con*

Available now at your favorite online retailer!

More Books by Janine Amesta

Love in El Dorado series

Book 1: *Striking Gold*
Book 2: *A Poinsettia Paradise Christmas*
Book 3: *Lucky Strike*

Available now at your favorite online retailer!

About the Author

Janine Amesta has loved reading kissing stories most of her life. She currently resides in Oregon with her husband and their pets, Hitchcock and Pippin. She studied screenwriting in college and her banter is influenced by the screwball romantic comedies of the 1930's. She's always on the lookout for the perfect line.

Thank you for reading

The Wedding Con

If you enjoyed this book, you can find more from all our great authors at TulePublishing.com, or from your favorite online retailer.

TULE
PUBLISHING